Immortal Air
A NOVEL

BY
Tracey Rombough

Cape Breton University Press recognizes the support of the Province of Nova Scotia and Canada Council for the Arts — Conseil des Arts du Canada — NOVA SCOTIA of Canada Council for the Arts Block Grants Program. We are pleased to work in partnership with these bodies to develop and promote our cultural resources.

Library and Archives Canada Cataloguing in Publication

Rombough, Tracey, 1962-, author
     Immortal air : a novel / Tracey Rombough.

Issued in print and electronic formats.
ISBN 978-1-77206-032-4 (paperback).
ISBN 978-1-77206-033-1 (pdf).
ISBN 978-1-77206-034-8 (epub)
ISBN 978-1-77206-035-5 (mobi)

     I. Title.

PS8635.O4728I46 2015   C813'.6   C2015-903572-4
                                               C2015-903573-2

Cape Breton University Press
PO Box 5300
1250 Grand Lake Road
Sydney, Nova Scotia B1P 6L2 Canada
www.cbupress.ca

Immortal Air

A NOVEL

BY

Tracey Rombough

CAPE BRETON UNIVERSITY PRESS
SYDNEY, NOVA SCOTIA

To my family

Part One

New Glasgow

1867–1869

Chapter 1 – 1867

The Launch of the *Pictou County*

Charley Cameron was on all fours. He tried to keep his back flat like a table, but his brother's feet pushed his shoulders down.

"Hold still." As George raised himself on tiptoe to reach the bottom branches of the beech tree, Charley felt the full force of his brother's weight dig into his shoulder blades.

"Hurry up now, George. I can't hold you."

"I can almost reach. I just have to grab…"

When the burden was finally lifted, Charley collapsed into the dust and dry grass of late summer. He looked up. His brother was hanging by one arm and extending an open hand downward.

"Come on now. Get up. It's your turn."

Charley stood up and looked over his shoulder. His mother was busy with baby Charlotte, and his twin sisters were talking with the McKenzie girls. He hesitated while he picked out the sharp stones and dried grass embedded in the palms of his hands.

"Come on now, while they're not looking."

Four years George's junior, Charley did not want his brother to think he was afraid, so he offered him his arm and George pulled him upwards. His feet scrambled for a footing on the smooth trunk. He struggled to pull his own weight to the safety of a lower crook in the tree. He didn't look down but looked upward at his brother's smiling face.

"Let's go."

"Where?"

George pointed up.

"Are you sure?"

"Just think of the view from there."

"What if you have a coughing spell? It's awfully high."

George continued to climb, snapping small branches as he went. He shouted down to Charley. "We'll be able to see the shipyard on Dalhousie Street. We won't have to run along the bank like the others." To George and Charley there was no grander event than the launching of one of New Glasgow's magnificent ships.

In the dense shade of the lower branches, Charley's feet tingled a bit and his hands became uncomfortably numb. He wanted to get down. It was too high and he had to admit it, or George would continue to coax him. "George, I can't...."

But George couldn't hear him. He ascended from one limb to the next, climbing higher and higher still. When he got close to the top, he poked his head out from the crown of glossy green leaves and the clusters of beechnuts to feel the warmth of the sun hit his face. A sudden gust of wind blew the branches and George swayed with the tree. He took a deep breath and exhaled slowly. He held the trunk with his left hand, and with his right he fished for his pocketknife in his trouser pocket. He held himself steady by straddling one limb like a saddle and bracing himself with his foot against another smaller branch. Confident that he was secure, George started to carve his initials in the grey smoothness of the trunk. Compelled by some greater force, he added "loves M. McG." underneath. He traced the initials with his index finger, brushed away the bark and then sat back smiling at his workmanship.

From this height, the town unfolded like a giant map. Stunted, misshapen figures milled about while the multicoloured squares of their picnic blankets spread out like a giant crazy quilt beside the river. George followed the narrow winding path of the railway as it snaked its way beside the East River. While it was no more than twenty yards wide at low tide, the river was deceptively deep. He looked to the west and saw the tall mast of McKenzie's latest ship, the *Pictou County*. At 1,400 tons, it was the largest cargo ship ever built in New Glasgow. George began to pick out familiar landmarks: McKenzie Mills, Jeffery McCall's shipyard, Riverside Cemetery, Marshall's Tannery, the Carmichael mansion on Temperance Street and the Black settlement on Vale Road. He traced the straight line of Prospect Street with his finger to see if he could find Maggie McGregor's house. Needless to say, she was one among thousands of tiny points blurred on the moving landscape of dots below. Closer to the expansive shadow of the beech tree, George heard Alex Munro call an eight-handed reel, guiding the dancers to turn away and cast off down the line. George focused his attention on the erratic orbit of one of the little dots – Johnny MacIntosh.

Tied to the trunk of a tree, Johnny ran in tight circles.
Deaf and dumb, the eleven-year-old flailed his arms
wildly. Johnny's parents fastened the rope around his
waist and left him in his own dark and silent world,
running round and round, while they joined the
festivities by the riverbank. In the distance George
heard the band start up and the crowd joined in a
rousing song.

"Up aloft, amid the rigging
Swiftly blows the fav'ring gale,
Strong as springtime in its blossom,
Filling out each bending sail,
And the waves we leave behind us
Seem to murmur as they rise;
We have tarried here to bear you
To the land you dearly prize.
Rolling home, rolling home,
Rolling home across the sea."

The crowd moved closer to the shore, and merchants made their way out of the stores on Provost
Street to the banks of the river. When the town clock
sounded the noon chimes, the church bells began to
clang. This was the signal to McKenzie's men to swing
their hammers against the holding wedges. Blow after blow, the heavy mauls fell with the precision of a
metronome. The men internalized the synchronized
metrical rhythm. Fathers, uncles and brothers stood
back from the launching cradle that smelled of fresh
cut timber and sweat. Captain George McKenzie, a
living legend, sat on a log in the shade, watching his
men work from a distance. Now and again he'd give a
shout if he saw one of the lads slacking.

"Put yer back into it, boy!"

Now well into his seventies, McKenzie had been a venerable seaman in his prime. The hero of bedtime stories and the topic of many a composition in school, he turned the boys of New Glasgow into men. Shipbuilding flowed through the veins of generations; the men harvested the timber, squared the logs, lay down the keel, launched the sleek crafts and navigated the dangerous waters to distant ports. McKenzie sat like a delighted grandfather as his men prepared for the moment of release.

"There she goes!" shouted George. Flags flew high and flapped in the wind as the massive vessel leapt gracefully into the deep blue waters of the river. Thousands of voices joined the chorus of bells so that the entire county shook with pride.

Charley's desire to witness the event overrode his fear of heights. Together the boys watched the *Pictou County* regally drift past. "Let's ask Mother if we can go to Pictou Bay to see her unfurl the sails before she heads to the strait." George began his rapid descent and was about to jump down when Jessie Cameron spotted her two boys.

"George Frederick 'n Charles John Cameron, get out of that tree this instant! Do ye want to murder yourselves? George, ye could get a coughing spell any time. Be careful now. And I expect ye to mind your wee brother." Her tirade continued until both boys stood before their petticoat-clad judge. George picked a few stray sticks from his shirt and listened. He thought better than to ask his mother if they could drive the team to the coast.

Jessie handed baby Charlotte to her youngest son and told the twins, Christina and Isabel, to pack up.

"George, hitch up the wagon. We're heading home. Where's your father?" When there was no answer, Jessie scanned the crowd and saw her husband drinking with men from the shipyard. "The rum is running freely. I doubt I can pull him away. George, get a move on now."

George wasn't listening to his mother; his eyes were fixed on the vessel drifting down the East River. He felt the wind fill the sails of his imagination and push him forward to distant lands.

Chapter 2 – Autumn 1868

A Proposition

The White School, an unassuming clapboard structure, smelled of linseed oil and chalk dust. Whether it was a matter of design or a shifting foundation, the hardwood floor, which was perpetually cold in winter, sloped upwards to the front of the room where the teacher's desk ascended to heights of intimidating authority. In his final year at the school, George towered over his teacher, Mr. Crestwick, both physically and academically. The little Englishman with black side-whiskers perched at the front of the room on a tall wooden stool like an omnipotent owl. At fourteen, George was already a full head taller than the man, who was a tightly wound bundle of nerves and knowledge. Perhaps in part to compensate for his lack of height, the schoolmaster had a sharp tongue and a nasty sense of humour. Many girls ran home at lunch vowing never to return. Among the students who felt the full force of Crestwick's criticism was Gertie McGregor.

"I am waiting, Miss McGregor." Crestwick tapped his fingers on his desk with exaggerated impatience and looked at the shrinking figure of a thirteen-year-old girl who sat in the second row. Charley and other boys stifled their laughter while she shifted uncomfortably in her seat.

"Umm…"

"Um is *not* an answer. Miss McGregor, I believe your time may be better spent embroidering the answer on a tablecloth."

On the verge of tears, Gertie ran out of the classroom and hid in the cloakroom where her intermittent sobs were audible above the children's laughter. George nodded to Crestwick and followed the distraught girl into the cloakroom.

"That man…" she started. "That man gives me the dithers."

"Gertie. Don't fret. Mr. Crestwick meant no harm."

"No harm? I feel like such a ninny." Gertie wiped her eyes with her sleeve. "It is fine for you, George. You're the smartest boy in the school. The man likes you, but he makes me feel daft."

George suppressed his laughter. He found it difficult to console Gertie when all along he agreed with Crestwick's assessment of her abysmal lack of academic prowess. Gertie McGregor was really the most vapid of minds. He was about to add to her misery with some clever comment when he realized that this conversation would no doubt be repeated to Maggie at the McGregor dinner table. He searched his store of empathy for something nice to say, some morsel of goodwill and compassion that would impress Maggie. In soothing tones he said, "We all have our talents, Gertie. When you are made to feel low, imagine Crestwick trying to embroider a tablecloth. If you gave him a needle and thread, I am sure he wouldn't know what to do. He's all thumbs."

Gertie smiled. "All thumbs and sideburns."

George put his hand on her shoulder and she melted under his touch. "I am certain that you will find your calling." His deep, soothing voice and his kindness fed the young girl's infatuation with the handsome scholar. To Gertie, he was Saint George – a brave soldier who tamed the dragon. Armed with George's advice, she resolved to tolerate her schoolmaster's sarcasm.

If Crestwick was hard on his students, he was equally supportive of their potential. It was the schoolmaster who first recognized George's talent as a poet. To satiate the boy's voracious appetite for reading, Crestwick loaned him volume after volume from his own collection. His admiration for the boy's facile memory and clever way with words led him to an indisputable truth. He knew George Cameron needed more than he could offer in New Glasgow. He took the course of George's education into his own hands, partly to spare him his own fate. There had to be more in George's future than teaching the Gertie McGregors of this world. It was time. He had summoned Mrs. Cameron to a meeting to discuss his plans for her son.

As the school day drew to a close, Crestwick pulled out his pocket watch, took note of the hour and snapped the cover shut as a signal to the students to put away their books. For months Crestwick had been preparing his speech for Mrs. Cameron with the zeal of a politician. However, he was not prepared for the maternal force that exploded from the small frame of this Scottish matriarch.

"What a day!"

"Please come in out of the rain, Mrs. Cameron." As she shook her umbrella at the door and leaned it against the woodpile to dry by the stove, Crestwick mounted his attack. "Your son George is a fine poet for his age. I see great things for him in the future."

"Poetry will not pay the bills, Mr. Crestwick, or feed his children. His father and I have our hearts set on the field of law. Master Ives, the English lad from Stellarton, has already established himself in the law school at Dalhousie University. A sharp mind like George's shouldn't be wasted writing rhymes. It's a nice...." She searched for the right word, then resumed. "Poetry is a pleasant pastime, but as far as his future is concerned, it is nothing more than that – a hobby."

It took Crestwick a minute to process the woman's thick brogue. He had not anticipated that she had given any thought to George's future. After all, the boy rarely spoke of home let alone his parents' interest in advancing his education. To Crestwick, George was his orphan protegé. "Indeed, Mrs. Cameron. That is the very subject of this meeting. Regardless, Mrs. Cameron, you owe it to George – to yourself as a parent – to see that your son will receive the finest education."

"Go on. I'm listening."

"There is a school of unquestionable reputation in Boston. All the fine young minds prepare for their graduate studies there."

"It will be bonnie for the boys to reunite with their sister Christina in Boston. She and the colonel have no children of their own. I shall write them immediately to tell them of our plans."

Crestwick hesitated. "The boys? Plural?" Then it occurred to him that Mrs. Cameron had misunderstood. He needed to clarify that it was *George* who would be attending school in Boston, *not* his younger brother. "Before you put the cart before the proverbial horse, as they say, George will need to prepare over the school year to write an entrance examination next fall. Mrs. Cameron, I cannot in good conscience make the same recommendation for Charley to attend the Boston Latin School. The entrance requirements are rigorous."

"Pardon me, Mr. Crestwick. I assure ye Charley is equally as quick as his brother. After all, he's only nine and it is unfair to compare the two. You tell them at this Latin school that it's the both of them or there's no deal." She looked down at the front of her woolen jacket and picked off a few stray balls of pilled lint. "Is there anything the lads can do over the summer to ensure their success with the entrance exams?"

"Yes, well, as a matter of fact there is. I have written to the school to inform them of my recommendation, and they have sent me this list of books. I know George has studied most of them, but for the ones he has not read, I can loan him copies from my personal library."

"That is very generous of ye, sir."

"They have also given George an appointment next August to write his examinations, but you will have to arrange his transport." Crestwick handed the letter to Mrs. Cameron. "It requires your signatures, Mrs. Cameron. Here," Crestwick flipped a few pages, "and here."

"I see. Well, I shall discuss the matter with my husband. I'm certain George and Charley will be prepared to take your examinations this summer." With that, Mrs. Cameron picked up her things, went to the school's side door and opened and raised her umbrella in one swift motion on the stoop. "Tut, the weather picked a fine time to pour cats 'n' dogs. Thank ye again, Mr. Crestwick. I'll be in touch."

George was oblivious to the complex manoeuvres behind the scenes of his own existence. In turn, Mrs. Cameron was unaware of the source of George's every waking desire and his muse: Maggie McGregor.

Chapter 3 – Spring 1869

A Game of Graces

George could not take his eyes off the slender silhouette framed by the window. Every now and again a crisp spring breeze caught her attention and she looked up from her book, smiled and returned to her reading. George traced the gentle features of her profile with his mind, lingering long on the lines of her graceful neck.

Behind him Gertie pulled his ear playfully. "C'mon, George. Let's go outside."

Entranced by the beauty of Gertie McGregor's older sister, he took no notice of the fair-haired child. Besides, he did not want to play with the children; he was beyond hide-and-seek and tag.

Frustrated by the lack of response, Gertie turned on her heel. "Suit yourself!"

"Hello."

"Pardon me?"

"I said hello, silly. I must say, you are a distracted boy."

Surprised by the mellow tones of her soft voice, George blushed. For an aspiring poet, the boy could not find his voice. Words refused to form in any meaningful manner, so he repeated, "Pardon me?"

"You know, Gertie can*not* stop talking about you. She entertains us at the dinner table with the tales of adventure you share with the class. She says you are quite the storyteller."

"Yes – I love to write." He had to turn her attention way from his age. It didn't have anything to do with who he was. "What are you reading?"

"Tennyson. Do you know him?"

George recited:

"Tears, idle tears, I know not what they mean,
Tears from the depth of some divine despair
Rise in the heart, and gather to the eyes,
In looking on the happy autumn-fields,
And thinking of the days that are no more."

"Delightful! I have never met a boy your age who could quote Tennyson."

"I am fourteen. I can also quote Virgil and Cicero." George was immediately embarrassed by his unnecessary boast. It was too eager, too proud. More than anything he resented Maggie referring to him as a boy.

"Gertie has never shown interest in poetry."

"She wouldn't. She still plays with dolls."

Maggie pulled the curtain to the side to get a better look at the children playing on the lawn. Her sister sent the beribboned hoop toward Charley, who caught the ring on the tip of his slender stick. Little Charlotte squealed with glee. "They look like they're having a grand time."

"I am not much for games. Besides they are playing Graces – it's a girl's game."

"Pity. Charley seems to be enjoying himself."

"He's ten." George wanted to change the subject. "I write my own poetry. Would you like to hear something I've been turning over in my mind?"

"Oh yes, please!" Maggie put her book aside and turned her attention to the serious boy who had now made a few tentative steps closer to her chair. He closed his eyes and recited the lines with such fervour that Maggie shook her head in disbelief.

"Thy sky is dim but yet I see,
Methinks, anear thy shore
The star that shines above the free
Arise to set no more:
And from that star a light doth spring
A light of heaven's own wakening."

Maggie clapped with delight then covered her mouth. "What a clever memory you have! Remarkable really. And such a lovely voice. Who wrote this? No, let me guess."

"I told you. I wrote it." George's brows came down, and his lower lip wrinkled under his upper lip, giving him the look of a petulant child.

"I didn't mean to...." She changed the subject. "Here, George, come look at my collection." She took him by the hand and led him to an ornately carved writing desk in the parlour. "Mother tells me that you will be going to Boston. How exciting for you and Charley."

George, trembling at her touch, gathered the scraps of his ego, cleared his throat and said, "Yes, it is a rare opportunity. Charley is growing homesick already, but I am looking forward to the academic challenge."

"Not to mention all the people you will meet."

Her beauty intoxicated George. His head was spinning. He tried to steady himself against the desk. "I am afraid that I will be buried in study for the next seven years – three at the Boston Latin School, and then I plan to study law."

"I do hope you will save time to write more poetry."

"It is part of my day, like breathing."

Maggie gestured to a beautifully crafted basket of lavender sweetgrass on her desk. Inside were stacks of letters and cards, each tied with a ribbon. "I have one hundred and seventy-six cards from all over the world. It's just a pastime, but I *do* love to write. Obviously, it's nothing like your hobby, but it brings me great joy."

George did not say a word. He was overwhelmed by the concrete testament to Maggie McGregor's popularity. Even if he did write her, he would be one among many – one among one hundred and seventy-seven to be precise. He was silent as she gently pulled a ribbon and let the bundle fall loose. He fingered the pile, pulled out one card at a time, gave it a cursory glance and flipped it over, reading card upon card of saccharine cheer. One card caught his attention. It was a familiar tinted print of a young woman fishing in the East River. It was the kind of postcard sold at the mercantile in New Glasgow to every tourist or visiting relative. The message was definitely scribed by a strong masculine hand of confidence and authority: *"Dear M – You may fish forever, but my flame burns low. G.S."*

George looked up and caught the crimson blush of Maggie's cheek. He waited for her to fill the awkward silence, but she did not look at him. Instead she busied herself by gathering the stray cards into a neat stack. George placed the card on the top of the pile with the message facing upward, and Maggie retied the bundle.

"Who is this mysterious G.S. whose flame is burning out?"

"Let's just say he is a man of sterling character."

Maggie's enigmatic response remained unexplored. They were interrupted by the shrill voice of George's mother.

"George! Do not bother Lassy McGregor with your poems."

"It's no trouble really, Mrs. Cameron…"

"I declare, he is the most single-minded of my children. He prefers the audience of adults. I tell him, 'George, there will be time enough in life for serious matters. Savour your youth while it's yours to enjoy.' My, now I'm starting to sound like a poet! Here I am scolding George for taking up your time, and I've been going on."

"George has been—"

"Goodness knows his wee brother Charley would love his company." Mrs. Cameron turned to her son who was red-faced and downcast. "Now, George, apologize to the lassy and scoot outdoors with the others."

"My apologies, Miss McGregor, for intruding on your reading." He gestured to the maroon leather volume on the table. "Tennyson waits."

"It has been no trouble, George. I enjoyed your poetry very much and look forward to hearing the piece when you have finished."

"Once again, lassy, my apologies." Mrs. Cameron held her son firmly by his shoulders and hastened him into the front foyer, out the door and onto the porch. Maggie could hear Mrs. Cameron's rambling reprimand continue as she and her son crossed the lawn toward Gertie, Charley and little Charlotte. George did not join the children; he sat in the shade and looked down at his feet.

Maggie's heart went out to him. His mortification was as clear as the frown that pulled at his features. *Such a serious young man. Such a handsome young man. Pity he is still a boy.* She headed out the door to join the children in their game of Graces.

Chapter 4

An Art History Lesson

The fair maiden shyly covered the beauty of her nakedness. George turned the page. The book was filled with detailed pen sketches of naked or nearly naked Greek statues. Why would Crestwick expose him to such an erotic display of flesh? Weren't there regulations to prevent the circulation of such sexual excess? Was this too part of his education?

Feeling the shame of guilt, George went to the door and closed it quietly, thereby crossing that fine line between art and pornography. It was like a switch turned on in his head. He retuned to his bed with the book. He unfastened his pants and began to tug fiercely as he imagined Maggie's firm white breasts and ample buttocks under his touch.

Charley opened the door wide, exposing his brother's intense study. "Whatcha doing there, George?" He didn't fully understand what was happening, but he sensed it had something to do with girls. He saw the pictures of the naked statues and gasped. "Whoa ho, George! Where did you get those? Does Mother know you have them?" He pressed in closer for a better look, but George slapped the book shut.

"Don't tell Mother, Charley. Close the door." As his brother went to the door, George buttoned his trousers.

"Tell her what?"

"Never mind. It's just that when you get older you will have feelings that must be – released."

"Do you mean like breaking wind? Because I already do that all the time."

"Something like that, only the feelings released are..." George searched for the right word, "er – private."

"There is definitely nothing private about breaking wind." Charley plugged his nose and wafted his hand in front of his face.

"The feelings are more pleasurable than that."

"Well, it looked painful to me. Your face was all twisted up, like this." Charley made a face that made George feel exposed and vulnerable.

"And like many private matters, Charley, I do not want you to share what you saw with Mother – nor anyone else for that matter. It's our secret bond as brothers that demands your silence. Are you with me on this?"

"Alright then." Charley grabbed a newspaper from George's desk, half expecting his brother to scold him for touching his collection. He began to scan the articles for something more interesting than George's private matters.

When George saw that Charley was now fully immersed in some story in *The New Glasgow Advocate*, he felt confident that his secret was safe. He opened Aeschylus and began to prepare for his extra reading.

Charley noticed that George had circled several advertisements on the last page of the paper. "Madame Gertrude Remington of West Troy, New York." Charley read the ad aloud, but stumbled over some of the bigger words. "Astrologist – som-nam-bu-list and clair-voy-ant." He stopped. "What's this stuff, George?" George wasn't listening, so Charley continued to read. "Madame Gertrude will de-lin-e-ate the features of the person you are to marry in a portrait of rare quality for fifty cents." Charley set the paper down and looked at his brother. "George? What's a," he paused to find the word again, "a clair-voy-ant?"

George looked at him over the top of his book. "Someone who can see the future."

"You mean like a gypsy?"

"More like the Oracle at Delphi."

"Huh? You believe in this stuff?" When there was no answer, Charley looked at the other circled advertisement. "Grows whiskers and mustaches on even the smoothest of faces. Used by the elite of New York, London and Paris with most flattering success. Miraculous results or your money will be cheerfully refunded. A dollar! Whoa!" Charley looked at George's naked upper lip and laughed.

"What's so funny, Charley?"

"Nothing." Another ad caught his eye. "George?"

"Yes?"

"Do you have any money?"

"Some. Why?"

"Well, I think I need to buy some of Dr. Grimstone's An-thel-min-tic."

"What on earth for?"

"Do you think I have foul-smelling breath?" Charley leaned over his brother's shoulder and exhaled into his face.

"Always!"

"Check my belly. Does it look distended to you? It feels hard. Touch it. Does it feel hard to you?"

"Anyone's stomach will look distended if you stick it out like that."

"Listen to this, George. 'According to the celebrated Dr. T.H.L. Grimstone, the tapeworm can grow to an indefinite length. It coils and fastens to the intestine.'"

"Disgusting, Charley. You don't have a tapeworm."

"Then explain to me why Mother says, 'Charley, laddie, ah cannae fill ye up. Ye must have a hollow shank!'"

"Charley, you eat so much because you are a healthy growing boy."

"Look at me, George! I'm all skin and bones! Where does all the food go? Cousin Dan told me he read that if I go hungry for a day or two and dangle raw meat in front of my face, the worm will come out my mouth and you can pull it out. Can we do that, George?"

"You are being ridiculous, Charley. Now you're making me ill. I'll have no appetite for dinner tonight. If you are that worried, tell Mother."

"I think I'm dying, George!"

"We all die, Charley."

"But I want to ride on a train and take the ship to Boston for our trip to see Christina. You know, George, Mother shouldn't have married off Christina like that. It's not right for Izzie."

"Colonel Moore is a good man, Charley. A war veteran."

"It's like taking away your reflection. You know Izzie cries at night?" Charley whispered.

"I know. I can hear her."

"Why can't she come with us to Boston?"

"Mother said Izzie must remain here and take care of Lotta and Father."

"I know I'd cry every night if you and I were separated," said Charley.

"Well, we won't be separated. We'll be together at the Latin school. But only if you study, Charley, or you won't be allowed to stay. You only have a few more months to prepare."

"That's lots of time. Besides, I've already told everyone at school that I'm going. They'll think I'm a liar if I don't stay in Boston with you!"

"Well, since you're dying, it won't much matter now, will it? Now leave me alone. I'm studying. You would do well yourself to do a little more reading in the textbooks and a little less reading about tape-worms."

"There will be time for all of that. I just want to go to Boston."

"You've decided to live then?"

"I'm hungry."

"Go in the pantry and grab a pickled egg before supper. But don't let Mother catch you or you'll be dead for sure."

Chapter 5 – Summer 1869

Casting Lines

One morning in July, the Cameron boys headed out before sunrise. George carried a pot-bellied creel of split willow and his grandfather's bamboo fly-rod, while Charley threw a burlap sack over his shoulder containing Mrs. Cameron's packed lunch of dried apples, scones wrapped in paper and a couple of hard-boiled eggs. At first they walked side-by-side in the steel grey silence of the morning. Charley had to skip every fifth step or so to keep up with his older brother until the boys reached the end of Sutherland Road; here they walked down single file through the woods, navigating over moss-covered roots and fall-en branches. George waited a few seconds every now and again, holding back the saplings as he went so they didn't slap Charley in the face when he let them go. The muffled thump of their steps on the spruce-scented path made it feel hollow underfoot. They reached the river's edge just as the sun climbed above the eastern bank of clouds. The water waited in its serene stillness for the first cast to break the surface.

"Looks like the rain'll hold off." The boys were startled by a young fisherman who had gotten to the shore before them.

Charley had never seen a Black person this close before. He stared with curiosity until George poked him in the back.

"Excuse my brother. He doesn't know better."

"Is awright. No harm done." The fisherman's smile melted away any insult.

Charley slid down the flat rocks until he was standing next to the boy who was full head taller than he, but otherwise seemed to be about his age. "Catch anything?"

"Them fish be steady runnin'." The boy leaned his pole against a large rock, bent down and held up a string of brookies and a couple of speckleds. He smiled again widely at the two white boys then returned the morning's catch to the cool water. He took off his sun-bleached bucket hat. "I'm Bartholomew Izzard. You can call me Bart."

"I'm Charley Cameron and that's my brother George." Charley gestured with his thumb at his older brother who handed him Grandfather Sutherland's pole. George drifted off further up the shore, but the younger Cameron, eager to make a new friend, stayed behind. Charley sat his sack down, baited his hook and tried to cast. He cast time and time again, got tangled in trees, caught a lot of the bottom, lost some bait and didn't catch any trout. He watched Bart cast a perfect loop and roll. "Where'd you learn to do that?"

"Pappy, he took me fishin' in brooks and ponds before I could walk. Times when I just enjoy casting, that's all. Enjoy the quiet. That's when you just enjoy nature. I think there's nothin' better than fishin' on a Sattiday mornin.'"

"Can you show me? I mean, how to cast like you?"

"Sure can. It'll take time though. 'Time 'n' practice.' That's what my pappy says."

Bartholomew knew where to go. "This late in the season the trout like to go deep," he explained. He watched the birds diving and pointed when a double crested cormorant hit the water with needle-like precision. "The stoneflies are out too," he said, and pointed out a few rises on the surface. "Cast over there, quiet like."

Charley imitated the subtle movements of Bart's wrist. He was getting better with each cast until he was startled by a sudden jerk on his line. A fish hammered on his bait and bent his rod in a sharp hook toward the surface of the water.

"Give 'er a good tug, Charley!"

Charley was so excited, he jumped up and down on the shore. When he eased up, the trout ran with his line a bit, so he gave it another jerk and started turning the reel in an awkward clunking motion. His grandfather had jimmy-rigged an old reel on a split bamboo pole, so it wasn't the smoothest or prettiest catch, but Charley didn't care. He had never caught a fish this size all on his own before. He was flushed with an exhilarating sense of independence.

Charley landed the ten-inch trout on the soft moss. "It's a beauty, isn't it?" Its distinctive sprinkling of red dots surrounded by blue haloes glistened along its flanks.

Bart grabbed the flip-flopping fish with two hands and held up Charley's prize. "That's a good catch, Charley. Lemme help. You pull the hook outta the mouth gentle. You gotta stringer? Never mind, you can use mine."

Charley was fascinated with Bart's delicate pink fingertips in contrast to the rich dark skin on the tops of his hands. He looked at his own freckled and cream-coloured hands with thin blue veins poking out under the translucent skin. He thought they weren't as interesting as Bart's hands. He watched the boy deftly thread the sharp stick through the gill of his fish and out the gaping mouth. Bart tied the loose end to a heavy branch that had fallen in the water. "They be fresh if they can swim a bit."

Charley wanted to show George his catch, but his brother had made his way upstream to the estuary and solitude. It wasn't that his brother was physically distant, but he was so deep in thought that it was as though he and Bart had ceased to exist. George was moody these days and sometimes downright sour. No fun. No fun at all. Charley watched his older brother take out his journal and write.

George always found the solitude of the river to be an excellent place to think. Inspired by a fish rising to the glassy surface, he began to write.

Dear little fish
All shining, shivering, silver in the brook,
Come from the rock's recess
Come to my hook.
See here I throw it,
And having seen my crook,
You and a watercress,
Dear little fish,
Shall make a dish,
I guess,
For any poet.

George fixed his gaze on the treeline across the water, emerging from the morning mist rising off the East River. He turned Maggie's postcard over and over in his mind until he became dizzy with delight and fear. A heavy stone sank in his throat; prickly adrenaline pumped through his arms and legs. His ribcage tightened so that the empty sacks in his chest ached for air. Maggie had caught him. He took a deep breath and exhaled slowly. He took another and another until he felt loose and calm. George closed his eyes. Who was this enigmatic G.S.? What was he implying by the reference to fishing? Was Maggie fishing for someone else? Was there another rival for Maggie's affections? He was that fish, hooked and gasping. Before he knew it, he found himself standing in the shallows. He was jolted out of his reverie by the cool water lapping around his ankles.

"You is scarin' them fish away with your stompin', George." When Bart got no response, he turned to Charley. "Best tell 'im he's scarin' the fish. Your brother don't fish?"

"Naw. He comes along because my mother makes him. He'll sit and write poetry all morning."

"He write poetry? Wha'?"

"That's *all* he does! That and think of his sweetie." Charley put his interlocked fingers up to his chin, tilted his head and fluttered his eyelashes. He twirled imaginary curls and puckered his lips like a fish. The two boys laughed. Bart slapped his knee and laughed so hard tears came to his eyes. He had never known someone white to be as funny as Charley.

"How come I've never seen you before, like at school or in town?" Charley asked.

"I lives on Vale Road, pass Brother Street. You know that street? We keep to ourselves. I goes to the First Baptist Church there. The reverend, he teach us at that church most days. I can read an' write some. There be about fifteen chillin there. My sister an' brother went to school in Guysborough before we moved here, so they teach me my letters and numbers. Mama and some o' the others petition the gov'ment to build a new school up at the settlement. She says, 'We pay taxes jus' like everyone else. These kids got a right to a school.' They is still waitin' though."

Charley opened his sack. "You hungry? I brought food." He shoved a triangular scone slathered in currant jam into Bart's hands. "My mother made these last night for the fishing trip. Good, eh?"

"They good. You tell your mama thanks." Bart's face was a sticky mess. "Charley, I got somethin' for you. Sit here."

Bart scrambled over the rocks to retrieve his cloth bundle. Charley watched his new friend wipe his hands on the back of his pants and pull from his bundle a frayed linen envelope tied with a string. Bart opened it carefully while Charley held his breath. "I want you to have my little brown troutie," said Bart. "I tied 'er myself."

"Beezer!"

"Wha'?"

"It's great! Thanks!" Charley examined the intricately tied fly. Bart had used a feather-thin piece of white rabbit's fur for the wing and wrapped it with fine white thread. He had trimmed a bundle of deer hair to form the head. It was perfect.

"Jus' put 'er there." Bart carefully hooked the fly to the brim of Charley's hat. "You practice some more and then you can use it good."

"Bart, you're a good friend."

Bart pointed upstream. "Looks like George has had enough of his poetry."

Reluctantly Charley reeled in his line, secured the hook to the eyelet and made his line taut. "Come on, Bart. We can walk together."

A sudden thought came to George as he, Charley and Bart turned up Temperance Street on their way home. Perhaps he could casually walk by MacKenzie's Millinery on Provost. Maggie might be there. She and her mother often shopped the millinery on Saturday. Perhaps he might happen to run into her. He gave Charley the pole and creel and told him to go straight home. "Tell Mother I have to mail a letter."

"Huh?" Charley juggled the equipment, but before he could say a word, George was making his way toward the centre of town. Charley didn't believe his brother had to mail a letter. He suspected it had something to do with Gertie McGregor. He put his gear down on the side of the road and turned to Bart and winked. Charley wiggled down the street after his brother like a girl and nearly split himself laughing. Bart laughed at Charley, but he knew their time was quickly coming to a close. They had reached that point in the road where they had to part ways.

"I live that way." Charley pointed down the street lined with clapboard houses, picket fences and garden gates. He didn't want to go just yet.

A scruffy-looking man staggered into the boys' path and swayed forward and back like a tattered rag blowing in the wind. He smelled of brown ale and piss.

"Whadda you think you're doin', talkin' to this white boy, eh?" he drawled.

"Charley, he my friend," said Bart.

"Is he now?"

Charley was afraid of the man. He could see that he was drunk – not the kind of drunk like his father and uncles. He was a mean drunk – all bluster and fists. And he was a lot bigger than they were. He had that glassy-eyed look – a look that meant he wasn't willing to let them go just yet.

The drunk pointed at Bart. "Why doncha' take yerself straight up the hill there, boy?"

The smile on Bart's face vanished and his bright eyes became vacant. He looked into the dirt at his feet. Burrowing a hole in the dust with his big toe, he looked over to his friend. He spoke in a whisper. "Can't no one tell you you ain't somebody, Charley. 'Member that, okay? I'm goin' home. Best I go 'fore there's trouble."

The drunk swayed again. "Why doncha git before I call Peachie Carroll to come git you and put you in jail for stealin' this boy's fish!"

Charley sensed his new friend's fear, so he kicked the stranger in the shin and shouted, "Why don't you just go to hell, you old buck-toothed bastard. C'mon, Bart. Let's get outta here." Charley left his grandfather's pole and creel and started to run down the street toward home. He stopped in his tracks when he realized that Bart wasn't behind him. He turned to see the drunk on the ground, holding his injured leg and shaking his fist at the heavens, cursing a blue streak. Bart was running in the direction of Vale Road. He had left his string of fish and bundle in the dust on the side of the road.

"Bart! Your fish!"

But Bart didn't answer. He just ran without looking back. Charley's heart sank. He didn't know whether it was the drunk man's cursing or the fact that Bart hadn't looked back, but he started to cry. He cried the kind of tears that come from deep inside. The kind of tears that refuse to stop even when you tell yourself that you are a ten-year-old boy, and boys your age aren't supposed to cry.

The drunk got up and staggered this way and that until momentum carried him forward down the street in the other direction. When he thought it was safe, Charley went back to pick up his brother's gear and his grandfather's pole. The string of fish lay by the side of the road, flopping feebly in the dust. Some of the smaller brookies had died the instant Bart dropped them, but Charley's prize opened and shut its mouth. Its black eye grew cloudy. A fly crawled across its speckled flanks and three or four buzzed around. Charley poked the fish with a stick and the fly took off and circled back to land on the fish again. It crawled into the open gill. Charley decided to leave it be. He wiped the snot from his upper lip with his sleeve and buried his face in the crook of his elbow to dry it off. He turned toward home but stopped for a minute to watch his friend disappear at the turn in Vale Road.

Chapter 6

Dangerous Waters

Maggie unfolded the paper George had slipped into her hand at MacKenzie's Millinery last Saturday. She had blushed when he tipped his hat and ordered a yard of white lace for his mother. In the privacy of her bedroom, she had read and re-read the playful lines several times before she refolded the paper and tucked it under her pillow. She read them again now.

> You and a watercress,
> Dear little fish,
> Shall make a dish,
> I guess,
> For any poet.

Maggie now knew it beyond the shadow of a doubt. She loved this boy; or rather, she loved this boy's mind. After all, he was fourteen. How could she separate that fact from the words she read and re-read? How could she distinguish between the chronology of his existence and the words of passion in this poem? Social convention tugged at her conscience for entertaining such scandalous thoughts. Try as she might to dismiss this contemplation as anything more than profound admiration, the nagging possibility that she was actually falling in love with him would not die. She rose to the challenge of his metaphors and turned his phrases over and over in her mind. When she closed her eyes at night, his clever conceits took her into his world. Into the poet's mind where she was lost in words – George's words.

When the townspeople saw the Cameron and McGregor children that summer, riding about town in the Camerons' wagon unaccompanied by their parents, no one gave them a second look. No one suspected that the fourteen-year-old boy held such private and adult thoughts about Mr. McGregor's eldest daughter; after all, the three younger siblings were always in tow. Charley and Gertie were often bored to tears with the conversations about Poe, Shelley and Browning. They would wander off to gather stones along the side of the river and skip them across the surface of the water, leaving their older siblings to talk. Charlotte was far too young to understand the intricacies of their conversation. She preferred to hold her brother's hand or ride on his shoulders. The ruse allowed George and Maggie unchaperoned time – time not granted to most young couples until they were wed. Like everyone else, Mr. G. Sterling had no idea that the object of his affection was falling in love with the Cameron boy.

George and Maggie felt the turn of the season press against them like a heavy door swinging shut. Both feared that once this door closed, it would mark the end of their physical time together. Five more days. George arranged outings and secret meetings in the woods between their houses. He made plans to propose to Maggie during an excursion to Bear Park in Albion Mines. Each word of his proposal was carefully crafted so that Maggie couldn't possibly say no. George's words painted a vision of their lives together. A vision so fair and wonderful. A world within their reach if she would only have faith. Faith and patience. He did not have a penny of his own to his name, so instead of buying her a ring, he secretly collected stray strands of her golden hair and braided them with the auburn strands of his own.

George spread the blanket on the ground and Maggie began to unpack the lunch. She spread her skirt wide on the quilt and watched her sister play with Charley and Charlotte. Every now and then, Gertie looked up at George and smiled.

The flit and chirp of a small bird above Maggie's head caught her attention. She followed the house sparrow as it hopped from branch to empty branch. *Chirrup, phip, phip*, it called. As she watched the tiny creature, she was certain the sparrow was watching her too. "Come with me," it seemed to say. Then it occurred to Maggie that she was staring at her own reflection. *I am a sparrow.*

"George, I am not a poet."

"No, my love – you inspire poetry."

"How can you say that, George? I am so plain – a common house sparrow, an everyday companion."

She fingered the stiff folds of her muted green and brown striped skirt.

"And you are beautiful to me."

"My sister is a swallow – sweet and beautiful. Look at her, George."

Clothed in a violet print calico, Gertie was spring made flesh. Almost fourteen, her breasts were distinct now under the fitted bodice. She was playful, youthful – full of life. Last night Maggie had rolled Gertie's golden hair into tight curls and tied them with rags. In the morning she carefully brushed the curls into soft golden waves that fell loose about Gertie's shoulders. Maggie wore her own hair parted down the centre and pulled back into a tight chignon at the nape of her neck – a suitable fashion for women her age, she thought.

Maggie was determined to turn George's head in another – more appropriate – direction. She squinted into the sunlight and caught her younger sister looking up the bank at them. Gertie had removed her shoes and stockings. She hauled up her eyelet petticoats and the hem of her dress into a fistful of violet folds and announced, "I'm going in."

Not to be outdone, Charley scrambled to the shore, rolled up his trousers past the knee and ran into the water, splashing Gertie as he waded deeper into the pond.

"Look at her, George. She adores you, you know. Why do you insist on casting your line in my direction? Why do you persevere in your affection for me? Her heart is so light and playful. I am a humble, dowdy sparrow. Look at her and look at me. If you're not careful, Charley will steal her affections."

"What is this nonsense? True she is beautiful, but she is a child and will remain a child in my thoughts always."

"How can you say that when she is but a year younger than you are?"

"No."

"It is a fact."

"She does not love poetry. She prefers to adorn herself in an outward show of ruffles and ribbons. Your mother really does indulge your sister's obsession with fashion. Though Gertie may appear beautiful, I assure you, she is not." George gently brushed Maggie's cheek with the backs of his fingers. "Did you know that the ancient Greeks associated sparrows with Aphrodite? You are my goddess, my divine inspiration, my familiar." He pulled her close and tried to kiss her, but she shifted uncomfortably, turned her face away and straightened her dress.

George looked at her intently, then leaned to kiss her shoulder. His kisses made their way from her shoulder to her neck and from her neck to her cheek. He turned her face toward him, and his lips pressed hard on her mouth.

Maggie pulled away. "George! Charley and Gertie will see."

"They are too busy mucking about in the pond, looking for frogs." They heard the splash and giggle of little Charlotte who was ankle deep in the rushes. Her dress was filthy. "See? They are fine." He took Maggie's hand in his and slipped the braided band on her ring finger.

"What are you doing, George? What if someone—"

George stood and pulled her up and into the bushes.

"We need to watch Charlotte."

"I can see her." George followed the children out of the corner of his eye while he smothered Maggie in kisses. He pushed his mouth against hers and put his hand on her breast. He was shaking.

"You're nervous. This isn't right."

"We need to find a time and place where we can be more intimate."

"Not here, not now." She pulled away and straightened her dress. She emerged from the bushes just in time to see Charlotte running up the bank in tears. Black leeches covered her tiny legs.

"George!" Maggie swept the child into her arms and carried Charlotte to the blanket.

George put his hand gently under his sister's chin to tilt her gaze upward, away from the hideous creatures. "Lotta, look up to the sky, my sweet. Keep looking at the sky. Tell me when you see a bird."

Deftly, with the flat of his thumbnail, George broke the seal at the end of each leech and flicked them away. George and Gertie joined them on the blanket and pressed close to see.

"Ew!"

Maggie held her finger to her lips and made a silent *sh*. Gertie began to whimper when she saw the blood. "Is she going to die?" Maggie shook her head slowly to catch her sister's eye.

"Bird!" Charlotte exclaimed between sobs and sniffles. "Are they gone?"

"One more, my sweet."

"You're so brave, Lotta." Maggie stroked the child's cheek. "So very brave."

On the way back, Maggie held the sleeping child in her arms. No one spoke. The only sounds were the clop, clop, whinny and snort of the horses as they instinctively headed toward home. Maggie kissed the top of Charlotte's head and rested her cheek on the child's hair. Gertie and Charley sat in the back of the wagon. They couldn't wait to tell everyone the ghastly details of their adventure at Bear Park.

Maggie turned to George who looked straight ahead in silence. She watched the muscles in his jaw ripple and clench. He gritted his teeth and kept staring ahead. He seemed so angry. At himself? At her? At the passage of time? She couldn't help but feel that this was an omen. A warning that they were treading in dangerous waters.

Chapter 7

A Fair Exchange

In preparation for his move to Boston, George hunted for his father's steamer trunk in the drive shed behind the house. The slanting shafts of morning light looked like sticks criss-crossing his path as he moved through the towers of junk and farm machinery, surplus this and that, forgotten until need propelled someone to search for something. Small eddies of fine dust rose and hung suspended like a twinkling curtain.

He spied the oak ribs of the tin trunk under discarded wooden crates and an old kennel of rusted iron bars and sawed flooring planks. When George was six, his father had ordered a farm dog all the way from Montreal to help with the cows in the lower pasture. James Cameron had seen the advertisement in *The Advocate* and promptly sent the company five dollars for a professionally trained, working collie, delivery guaranteed within the month. Anticipation turned to disappointment for George when the promised farm dog did not come.

"Foolish! That's what I say. Sending solid earned money through the mail to God knows where. And for what? A bitch?" Mrs. Cameron stabbed her needle through the white cloth as she worked the delicate white loop around an intricate pattern. "Why in heaven's name ye felt the need to send out for a dog is beyond me when ye can get one of the Mi'kmaq mixed breeds for a handful of beads if it comes down to it. Have ye forgotten we have Louise's wedding in a few months' time?" She huffed heavily. No response. She looked over her spectacles at her husband, but he remained at the window, looking out across the pasture. She knotted the thread and clipped it closely with her silver scissors. Jessie Cameron tutted her tongue and shook her head again. "Solid earned money. I never heard of such foolishness."

After waiting three months for delivery of the dog, Mr. Cameron decided he had been swindled. He wrote a stern letter to the company, threatening legal action. When they got notice two weeks later that their delivery had arrived at the train station, George pleaded with his father to take him along.

In the station yard the porter directed the Camerons and four other buyers down the platform. Before they got within fifty yards of the train car, they heard the barking. The porter slid a heavy metal bar and opened the train car. A putrid olfactory wall of canine urine and dead meat assaulted them. George gagged. He had to step back for air. Vomit rose in his throat and he spat it out. The barking, once muffled by the iron door, now rose to a deafening chorus of staccato jabs and high-pitched howling. George felt each yelp erupt in his chest like a hollow explosion of despair. He put his hands up to his ears, but he could not silence the vibrations in his temples. The man looked at the cargo manifest and compared it to James Cameron's bill of sale. He walked to the back of the car, double-checked the number and with another sliding click of metal, he opened the crate door.

"There she is."

The collie cowered in its crate. Its black and white fur, caked with dried feces and straw, looked thin and mangy. Deprived of the opportunity to move freely in the wooden box, the dog's muscles had atrophied to the point that she shook uncontrollably when she tried to stand. Without human interaction for God knows how long, the creature did not respond to George's father when he tugged gently on the rope to coax her out. Fear emanated from that box. The collie shut its crusted eyes against the daylight and retreated to the back of the crate.

"Poor thing," said Mr. Cameron. "Must be hungry and scared. Give her time. She'll be right as rain when she sees the farm."

Unaccustomed to any expression of tenderness from either of his parents, George looked up at his father. He expected to see some sign of anger or evidence of disappointment, but James Cameron wore the mask of Scottish Presbyterian indifference that over the years had become his face. After all, he needed to meet his wife's critical eye when he took the dog home.

James could not be more mistaken when he thought time and fresh air would make a difference. After two weeks, the collie was still listless and timid. At night she howled so plaintively that two-year-old Charley joined in with wails until the entire Cameron household was wide awake. James went out to the back step, untied the dog from the newel post and led her inside by the woodstove. The howling stopped when the dog collapsed in a spent heap of vocal exhaustion. George and Charley peeked out through the spindles on the landing. Louise tried to coax her brothers back to bed, but they held firmly to the spindles. Curious and sleepy, they watched their father sit cross-legged on the floor beside the dog, feeding it dinner scraps and talking in a low and calming voice. "There now, lassie. It's time for quiet."

"Is she alright, Father?" Louise's voice was barely above a whisper.

James tied the dog to the leg of the kitchen table. "There's nothing to see, children. Get back to bed." He followed them up the stairs and went to his room.

In the morning the Cameron household was wakened by the clamour of crashing dishes. Eight months pregnant with Charlotte, Jessie waddled into the kitchen, wide as she was tall. "Jesus, Mary 'n' Joseph, what a racket! The devil has upturned the table and goosed my best dishes. Out with ye! Get out now!" Jessie picked up the broom and chased the dog out the kitchen door and into the pantry. The dog, still tied to the leg of the table, went crashing out of the room, trying to escape a swift swat from Mrs. Cameron's broom, but was jerked back when she ran out of rope. She howled in despair. *Thump thump thump thump.* Mr. Cameron took the stairs two at a time to see the source of the early morning uproar.

"What's the racket? Settle down, Jessie, or you'll have the baby on the kitchen floor!"

Mrs. Cameron, out of breath and drained of patience, lowered herself. She started to pick up pieces of her broken breakfast dishes, but Louise and the twins quickly set to picking up all the shards.

"You'll not be bringing that she-devil into the house again! Do ye hear me, James Grant Cameron? If ye do, you'll find yourself sleeping out in the barn with it!"

George swept the kitchen floor so his mother could proceed with preparing breakfast. Charley was more hindrance than help. He struggled to keep the dustpan steady as George manoeuvred the broom. They took their seats at the table and sat in complete silence. They knew better than to ask their mother if they could play with the dog, though they were both itching to do so.

After James milked the cows and led them down to the creek, he came up to the house. "Jessie, I'm taking the dog down to the pasture. Maybe she'll do better doing what she's trained to do."

George tugged on his father's sleeve. "Can I come?"

"Suit yourself. Doesn't matter to me one way or the other."

"Put your boots on if you're going down to the pasture, George."

"Mind your mother, do ye hear?"

"Yes, Father." George pulled on his boots and trotted alongside his father and the dog.

"It'll take some time for her to get used to what's expected of her." But when James introduced the collie to the cows, the dog put her tail between her legs and hid behind George. She spooked the cows so badly with her plaintive howl that they headed into the woods on the perimeter of the Cameron property.

"Goddammit! Good for hee-haw." Mr. Cameron chased after the cows and tried to corral them back to the pasture. All the time in the world would not change this dog's mind. She hightailed it up to the house and didn't look back. Out of breath, George chased the black and white blur through the field. The dog curled up by the back step and waited for the boy. George collapsed. Sweat plastered his auburn curls to his brow and tiny beads of perspiration formed on his freckled nose.

"Not your cup of tea, eh, girl?" He put his delicate white hand on the dog's snout and stroked the soft fur. The dog pounded its tail in rapid beats and nudged George in anticipation of more affection. George pulled the dog close and hugged her around the neck. "I'll call you Patches."

"There will be no names for this boot. It's decided. I'm sending her back on the next train to Montreal." George looked up. His father stood so tall in his anger that he blocked the sun.

"Please give her one more chance. I know she can do better. I'll help her. Just give us one more week."

Mr. Cameron didn't answer. He went into the house. George could hear him quarrelling with his mother in the kitchen, so he walked to the drive shed. He turned and slapped his leg several times until Patches joined him. Oblivious to any short-comings on her part, the dog followed the boy to the well. George pulled the handle until water sput-tered and spat on the ground. He cupped his hands, splashed his face with cold water, then pumped the handle again. George held out his hands. His com-panion sniffed, hesitated, then lapped up the small boy's offering.

And as quickly as the memory had emerged, it was gone. Only a faint trace of Louise's features lin-gered. His older sister had died a year later, months after her wedding. George lifted the dog crate and placed it on the ground. He couldn't remember if his father got his five dollars back, but he did get rid of the dog, much to George's dismay. The memory of Patches stirred George's deep longing for something soft and beautiful in his life, for some genuine af-fection.

He began pulling on the trunk, but it wouldn't budge. He opened the lid to discover that it too housed more stuff. He started to unpack papers and smaller boxes from the trunk, setting them in an empty crate.

A faint rapping on the side of the shed startled him. He looked up to see a human triangle standing in the frame of daylight. A middle-aged Mi'kmaw woman stood with two small children clinging to her skirt: one Mi'kmaw and the smaller one Black.

George tossed a handful of newspapers on the dirt floor and approached the curious tableau. The woman was dressed in a red and black blanket fashioned into a jacket and belted at the waist with rope. The collar and calf-length hem were decorated with soft caramel-coloured leather trim. She wore a brightly beaded cap with a distinctive double curve. The woman held something up, but from the shadows of the drive shed it was nothing more than a silhouette against the light. In an exaggerated pantomime, she coaxed George to come outside where she presented him with a mauve braided basket with a snug-fitting lid, similar to the one Maggie used for her collection of cards. Another figure stepped into the rectangle of light. She approached George and spoke with the distinct and poetic precision of a stage actress.

"*Kwe'*. My name is Mabel, and this is my mother, Madeline Selome." George guessed that the young woman was about twenty years old. She pointed. "This is my sister, Margaret. Behind my mother, you will find our shy little Sophie. My sister and I take care of Sophie when her mother is at work in town." The child, who couldn't have been any older than three, buried her face in Madeline's skirt.

George knelt down to speak to the little girls, but they retreated further behind the woman and giggled at the handsome young man. He looked up at Mabel. "You speak English well."

"*O'wela'lin*. My mother would like to exchange her basket for some food."

"Wait here." He gestured for the woman to sit on the back step and turned to her daughter. "I will be right back." He disappeared through the back door to ask his mother for some food.

The two women and their young charges could hear Mrs. Cameron's disembodied voice travel through the house and out the window. They knew that tone. Mabel looked at Madeline and motioned to leave, but the older woman gently put her hand on her daughter's arm. They sat and waited for the young man to return. Madeline Selome knew that the Great Spirit created all people equal. She also knew that her baskets had value and was not ashamed to offer them in exchange for what her family needed.

"Tell her to come back another time. I am needing no baskets today."

"But Mother—"

"Another time, George. Now go on with ye. Can't ye see I'm busy with tea?"

George felt a sudden itch at the back of his neck and he scratched it violently. His mother's lack of interest in the woman's handiwork bothered him; however, having entered into many a quarrel with his mother, he knew when it was pointless to argue. Behind his mother's back, he grabbed two jars of preserves from the root cellar to spite her. He knew they were inadequate to compensate Madeline for her hours of fine weaving. He really wanted, no, he needed the basket. George had heard that, to the Mi'kmaq, sweetgrass is sacred – to him it was everything divine. It reminded him not only of Maggie's basket, but also of the precious moments tumbling in the grass with his beloved. On windy nights, they could smell the coumarin in the sweetgrass that danced and swayed in waves on the brackish shores between the saltwater of the Northumberland Strait and the fresh water of the East River.

When he opened the back door, he found Madeline and Mabel as he had left them, serene and patient in air heavy with the scent of his inordinate longing. Perhaps he wanted it too much. His mother's reading of Exodus resounded: "Thou shalt not covet." He wanted this basket to remind him of a homespun promise. In it, he would keep the letters he received from Maggie.

The preserves were not enough. Desperate now to have the basket, he gestured for Madeline to remain seated while he went back to rummage through the steamer trunk. There had to be something in this jumble of forgotten items – something worthy of exchange. He noticed a blue velvet pouch tucked into the corner of a smaller box of thread and wool. He pulled open the knotted cord and found a tarnished pair of antique sewing scissors. Hand-forged and stamped with pivoted blades and elaborately decorated handles, the scissors had come over from Scotland on the *Hector*. His great-grandmother Janet had given them to her daughter who in turn gave them to Jessie Cameron. Useful. Beautiful. Satisfied that this was a fair trade, he handed the woman the preserves and the velvet bag containing the scissors.

"*Wela'lin.*"

"My mother thanks you. She loves these berries. This fruit will be a delicious treat for us. *Wela'lin.*"

"Tell her that I will cherish this basket. It will remind me of home." He lifted the basket gently and inhaled its sweetness.

The woman smiled and nodded. She opened the velvet bag and pulled out the silver instrument. She looked pleased. She inserted her thumb and forefinger into the handles.

"My mother cuts thin strips of sweetgrass for her weaving. These scissors will be very helpful when she prepares the dried grasses for basket weaving."

The older woman pointed at the steamer trunk and said a few words in her native tongue.

"My mother says that you are going on a journey soon. A journey that brings you great excitement and great sadness."

"Yes … I am going to school in Boston." George spoke directly to the mother and then waited for Mabel to translate before he spoke again.

The woman frowned and pointed to the deep line that formed between her brows. She spoke to her daughter again in urgent tones, but Madeline hesitated. The mother waved her hand at her daughter and pointed to George.

"Pardon me for being forward, but she insists that I tell you this. She says you worry too much about things."

"This is true. I am leaving my loved ones."

"Your friend will be saddened when you leave."

"*Wantaqo'ti.*"

And with that final wish for peace, the women walked down the driveway and turned onto the road in the direction of the shanties by the river. Away from the public eye, the little girls danced in the dappled sunlight, weaving in and out like the fine braids of sweetgrass. Clockwise they circled with quick, shifting steps around Madeline so that their forward progress was slowed to the measured movement of ticking gears. The ribbons of their laughter trailed behind them, floating back to George like whispers. *How beautiful*, he thought, *to be free of expectation*.

As he stood on the porch and watched the parade of retreating figures, the full weight of his own departure became as tangible as the basket in his hands. It was a fair exchange – his secret defiance against his mother's indifference toward their sacred weaving, a ceremonial cutting of ties. Now, further down the road, the group – barely recognizable as human forms – drifted into the amber light. Their shapes blended with the curves of the distant land in an abstract configuration of pastel dots gliding imperceptibly into George's memory. They hovered for a brief moment on the horizon. The tall girl looked over her shoulder at the disappearing farmhouse. George blinked once and they were gone.

Chapter 8

Sunset Promises

In the amethyst of dusk, Maggie and George sat on the banks of the East River. She had agreed to meet with him alone one final time before he left for Boston. She had one sole purpose: she needed to let him down gently. If she was careful, she could make it seem like *he* made the decision to part.

"Our love will set like the end of this day." Though deeply moved by George's devotion to her, Maggie doubted his affection would last. She thought it best to make a clean break now, but George persisted in his devotion.

"Never."

"How can you be certain that time will not dim your affections?"

He kissed Maggie's hand playfully. "All you must know is that I love you wondrous well."

Maggie stroked his forehead and ran her fingers through his auburn hair. She forced a smile when she looked down at his beautiful grey-green eyes. Seven years stretched out before her like an eternity. She needed to convince him that this was goodbye.

"You must be excited for tomorrow."

"I wish that tomorrow would never come."

"I feel so old, George. When we meet again I will be twenty-five. Perhaps you love me now, but time has a way of—"

"Before those seven years are up, I intend to return and make you my bride. You say that you are older…" He paused for a minute to gather the threads of his argument. "I say to you then, look at Elizabeth Barrett Browning. She was six years Robert's elder. She doubted their union just as you do now, I assure you. Poets do not live in the ordinary world. We dwell in a place where time has no meaning."

"George, we must be realistic."

He looked into her violet eyes, two mysterious gems fringed by dark lashes. She pulled the pins and ribbon that tied her hair back, and a shower of summer gold fell loose on either side of her troubled face. He needed to prove to her that she was his only thought. His only love. He turned to poetry.

"Your name with mine entwined as queen and king,
Lords of the earth, of love."

There was urgency in his movements that evening. Maggie could sense it. In two days she would wave goodbye to George at Pictou Station. Goodbye to her internal struggle. She would close this chapter. She would no longer hear that voice penetrate her whenever he spoke, the words that had kept her buoyant on a sea of uncertainty over these past few months. Then George whispered in her ear and she began to melt.

"Mine own! Mine own, my beauty, mine to bless;
To keep and have and hold,
To love, till love itself grow old,
And the dark scythe-fiend's ruthlessness
Have put the grey above the gold;
Nay, even in death my love alone,
Still loved, still lovely, still 'mine own!'"

The last of her resolve melted. Maggie was lost in George's words and held captive by a world separate from her own life. Again he pulled her into the safety of the shadows. In the late afternoon darkness of the woods they lay in an awkward embrace, listening to the steady rhythm of their breathing. It was a sweet, strange sound. Two lives mingling with each breath. He touched her and all was lost. They were two innocents on the first step of a long ascending stair. Climbing further and further together until at the very height of the stair he collapsed with divine exhaustion.

"Your love is all."

That night George could not stop smiling. His heart took flight. He replayed the sensory tune of their embrace over and over again like a music box in his mind. He whistled incessantly until Izzie asked, "What's wrong with you?" At dinner George ate two large helpings of his mother's steak and kidney pie and a second helping of pudding. Satiated, he went to his bed and read the poetry of E.B.B. until he could no longer keep his eyes open.

Your love is all.

On the other side of town, Maggie had snuck in the back door of the house unnoticed and ascended the stairs reserved for the servants. She removed her soiled garments, washed herself in the water closet then walked straight to her room and shut the door. Her temples pounded. Startled by knocking, Maggie raised her head to hear her sister's muffled voice on the other side of the door.

"Maggie? Mum sent me up. Dinner is ready. We're waiting for you. Open the door."

"Go away, Gertie. Tell Mother I am not well."

A crippling headache blinded her for the rest of the evening. She woke the following morning with the same excruciating pain. The next day when George and Charley called upon the McGregors, Gertie came to the door to tell them that her sister was confined to her bed.

Maggie listened at the top of the stairs. No one could see her in this state. They would know for certain that she was now different, a fallen woman caught by a boy of fourteen. When they left, she returned to her bed. In the silence of her own room, without the hypnotic spell of George's poetry, she could think clearly. The truth of her depraved actions became a shout louder than she could stand. The complexity of her moral choices weighed heavily on her soul. When she looked in the mirror, a wild gypsy stared back at her. She was a reflection of a wandering soul. How could she have let this happen?

"Maggie? George and Charley Cameron are leaving tomorrow. Don't you want to say goodbye?"

Pretending disinterest, Maggie casually told her mother that they really weren't that close.

Chapter 9 – August 1869

Leaving New Glasgow

When Maggie did not come to the station, George became frantic with worry. What had he done wrong? He had merely shown his love for the one person in this world who understood him. Maggie was his only. There would never be another.

Gertie McGregor appeared and hand-delivered a letter to George. Everyone at the train station assumed that love had blossomed between Gertie and George. It was no secret that Gertie was infatuated with the handsome Cameron boy. After all, George had walked Gertie home each day after school this past spring and visited at the McGregor place for an hour afterwards. And they had spent the entire summer in each other's company. "What a lovely match," they would say.

"Maggie asked me to give you this." Gertie, though jealous of the time George devoted to her older sister, accepted the fact that Maggie was a better match. George's intelligence intimidated her; besides he was a terribly moody boy who preferred study to play. She kissed him on the cheek and whispered in his ear, "That's from Maggie too." They both blushed under the watchful eye of the townspeople.

"How adorable!"

"What a lovely young couple," his Aunt Margaret gushed.

"Don't forget your sweetheart, Georgie." Everyone let out a collective sigh for the parting of these two steadfast companions.

George slipped the letter into his jacket pocket. He whispered in Gertie's ear, "Tell your sister that I love her wondrous well."

Not being able to say goodbye is worse than the goodbye itself. As George and Charley pulled out of Pictou Station with their mother, the Cameron cousins and a few of Charley's friends raced along the track until the train picked up speed and gradually disappeared into the distance. Jessie Cameron sat across from her boys. This was the hardest part of all for George, hiding his profound despair from his mother. Of course Charley wept openly; he was not as keen on academic glory as George.

Mrs. Cameron did not say a word. She knew her younger son would cry himself out and eventually get distracted by the adventure ahead. George was another matter. She had figured out that the supposed link between Gertie and George was nothing but a ruse designed to throw the town off the scent of his infatuation with the elder McGregor daughter. She witnessed it grow with each of their serious conversations about his poetry. She recognized the look of love in her son's eyes as he followed Margaret's every movement. And she knew that smile that passed between them was more than courtesy. She felt more confident in her decision to leave New Glasgow. George did not need the distraction. George tried to channel his sorrow through Charley's tears and keep an outward calm, but the suppression of his unhappiness built up in his lungs until they ached. He could feel his airway constricting as he gasped for air. It was as if he was denying himself life, for in those moments away from Maggie, there was no life.

Sensing her son was on the brink of an attack, Mrs. Cameron shooed Charley out of the seat beside George.

"I know you're down, son. It's a hard thing for ye boys to leave the only home ye have ever known and move to a strange town, but I assure ye, this pain will ease with time. Now, George. You'll need to breathe the way Grandmother Sutherland taught ye. Lord knows she had to help my father through many a spell." She took a bottle from her bag, uncorked it and handed it to George. "Drink this and it will calm your nerves. Ye will need your rest, George. Ye have examinations to write."

George grabbed the bottle from his mother's hands and took three large gulps of the bitter-tasting liquid. It did not take long for the narcotic to take effect. It seized his senses. The image of Maggie became an ethereal wisp of golden light fading into darkness.

When George finally regained consciousness, they were in Halifax. It was a beehive of activity. He felt jostled by the bustle of people on the platform and grabbed his mother's hand so they wouldn't get separated. They had a one-night stopover in Halifax before the *Alahambra* departed for Suffolk Port outside of Boston. Two people in the sea of faces waved frantically to catch their attention. Reverend Grant and his wife embraced the three familiar travellers and guided them to a quiet spot. "I'll instruct the men to forward your trunks to the Halifax port for tomorrow's boarding. Meanwhile, you must join us. There is plenty of room at the manse for all of you."

"We thank ye kindly for your generosity, Reverend Grant." Jessie Cameron turned to the reverend's wife, whom she had known most of her life. "It is so good to see you up and about, Jessie. I heard ye were feeling poorly, but ye have a fresh glow in your cheeks this evening. And Reverend Grant, how is the congregation at St. Matthew's?"

"Growing every Sunday."

Jessie Grant turned to the two boys. "You must be hungry after your trip."

"Yes, ma'am."

After a hearty dinner, George excused himself from the table and went to the privacy of his room. He pulled the letter from his jacket. He followed the delicate filigree of her hand and inhaled the scent of lavender fields. He turned up the lantern in his room and opened the letter.

August 25, 1869

My dearest G,

I realize that I have been distant of late, but I am drowning in dry tears of my own making. I shall do my best to hold the memories of our time together in my heart and promise to ease our time apart with a steady flow of letters from port to port. From heart to heart. Please continue to share your work with me for every word is committed to my very soul and when I read your poetry aloud, I am with you. Mind and body. I have enclosed a photograph for you to remember my face when the memory of me gets jostled with all the new faces you are sure to meet. I shall miss you more than words can possibly tell, so I shall close this letter with the hope that time will pass quickly until we meet again.

Forever Yours,

M –

These simple words buoyed his sinking spirit and bolstered his determination to return to New Glasgow a man of distinction. He vowed to make her his bride. The gentle hand that penned this letter gave him the courage to make it so.

Part Two

Boston

1869–1882

Chapter 10

Cicero and Ginger Nuts

Stalwart and proud, Headmaster Gardner stood at the entrance of the Boston Latin School on Bedford Street to greet the class of 1869. His presence was a sober reminder that once a boy passed this threshold he belonged solely to Gardner. The headmaster shook each young man's trembling hand firmly as the new students filed into the building. It was under this man's guidance that George Cameron would grow into a scholar and a gentleman. It was Gardner who would shape the course of George's days for the next three years. It was Gardner who laid out the curriculum and upheld the standards of distinction expected by parents. And it was his hand alone that flogged wayward boys who preferred to dwell in mediocrity.

School began promptly at seven o'clock. George sat stock straight in his assigned seat in the second row to await further instruction. No one dared to exhale until Dr. Moses Merrill made his way to the polished wooden lectern at the front of the room.

The instructor opened his Latin book and began to conjugate verbs. He paused and there was a punishing silence.

"*Num negare audes*?" Merrill repeated the present and past of the verb while the boys scrambled with their books and flipped pages to locate the first lesson. This time when Merrill paused, the boys filled the gap with tentative voices. "*Sum, es, est sumus, estis, sunt. Ero, eris, erit, erimus, eritis, erunt.*" This mechanical chant bored George; he had learned his irregular verbs two years earlier. He scanned the room to measure himself against his peers.

Merrill spotted a boy in the second row mouthing the chorus of verbs. He hit the lectern with four taps in rapid succession. There was an awkward suspension of sound again when Merrill closed the Latin primer and opened Cicero.

"*Historia magistra vitae et testis temporum.*" Dr. Merrill paused and traced his finger down the register of new students until he rested on the alleged culprit. "Master Cameron. Translate."

All eyes were upon him. George cleared his throat. Without hesitation and quite certain of Cicero's speech, he said, "History is the teacher and witness of the times." He felt his ears burn under the scrutiny of his classmates. He had translated lines of Cicero by heart when he was twelve and recited them with eloquence. He was certain that his translation would leave the class in awe of his brilliance. As soon as George finished, Merrill moved on. "*Mea mihi conscientia pluris est quam omnicem sermo.* Master Edmunds. Translate."

A striking young man stood up in the first row. George found his profile to be reminiscent of ancient

Roman coins. He was well proportioned and George could see the ripple and bulge of his muscular frame under his crisp white shirt. The young man repeated the Latin phrase, and in a clear, deep voice offered his translation. "Sir, 'My conscience is more important to me than any speech.'" He glanced at George with a smug expression and sat down. While George's eidetic memory had astounded his teachers back home in New Glasgow, here at the Boston Latin School such rigour was commonplace and impressed no one. George flushed crimson when he realized his very public gaffe in etiquette. His failure to stand during his recitation sent him reeling in another wave of doubt.

At eleven o'clock Merrill escorted the boys to the dining hall where Headmaster Gardner addressed the fresh faces of fall. In Pictou County George and Charley were in the same schoolhouse; now Charley joined boys his age in junior class and George sat among the seniors in the back row of the hall. Gardner, dressed in long black robes, took his place at the front of the hall for prayer. The giant bat was flanked on the right by a serene marble statue, a gift from the school's graduates in memory of those sons of Boston who had made the ultimate sacrifice in the war. In one hand, the radiant woman held a shield, and in the other a laurel crown dangled from her slender fingertips. To Gardner's left the gallery of previous headmasters stared down at the new class with stern disapproval, a look that made even the pious among them squirm with moral inadequacy.

Head bowed and eyes cast downward, George listened to the prayer rapt with solemn admiration for the deep voice that reverberated within the rich oak walls. Mingled with George's sense of awe lurked that gnawing fear. Forever a tug of war within. *Do I belong? Am I worthy?* Fear of failure has a way of pushing some young men to achieve greatness while this very apprehension has a way of paralyzing others under the weight of expectation. George wiggled his toes in his new leather shoes to assure himself that he was not frozen. He took a deep breath to crack the thin layer of ice that spread across his chest.

Dismissed from lunch, the boys revelled in their freedom outside in the yard. In his first few weeks at the school, George joined the boys in the schoolyard, enacting mock battles while Charley shot ring taw in the dust with the younger boys. Charley steadily rose in popularity during the lunch recess, but his older brother soon withdrew into a solitary world of study and poetic contemplation within the confines of the Dixwell Library.

The library's walls were lined with well-worn volumes of George's favourite poets and historians, all housed behind glass on rows of wooden bookshelves, all waiting for him. The French windows rose from these cases to the ceiling, allowing a certain slant of light to spill onto the checkered floor beneath his feet. At times George thought the boys in the library looked like chess pieces as they sat in straight-backed chairs, pawns of parental expectation.

Within these walls, he indulged in his passion – writing. Most days it was a scrap of thought stirred by his daily walk past the wharves on the Charles River, or it was a sudden spark inspired by the great minds he studied in class. Sometimes he could not wait to retreat to his private sanctuary to read the letters he hid from his family – the letters from Maggie.

One lunch hour partway into the term, George looked out the window at Edmunds, Crittington and the rest of the senior students who had organized a game of bandy in the far corner of the field. *Boys.* He returned to his table and opened his journal to write.

> I know not if it be her eyes,
> Outshining all the stars that rise
> With their deep splendour calm and true,
> That makes me love her as I do:
> The only thing that I can tell
> Is that I love her wondrous well!

When Maggie neglected to respond promptly to his letters of effusive affection, he dragged his younger brother with him to share his sombre mood in his sanctuary. Charley agreed to go to the library, but he refused to join George in his melancholy mood.

"Come look, George."

George turned in his chair to see Charley on tiptoe peering through the glass cases in the middle of the room. He was examining the scale models of the Parthenon and the Coliseum.

"I shall visit both of these places some day and poke about the *real* ruins. Gladiators fought to the death in there, George." Charley turned his thumb down in a grand display of power over imaginary men. "I am positively bored to bits. Let's enjoy the day." But George refused – again. Despite Charley's frequent implorations to join him on the playing field, the elder brother favoured the solitude of his little corner of the library to the company of the other boys.

"All you do is study."

"Isn't that why we moved here, Charley?"

"Very well then. Suit yourself." His brother's preference for dusty books over raucous laughter and rough play was beyond Charley's comprehension and patience. He stopped inviting George and left him to the fortress of books that he erected to wall himself in.

In the winter months, George and Charley trudged through banks of snow each morning from Franklin Street where their brother-in-law, Colonel McLelland Moore, dropped them off on his way to work at the publishing house. Many of their classmates, who came from the opposite direction on the hill, brought their sleds to school.

"Can we get a sled?"

"Charley, it is perfectly flat from here to the bridge. I'll end up pulling you most of the way."

"We could take turns!"

George did not answer and the matter was dropped, but this didn't mean that George did not *want* a sled. On the contrary; he did very much. He remembered the exhilaration he felt when he and Charley were children sledding down Mountain Road. It was just that a sled was an impractical expense at this time and a distraction.

The other boys coasted down Beacon Street to School Street and then from Tremont to Bedford. Whizzing down Tremont, they shouted the school's motto, "*Sumus Primi!*" much to the ire of early morning employees of the Parker Hotel who were on their way to work on School Street.

One morning, the reckless boys blew frozen kisses at the chambermaids as they flew down Tremont, dodging pedestrians as they went. After a near miss, the laundress shook her fist at the boys. "I'll tell yer Master, you little buggers!"

The next day, the boys from Beacon Hill ran into a nasty surprise. The merchants had got together and spread ashes on their sled path to discourage any further spectacle. When the lads arrived at the school carrying their blackened sleds and trudging in yellow snow on their soot-covered boots, the headmaster promptly sent them home. The following morning various alumni of the Latin school, all of notable standing in Boston, arrived at Gardner's office before the morning bell to rectify the situation.

"If it was a tradition accepted by Boston merchants when the likes of Hancock and Franklin made the celebrated sled ride to school, then it is – by God and by country – perfectly acceptable for our sons and nephews to do the same!" That was all that was said. No more ashes were spread on the freshly fallen snow on Tremont, and not a single one of the mischief-makers received the dreaded misdemeanour blot on his record.

George and Charley watched the boys careen down the hill and stop at Gilbert's Grocery. The proprietor spoiled these young rascals with free ginger nuts and soda pop. He laughed delightedly when they called him Uncle John like their fathers had done before them. As a matter of fact, this common merchant was so respected by Boston's finest, that when the City, in its wisdom, desired to widen the streets, Gilbert was paid to move his establishment back. The required move of five yards from the designated road was achieved by rolling the brick structure incrementally on cannon balls. He was not a great man, nor was he a learned man, but he was liked. He was universally well liked.

George, however, never felt at ease taking Gilbert's ginger nuts. He would smile politely and give the grocer the obligatory nod when he passed the store. One afternoon, Gilbert stopped George and his brother on their way home. Charley eagerly accepted the nuts and sat on the concrete stoop munching away.

"Why don't you take the ginger nuts like your brother here, eh?" Playfully he took Charley's cap and tousled the boy's curly hair.

"Oh, I couldn't possibly."

"What? You don't like 'em?"

"It's not that, sir. I like them well enough. It's just I don't want to spoil my dinner." George gave Charley a reprimanding look. "My sister Christina would have a fit. I shall never hear the end of it." George tailored this lie to suit the time of day. "Thank you very much for the offer, Mr. Gilbert, but I had a substantial breakfast." Or, "My stomach is unsettled after lunch, sir." He kept this up until Uncle John stopped asking. Even though he was mildly insulted by the boy's indifference to his generosity, he didn't say a word to George about it. He told his wife that he had never met a boy who wouldn't eat a handful of ginger nuts. He thought it odd.

The truth of the matter would have puzzled Gilbert even more, for George wanted nothing more than to accept the proffered treat. He often imagined what they would taste like and asked Charlie to describe them for him. How he wanted to taste just one. He never did. It was almost as if George denied himself this indulgence to test the strength of his willpower. The time at the Boston Latin School was a trial to determine his strength against the temptation of something sweeter.

His repressed desire for Maggie was not wholly exorcised by his studies. It was kept in constant check until he built his walls, book by book, around him. Then and only then would he retrieve her photograph and the delicately scented pages from Pictou County. They smelled like home, and he inhaled the perfume of sweetgrass deeply. Some of the pages were so dog-eared that the worn words were actually illegible, and the pages wrinkled like limp cloth. He read them over and over, weighing each word and wondering what subtext lurked under her clever phrases.

George took a freshly printed postcard from his jacket. The pen and ink sketch of Boston Latin School was one of five Gardner handed out to every boy, the headmaster's way of spreading the good news of the school's success. George took out his pen and dipped the nib in the inkwell. He paused and searched for the right words. He squeezed his eyes shut. The message had to be cryptic since many eyes would read the card before it was delivered into the delicate hand of his beloved. He opened his eyes and wrote: *You will be pleased to know that I am burning the midnight oil.* Surely she would register the contrast to G.S.'s lowing flame? It was the perfect symbol of his undying love for her disguised in the half-truth of study.

George was giddy beyond recognition when he received letters from Maggie, in which she poured out words of affection and longing. Then there were the endless weeks when no letter came at all. During these lulls in correspondence, George was held in a heightened state of anguish. In these moments, he wrote page upon page of passionate poetry with such intensity that the librarian cautioned him to calm down.

> Yes, love of mine, and fair as any fair
> Song of my soul, and soul of all this song!
> I will forgive thee, though thou makest bare
> And bleak my life: yea, by thy glorious hair
> And violet eyes, I will forgive the wrong.

"Master Cameron. You will burn yourself out with such study. Some fresh air will do you good."

Startled by this unsolicited advice, George peered over his copy of *The Iliad* and forced a congenial smile. "I appreciate your concern. With all due respect, sir, I must take this time to study, for I have chores to do in the evening hours. It is more a matter of necessity than desire." Of course this was a lie. His mother had given Christina strict instructions to free the boys from any unnecessary work while they prepared for their future professions. School was their only focus. She had spared no expense to send them to Boston, and she expected a handsome return in her later years when she could boast of her sons' achievements.

"I see. I am sorry that you are burdened with work at such a critical time in your young academic career. I know full well the demands of the school, and any additional commitment could cause mental strain. Nothing need be said, young man. Carry on."

When the scholar returned to his postcard, he was hit by a sudden inspiration. Perhaps Maggie needed some proof of his affection. Perhaps this explained her sudden silence. He had denied himself the pleasure of the ginger nuts – did that not confirm his fortitude against any other temptation? He would write and tell her of this show of strength. No, no. That would be childish. A spoken vow in a rushed farewell beside the East River – was it enough? He fidgeted as he thought of the juvenile romantic gesture of his promise ring. After all, two strands of woven hair could easily unravel or be lost. He knew in his heart that his word was his bond, but time and distance may have weakened her resolve. She may doubt his fidelity. He traced the initials *G.S.* over and over until the letters formed an angry blot of ink on the page. Of course he could not insult her by asking. He did not want to be perceived as a jealous lover. He needed a lasting symbol stronger than a braid of intertwined hair to secure her affection. A ring.

It was this realization that set in motion George's next mission. He would transform his lie to the librarian into a truth. He would take on a job to save up for the purchase. If he combined his earnings with his allowance, he would have enough to present Maggie with a real ring. He would return to New Glasgow in three years' time, before he commenced his law studies. It was settled. He would speak to his sister's husband when he got home that very evening. Surely McLelland would know of something – anything – he could do at the printing house to earn the money.

He pasted a three-cent stamp in the corner of the postcard, gathered his books and set off to the postal box on the corner.

Chapter 11

The Ring

George was certain Colonel Moore would help. He resolved that on the way home he would pull him aside and ask. Charley mustn't hear the conversation, or he would let it slip at dinner. Charley couldn't keep secrets very well. All George had to do was to assure McLelland that he would keep up with his studies. No one would be the wiser. George was confident that he could pull it off. His mother need never know. George also knew that asking his brother-in-law to keep a secret from his wife put Colonel Moore in an awkward position. He regretted that, but if he wanted to earn enough money to buy a ring and secure his future with Maggie, he had to ask for McLelland's assistance.

George and Charley had grown to love living with their sister and her husband. There was a humble greatness about Colonel Moore. McLelland and the boys rose each day before the sun, scraped together a breakfast of sorts and headed across the bridge together to catch the horse-drawn trolley car into the inner city. Colonel Moore always parted with a warm smile and a formal salute at Devonshire and Franklin where he left the boys to make the rest of their journey on foot. From there McLelland disappeared down the street to work a ten-hour day at J.H. Bufford's Print Publishing House. In the early days when the boys missed their parents and sisters in New Glasgow, this daily routine with the Colonel gave George and Charley a certain sense of comfort and security.

There was one morning in particular when George discovered the true measure of the man he called his brother-in-law. On the verge of sleep, with heavy lids and nodding head, George listened to Charley and McLelland chat during their daily commute. George leaned against the trolley cart and tried to sleep.

When he was twenty-four, McLelland Moore had served with the 28th Regiment Massachusetts as Colonel, a fact that only served to fuel Charley's imagination and curiosity. At ten years of age, Charley was forever pestering McLelland to share stories from his time in the Civil War. Reluctant to share the horrors of this part of his life with anyone let alone with his wife Christina, McLelland would dismiss his service with quick and humble excuses. "No one in their right mind wants to hear my stories because mostly they are all about waiting, smacking mosquitoes under the hot sun and then waiting some more."

But on this chilly late October morning, in part to satisfy Charley's incessant pestering for all things related to war and in part to exorcise an inner demon, McLelland let his guard down. "There was this one lad by the name of Johnny MacDonald who reminded me a lot of George. He was a Canadian farm boy, originally from your neck of the woods. When I met Johnny, he wasn't much older than your brother sleeping there. The army tends to turn a blind eye to young men when they are eager and strong, so this boy made it into my regiment. I took to the boy right away. He had this funny way about him that eased the tension a bit. I tell you, Christina woulda loved him. You know how much your sister likes to laugh.

"Well, as most boys do, he wanted nothing more than to prove himself a man, but I could tell he was homesick. Mind you, that's nothing you mention aloud to your men even if they were really boys. Feeling vulnerable is a real private thing, Charley. You got to respect that, do you hear? Anyway, he spent most of his down time writing letters to his sweetie and to his family about the day-to-day life at the camp. We were held up just outside Secessionville for a couple of sweltering days in June of '62. As time dragged on, I think he came to realize that he was in way over his head. He got scared. The sounds of battle are deafening, but when the shelling finally stops, the cries of the dying are far worse. By the time the shelling started the next day, Johnny was all jittery and the like – not a good state to carry a gun, you see? He told me one day that he'd never killed anyone. Oh, he had seen death on the farm, but that's far different than taking the life of someone you know has a family waiting for them back home. He asked me what it was like and how to do it without feeling bad for the one you killed. I told him when the time came he'd know. He'd feel it 'cause it would be kill or be killed, as they say. I tried to assure him that when the time came he'd give a good account of himself."

"What happened to him?"

McLelland's voice became low and respectful. "He died the next day, Charley."

"Fighting? And did he give a good account of himself?"

"He gave as good account as any of them. I doubted he could carry a gun, so I gave him the honour of carrying the colours."

"You mean the flag, right? What then?"

"I think you're too young to hear about that. Let's just say he died quietly on James Island just after sunrise. That's a nice way to go, with the colours all soft and pretty."

"Did he say anything? I mean, did you talk before he...."

"He asked me to write his family when I had the chance and tell them he loved them very much, and I did." McLelland shook his head. "The boy died carrying the colours of a country that wasn't even his."

Under the lids of feigned sleep, George watched his younger brother console the Colonel. Charley patted the man on the back softly, and they sat in silence the rest of the way to Franklin Street. George wondered if he would give a good account of himself in his lifetime. He wanted so desperately to be heard. To be remembered in a heroic light.

Charley touched George on the shoulder and gave him a gentle poke. "Hey, George," he said quietly. "It's time to wake up."

George pretended to wake and smiled at his brother. Neither of the boys asked McLelland about the war again.

Almost three years later, George stood looking in the front window of Shreve, Crump and Low. Tucked among their display of engagement rings, a sign written in gold cursive read: "She will always say yes." George looked at his reflection in the store window. He had grown since he left New Glasgow. It was more than his height. He was fuller in face and broader across the shoulders, but it would be perceived as a boast to write to one's beloved of such physical changes. No. She had to see and touch him in the flesh. How he longed for Maggie's embrace.

Working three nights a week at the printing house with Colonel Moore, George had managed to save enough money to make the greatest purchase of his young life. He had visited Shreve, Crump and Low every week with his meagre earnings in hand. When George stepped into the shop, Shreve greeted him with good cheer.

"Georgie boy! Come to make another payment?"

"Another month's allowance and a little extra too."

"You know, Georgie, when you first came in the shop three years ago, I'll be honest, I had my doubts. We see many a young man in our business."

"None, I assure you, as determined as I."

"She must be something special."

"May I see it again?'

Shreve nodded and retreated behind a red velvet curtain. While he was in the back, Crump came out. Crump was the eldest of the three partners. A jeweller's loupe dangled from the chain around his neck. It was he who set the gemstones and inscribed the bands with a steady hand. "Master Cameron," he said. "It is almost yours. Shall we inscribe it for you?"

"Yes. No wait, not yet. I have to compose the exact words."

"Well, not too many, eh, George? I know you're a poet, but there's only so many characters I can fit on the inside of the band."

Shreve came out with a blue velvet box. He opened it with a flourish to show the young man. It was an 18 karat gold band adorned by a single small ruby surrounded by diamonds. The clerk assured him that the setting was quite fashionable in London and Paris. Crump added that anyone "in the know" would recognize George's choice as *de rigueur*. The small clusters of diamonds formed two perfect filigree constellations on either side of the central setting. *Yes*, thought George, *this is the one*. He bathed the suffering and sacrifice over the long months of restraint in a heroic light.

"She's a lucky girl!"

"Quite the contrary, Shreve. It is I who is lucky."

Crump examined the gemstone with his loupe. "I gather by your plastered grin that you are confident that her answer will be yes. When are you going to give it to her?"

"I enter Boston School of Law in the fall, so I plan to go home this summer and bring my fiancée back to Boston."

Low, who had remained silent to this point, chimed in. He rose from his stool behind the counter. "This summer? Another four months from now? That's a long time to wait and a fair way to travel."

"Time and distance are love's true test." George handed the box back to Shreve. "Two more payments, my fine fellows. Keep her safe for me."

Over the years George had also saved his modest allowance. Unlike the other boys at the Boston Latin School, he did not spend his allowance on new clothes or shoes. He continued to wear the jacket his mother had bought him the fall they left Halifax. He sported it even though it was long out of fashion and the shoulders could no longer accommodate the breadth of his frame as he grew into manhood. Instead of buying new books in the fall, he borrowed the volumes from his peers and read in the library during his lunch break. He went without many things in those years away from New Glasgow, in those interminable hours away from Maggie.

He took secret pleasure knowing that Maggie sat at her writing desk in her room composing sentences for his enjoyment. At first these thoughts of Maggie's fidelity dissolved the time and distance between them. But as time went by George grew anxious. With the ring in his hand, he had a renewed sense of purpose. A rekindled certainty that she would be his.

On the day he made his final payment, he celebrated silently. No one could know about the ring, not even Charley. Crump told Shreve to wrap up the purchase. The clerk put the blue velvet box in a slightly larger cardboard one and gave it to George. George did not engrave the ring for Maggie. He didn't have the chance.

Chapter 12 – Spring 1872

A Mother's Visit

Charley climbed the stairs to the bedroom he
shared with his brother. He threw a pile of letters on the dresser. "Hey there, Georgie." His brother
greeted him with the usual indifference of siblings
who have shared close quarters for too long. He
grunted and continued to study. Charley threw a
sock at him to get his attention. "There's another letter here for you from home. By the smell of it, I'm
sure it's from your sweetie."

"Where?"

Charley pointed to the dresser. "There's one
from Mother too, if you're interested." He laughed,
but George took no notice. He was desperate to read
Maggie's letter. The intervals between their correspondence had grown greater and greater until he
scarcely heard from her at all. Charley was talking to
him, but he heard nothing. Instead he retreated to his
bed and opened the letter.

My dearest George,

I have accepted Mr. Donald McQuarrie's proposal of marriage. I share this news with you in advance of telling our family and friends out of the sincere respect and love I hold for you. I want to tell you lest you are tortured by broken gossip or vicious rumour. The decision to marry Donald was not an easy one. For months I weighed his offer with a heavy heart, knowing that my choice may break yours. I have been suspended in an unnatural state of uncertainty. Our difference in age grows greater as each season passes. I cannot sleep, for my fearful imaginings have made me ill. Each night I have a dream of recurring horror. I see myself. I am an old woman sitting on a bench at Pictou Station, waiting for a train. I wait and wait and wait, but the train never comes. People point at me and whisper "Spinster." George, I am getting older and want to have children. I could wait no longer. I wish you the best in your academic pursuits in Boston. You are a tender soul, and I am certain that you will love again.

With all my love and respect,

M –.

George gasped for air. *Donald McQuarrie? What happened to Sterling?* He repeated again: *McQuarrie. The carpenter from McKenzie's shipyard?* And then aloud, "He is not worthy of her!" He ripped the letter into pieces.

"What is it? Breathe, George. Remember, slowly in. Look at me, George. George?"

"It's Maggie. She's accepted Donald McQuarrie's marriage proposal."

"Who is Donald McQuarrie? Why do you care?"

"We were engaged."

"What?"

Charley picked up the pieces of the discarded letter and read the torn scraps of paper: "… in advance of telling our family and friends out of the sincere respect and love I hold … cannot sleep … fearful imaginings … certain you will love again."

Charley looked up at George who was now inconsolable. Gutted by a grief greater than words could convey, George wept. Charley tried to reach his brother, but he drifted further and further away from him. "I didn't know. I mean, I thought you and Gertie…." George grabbed his brother viciously by his shoulders and looked him in the eyes with such a wild desperation that Charley pulled away in fear.

"No one must know. Promise me, Charley. For once, Charley, can you keep a damn secret?" George paced back and forth in the small room. "Leave me alone. Get out! I need to be alone."

"But George, you shouldn't be."

"Get out!"

When Charley shut the door and descended the stairs, George opened the small blue velvet box that was hidden under the mattress. *Sincere respect?* He snapped the box shut. He crossed the room, opened his father's steamer trunk and buried the ring under his old clothes. The clothes from childhood. The clothes that no longer fit him. His immediate reaction was to write her a letter to ask if there was some mistake. But no words came to mind. Maggie was suddenly dead to him.

In the days that followed, on more than one drunken night, George contemplated throwing the ruby ring into the Charles River. Another letter from Maggie arrived in the interim; still he had not found the words to write her back. But the poetry poured out now. Angry words, vicious phrases, short bursts of venom.

> Could I but be the thing thou art,
> Or rather that thou seem'st to be,
> A thing of dull or deadened heart
> I deem it might be well for me.
> Could I, as thou hast done, forget
> The pleasure and the promise flown,
> I should not be as I am yet,
> A creature desolate and lone.

Try as he might, Charley could not move his brother to talk to him. He listened helplessly as George cried at night. Something was terribly wrong and George's family was desperate to remedy the situation. McLelland and Christina were nervous. After all, Jessie had entrusted them to guide and shelter her boys. Perhaps this mood would pass. Of course, they knew nothing of George's secret engagement. At first they suspected that it was the rigour of his studies that weighed on his spirit. The Colonel confessed that he had secretly given George extra work at the printing house. He regretted keeping secrets from Christina, but George was adamant that he could handle the extra hours. And based on his grades, he seemed to be keeping his end of the bargain.

After weeks of George's distracted behaviour Colonel Moore called Charley to his study. "Charley, are you certain you know nothing of why your brother shuts himself up in his room?"

"I wish I knew. He rarely talks to me anymore."

Colonel Moore eyed Charley carefully. He was certain that his young brother-in-law knew something. "He hasn't been to school in weeks. His final exams are coming up. He quit working at the publishing house. No word. He just stopped showing up."

Charley squirmed under his brother-in-law's inquisition. He had promised George to keep the nights of private drinking quiet.

"It might – and I don't know for sure – but it might have something to do with a girl."

Christina joined her husband's inquisition. "The letters from the School of Law are all unopened. This is not like your brother. I must write Mother."

"I wouldn't do that, Tina. He'll be fine."

"Really, Charley? He is drinking tonics every night until he passes out. You need not confirm or deny it. I see the empty bottles in the trash. It's been weeks. McLelland, I told you working at the publishing house was too much for him."

"Christina," George insisted. "He was determined, said he needed the money."

"But Mother pays for everything."

"Listen. I didn't think. I mean, he's been fine for the past three years. Maybe there's something to this girl business."

Christina was unconvinced. "He's never even mentioned anyone. Charley?"

Charley shook his head. "Please don't ask. I promised."

"I should call Putnam," offered McLelland.

"He'll just prescribe more tonics," said Christina. "George doesn't need to sleep. He needs to get out of bed. I will write Mother."

McLelland dreaded the aftermath of the inevitable. He and Christina telegraphed the Camerons by Western Union, and within the week, they arrived in Boston to get their son back on his feet.

The moment Jessie saw her son, she knew the cause of his distemper. She had long believed his affections for Margaret McGregor were more than a passing crush. She was pleased when she heard that the charming Mr. McQuarrie from the shipyard had proposed to the daughter of their dear friend Mrs. McGregor.

As the chief architect behind the grand design to relocate George to Boston, Jessie saw a crack in the foundation she had laboured so long to construct. She took this setback as a small personal defeat and felt determined to rectify the matter immediately. After all, the cost to set her plan in motion must be recouped somehow. It was for the future of the family that she took it upon herself to set things right.

Mrs. Cameron eyed her son carefully. He was pallid and perspiring at the temples; his eyes were anxious. Gasping for breath, his shoulders heaved.

"James, do you have a cigar on ye? Light one up so we can get some smoke into his lungs."

Grandfather Sutherland had sworn by cigarettes laced with deadly nightshade, yet James felt it was country hokum. He lit his cigar, took a few deep puffs then reluctantly handed it to over to his wife.

"I know ye have your doubts, but I assure ye, Grandfather Sutherland swore by the cure. He should know; he suffered his whole life." Mrs. Cameron sat her son on a hard wooden chair. "Lean to the future, son." She placed her hands below the ribcage, over the small of his back. "Now breathe slowly in through your nose, down to my hands. Keep your shoulders forward. Take the smoke into your lungs. Just breathe in slowly down the length of my hands. Now breathe out slowly."

For all of her bluster and vanity, Mrs. Cameron knew how to help George. She had watched her own mother do the same with her father when he suffered asthma attacks. Breathing out was the hardest part for George. Letting go of it all.

"Better? Yes? My darling, it's natural to mourn the loss of love, but ye know we have all felt the sting of one-sided affection."

"But Mother, we were engaged!"

"Pooh-pooh! At fourteen? George, neither of you could see such an agreement as binding. No actual jointure was made." She was surprised that her son held on to the memory of Margaret McGregor. Why was he pining over a simple country girl? And an older woman at that! While her words were superficially sympathetic, they were also tainted with the hypocrisy of her own delight. A common woman from Pictou County was certainly no match for her son. "She is, after all, four years older than ye, dear. Ye couldn't expect her to remain true to such a whimsical proposal."

"She will change her mind when she hears that I have been accepted to Boston Law. I'll be eighteen this fall. I am a man in my own right. She needs to see how I have grown."

"Well, that is the very matter. Ye've not been accepted yet, George. Ye must finish your entrance exams for Boston Law. Besides, McQuarrie is a decent choice for a woman with limited choices."

"No more about McQuarrie, Mother!"

"Mr. McQuarrie proposed. She accepted. It's done. They were married two weeks ago Saturday."

George threw himself on the bed and buried his face in his pillow. His sobs shook his shoulders so violently that his father sat on the bed and patted his son gently. "You will make yourself ill, George."

"I don't care."

His mother grew increasingly impatient with her son's tantrum. She began folding the laundry that littered the floor. "Now ye can set your sights on one of the charming women from Beacon Street."

"Jessie. Now is not the time." Mr. Cameron was more sincere in his condolences, yet he was a practical man who knew very well when to move on and when to deal with the most urgent matters at hand. "George, your sister told us that ye haven't had a good meal in days."

Jessie looked down at the heap that was her son. "Wash up 'n' shave. Change into something more appropriate for the Parker. I hear the pie is divine. James, let us leave George. We shall give ye a few minutes to pull yourself together." With that the Camerons descended the stairs to wait in the front hallway.

George did not want to pull himself together. He wanted to wrench himself apart limb from limb. Explode. Disappear. Anything but face a future without Maggie. He bit the end of his pencil to sharpen the blunt lead tip. Feverishly he searched the mattress for his journal. Satiated by this outburst, he buried his face in his pillow and held his breath. He wanted nothing more at that moment than to disappear into the linens.

What new found pain is this
So cutting, keen of edge?
It seems there was a Judas-kiss
And is a broken pledge.
What pain?

When George did not come downstairs, Mrs. Cameron turned to her son-in-law. "It looks like we'll be needing the services of your doctor after all. Would ye mind giving him a call? Sooner better than later, my dear Colonel."

Hours passed in the tension of a silence thick with accusation. Mrs. Cameron's disappointment lingered at the end of each sentence like a suspended question mark. When Putnam arrived, Christina directed him to George's room. She knocked, but there was no answer. "George?" Christina opened the door slowly to see her brother buried under blankets and crumpled papers. Wading through cast-off clothing and stacks of books, she brought the doctor to his side. She excused herself and shut the door behind her.

During his physical exam, Putnam occasionally gave George instructions. "Breathe in, George. Hold. Exhale."

George was vaguely aware of someone's presence, but he remained mute. As the physician poked and prodded, George turned over phrases in his mind. He wanted the man to leave, so he could dwell on the anger of the lines –

She won my heart, and wore
To please her woman wit
It for a day, or some-thing more,
And then discarded it.

The doctor fastened the two buttons on George's shirt, and tucked his stethoscope back in his bag. "You would be well advised to take advantage of your sister's fine cooking. I'm sure she can feed whatever is unsettled in your heart." He pulled a brown bottle from his bag, shook it rapidly and cracked the seal. He poured a generous dose of camphor into a small silver cup. "Drink a cup of this tonic three to five times a day for your depressive mood." He directed his patient to swallow the bitter fluid. The sticky yellowish liquid dribbled down George's chin. Instinctively, he wiped it with the back of his hand, closed his eyes and waited for it to take effect.

"How do you feel now? Better, yes?" When there was no reply, the doctor turned to the bed to examine the reams of foolscap scattered across the sheets.

> And can I pardon this,
> Nor from my manhood fall,
> The broken vow, the love, the kiss?
> I will forget them all.

He flipped through a few pages and shook his head. "Colonel Moore tells me you're going to law school. A lawyer poet? There is nothing more dangerous to a temperament like yours than to dwell in feeling." Receiving no response, Putnam turned to leave George's room. He stopped and looked at the young man who was still sitting on the edge of the bed. "Though fashionable for poets, melancholia is disadvantageous to your good standing in the field of law. You need to remember that you are a man now, George. You'll need a stiff upper lip if you want to make a name for yourself in this town."

George laughed when the doctor left the room. He wrote in his journal:

My friends, here's a potion
Which I have a notion
Will cure all the ills that are under the sun;
There is nothing fitter
Than this new stomach bitter
Till at long last they let him
I mean by that last the poor fellow they bled
But nothing relieved him
And the poor bard believed them
That in less than a week he would surely die.

Downstairs, Putnam gestured for the family to remain seated while he shared his diagnosis. "Your son must rebuild his broken constitution. His wasted frame, derangement of nerves and palpitations of the heart will all respond well to a strong camphor elixir." He handed the open bottle to Mrs. Cameron and scribbled instructions on a card. "He must have fresh salty air. However," Putnam paused to construct a diplomatic frame for his next observation, "while this route to wellness, in my professional opinion, is unparalleled, I am afraid that your son's cure rests in his mind, not in his body. I can do very little to help him if he does not want to help himself."

"What do ye mean by this?" Mrs. Cameron fanned herself briskly. "Doctor, I assure ye my son is perfectly sane. To suggest otherwise is quackery!"

"Mrs. Cameron, I assure you, I do not take such a diagnosis lightly. In my discussions with George, there was an evil foreboding in his thoughts. His total aversion to all society, his love of solitude, his intemperance and his fascination with pernicious thoughts will hasten him to an early grave if you do not get him away from the city for a rest cure immediately. I suggest Tybee Island. There is an outstanding clinic there."

"But George has his entrance examinations…."

"He has no mind for examinations, I am afraid. It will be weeks if not months before I can restore your son to health. It is beyond my control. I must convince him first to accept that his life has worth." Before he could finish, his eyes opened wide and amazement swept over the facade of his professional countenance. Like a ghost of his formal self, George leaned against the banister as he made his way down the stairs.

"Mother." George took a deep breath and a few more steps toward her. "I will be fine. I must write my examinations. I promise to take your tonics if they don't cloud my vision or jumble my thoughts." He made his way across the room with great effort. "Father, you are right. You are all right. I am making myself ill. I shall take your rest cure, after graduation. I have come this far. I cannot – rather I *will* not – waste any more precious energy on the matter."

George gritted his teeth. Words were churning in his mind, snaking through his thoughts. They wrapped around the moment and choked out his reason. Words parallel to this universe.

> And can I pardon this.
> Nor from my manhood fall,
> The broken vow, the love, the kiss?
> I will forget them all.

Anger replaced despair. Visions of McQuarrie's flawless shining stone on the long taper of Maggie's finger blinded him with rage. "I will not allow news of my capricious fiancée's engagement to another man ruin me." His voice trailed off into tears, but he steadied himself against his brother Charley. "It's done."

Chapter 13 – November 1872

Beyond the Smoke and Flame

George buried his grief in his studies. He finished top of his class that spring and started at Boston Law in the fall. He put off his promise to his mother to take Putnam's rest cure, and Jessie was so pleased with his academic achievements that she allowed him to do so.

George and Charley were lying in their beds reading on a quiet Saturday evening when they heard the clanging of distant bells. The boys had grown familiar with the sounds of the city, so George kept reading. The bells, though a distraction, did not break the young man's focus.

"George, you better look." When his brother did not move, Charley insisted. "Let's go outside and get a better look. C'mon."

Impatient with his brother's indifference, Charley grabbed a blanket from the bed, shoved his feet in his shoes without unlacing them, and *clop, clop, clop*, he was down the stairs and out the front door. He stood among a small crowd gathering to see an orange ball glowing above the fragile black skyline. Thin shafts of flame flickered in their eyes. Their mouths hung open in awe and disbelief. It sounded so close. The bells were deafening.

George heard his sister and brother-in-law bustling about on the main floor. He peeked out of his room and down the stairs to see McLelland pulling on his leather army boots. As a military man, it was expected that Colonel Moore and the other members of his regiment would do whatever the local police and fire departments needed of them. George put away his books, got dressed and slipped out the door to join Charley on the street below.

"It must be a big one," the Colonel said to his wife. "We'll be pulling the equipment tonight. I doubt that the fire will jump the river, but you never know. I'll send word if they're going to evacuate this district. Organize some valuables that you can carry."

"Do be careful!" said Christina. She helped her husband with his heavy jacket then followed him outside. When she looked toward the north, the cityscape was a silhouette of black spires and looming shapes against a backdrop of roaring flames. She stood at the door and watched her husband head down the street. "Stay safe!" she shouted after him.

"Good luck!" Charley shouted to McLelland. He tugged at George's sleeve. "Whoa ho ho! That is massive! It looks like it is in the direction of Bedford Street. No school for me tomorrow. C'mon, George. Let's go to the bridge."

Transfixed by the flames, George didn't argue. Like many others from Fourth Street, the brothers moved toward the channel to get a better look. Christina saw them heading down the street and shouted,

"Keep your distance, do you hear?" But her words were swallowed up in the growing din, and the boys kept walking toward the flames. She put her hands to her ears to muffle the incessant ringing of bells and wailing cries of the neighbourhood children. "Not too close, boys!" But they were long gone.

Closer to the fire the crowd was standing spellbound, watching the heat explode glass panes, which crashed onto the street below. With textiles filling the basement and another five floors above, the Klous Building was consumed by the ravenous fire in a matter of minutes. It travelled up the wooden elevator shaft, igniting everything in its path – wool, bundles of hosiery, cases of gloves and lace. A bright orange tongue licked into every corner. The wooden mansard roof only fuelled the hungry flames as they leapt across the narrow streets onto other buildings. Flying embers and cinders started fires on even more roofs until a five-block area was entirely ablaze.

Six blocks from the centre of the inferno curious onlookers and frantic proprietors could feel a solid wall of heat pushing against them. McLelland and the men from his regiment worked frantically to push the line of onlookers back beyond the widening path of the colossus. "Get back!" they shouted. "Let the firemen do their job. Back it up!"

Firemen arrived in teams, pulling the heavy pumps in place of the trained horses incapacitated by equine flu. Chief Darnell and his men aimed limp hoses at the buildings' crumbling facades. Without adequate water pressure, the upper regions of the structures were unreachable. Insubstantial streams of water spat upon the giant's feet and were reduced to hissing mist. The fire began a steady march toward the water.

The crowd of thousands, the Cameron boys among them, was completely dwarfed by the sheer magnitude of the all-consuming inferno. Fear and excitement mixed in an intoxicating elixir, and like everyone else, George and Charley stood in frozen awe. They watched as the fire chewed into the skeletal structure of each building, the bricks and stone crumbling in sheets and sliding to the ground in a splash of red cinders. Business after business swayed and collapsed, rafters and timbers crashing in flaming heaps.

By ten o'clock Mayor Gaston turned to explosives to starve the flames of fuel. *Boom! Boom!* More structures collapsed. Gas supply lines ignited the street lamps, sending them soaring like rockets and raining down sparks and glass in all directions. The earth shook ominously underfoot and the skies were now blackened with thick clouds of smoke. Sixteen hours after the fire had started, Darnell and his men succeeded in creating a dead zone of exploded buildings that contained the firestorm within a circle of its own destruction.

Sometime in the wee hours of Sunday morning, George and Charley made their way back to Fourth Street. Once the adrenaline drained from their bodies, they were exhausted. They didn't speak. Words seemed far too feeble to address the devastation they had witnessed that night. On their way home, they passed miserable piles of housewares and clothing dragged to the safety of the streets behind the fire's path. They were amazed to see what people had chosen to salvage when faced with the possibility of losing everything. Feather ticks, tintype albums, leather-bound family bibles, pots and pans, decorative lamps and braided rag rugs – all thrown into the street, so that the boys had to navigate around these cairns of human junk. As the sun started to rise over the channel, the boys climbed the stairs and collapsed.

The new day brought the sobering reality of the night's horror. Sixty-five acres of Boston's prime business section reduced to rubble. George later learned that the establishment on the corner of Summer and Washington, known as Shreve, Crump and Low, had been destroyed the day *after* the Great Fire. On Monday, the jeweller where George had purchased Maggie's engagement ring was reduced to cinders by a coal gas explosion. George took it as a definitive period at the end of the sentence that was his engagement to Maggie.

The black smell of wet cinders lingered in Boston for months. Yet from the ashes the city rose again, vital and stronger within a year and a half of the disaster. While words failed George to capture the horror of the Great Fire, in the days and weeks afterwards, in the poetry of Oliver Wendell Holmes he found solace and the strength to rebuild his own devastated life. Like the city, his love was reduced to ashes, but Holmes' poetry encouraged him to "teach his half-fledged soul to fly again" and assured him that from the ashes, "love will come again."

Chapter 14 – Late September 1873

Tybee Island, Georgia

In the months that followed the all-consuming blaze, soot settled in every crevice of the city. The smell of charred, wet wood lingered. George's fits fell hard one upon the next. His hatred for Maggie manifested itself in the smell that assaulted his nostrils until the ruins became synonymous with his own loss. He tried to concentrate on his studies in his first year of law school, but his spells became so bad that he coughed up phlegm tinged with streaks of red.

"Ye need to take in the salt air of Tybee just as Putnam insisted over a year ago. Need I remind you that he prescribed the cure, yet you have chosen not to listen, and your health grows worse? School can wait."

"Mother, I have told you on numerous occasions that they may not let me back in. Every sacrifice I have made in life has led me to this point."

"Well, ye cannot stay. All the sacrifice in the world will not matter one whit if you're not well. I am not going to watch my son suffocate before my eyes. It's settled. I'll make arrangements for the train to Georgia."

The beach was all but empty now. When he arrived on Tybee it was the end of the season, so only the die-hards remained. They waved goodbye as the last of the summer crowd boarded the steamer for the one-hour trip to Savannah. When no one showed up to meet him, George asked a local for directions to the Strand Cottages. The resort had been erected twenty years earlier as a vacation destination during the summer months, but as more people had gravitated there for the rest cure, the proprietors had decided to hire a doctor full time and a staff of nurses to tend to the needs of patients with severe respiratory ailments.

After strolling a distance on the beach, George sat in the sand and pulled off his shoes and stockings, rolled up his trousers, then stood and let his jacket fall from his shoulders. He strolled a little further and stopped for a moment, synchronizing his breathing with the inhale of rushing water and the exhale as the shore sighed a drawn-out breath. The water washed back to the sea in rivulets over the dark sand. He tasted salt on his lips and took a step toward the water. When he looked down at his feet, they disappeared, so it looked like he was standing on two thin stubs. Now he felt at one with the sea. Sinking ever so slowly. He looked to the southwest where a curved wall of cloud crept forward at a steady pace. The low slanted shafts of sunlight became ladders that George climbed in his imagination.

"Hello there! Couldn't wait, eh?"

George turned to see the flap of a loose blue shirt and tan trousers in the wind. He presumed it was Rhodes, the proprietor of the cottage resort. George offered him his hand and the man shook it enthusiastically. His sinewy, muscled forearm reminded George of driftwood. Two piercing blue lights looked back at him under the wrinkles of smiling eyes. "Your mother wrote to us and said that we should expect you today." Rhodes was a sturdy, tanned man a little under six feet. Curls of sandy grey hair caught the wind, giving him the rugged look of a sailor. "Sorry I missed you. There was such a crowd on the dock. Hard to say who was coming and who was going. Some residents are leaving on account of the storm headed our way." He pointed to the southwest.

"Storm?"

"Not too bad; it blows in and out and life goes on, eh? Who knows. It may be a strong wind and a lot of rain. We're prepared either way." Rhodes hesitated and looked up and down George's frail frame. "My wife has set out a light lunch on the veranda if you're interested."

George gathered his clothing, which was spread out on the beach like long strands of seaweed. The wind picked up and stung their faces with hundreds of tiny pinpricks as George and Rhodes headed up the beach toward a large, open-air pavilion.

"You'll spend many an evening out here." Rhodes gestured to a large, gleaming white dance hall framed by playful lattice and filigree. "You'll see. Not tonight though. Tonight we'll watch the storm come and go from under the veranda, and you can rest from your long journey." He led George up the main path to the large pale yellow building with wraparound verandas

– one on each of its three floors. "This is where the chronic patients stay. There are ten of you at present." He showed him to his private room on the second floor.

Before the proprietor left, George stopped him and said, "I am not as sick as this. I mean, I do not require a nurse or a doctor."

"Well, according to Dr. Putnam's letter, you do. If you are well enough to join us in the main dining area, it is down the stairs and to the left. If not, I'll send Mary with a tray."

"I shall be down after I wash up."

"Mary put a fresh basin, towels and some soap in the water closet." With that, Rhodes gave a mock salute and closed George's door.

Alone now, George removed his trousers and let them fall to the floor around his ankles. Again, he looked down at his feet, and it seemed as though he was sinking into grey flannel sand. *How my ankles are growing thin*, he thought. On the periphery of his field of vision, he caught a quick movement and grew embarrassed by his state of undress. He walked toward the water closet. "Who's there?" When there was no answer, he stood in the doorframe and saw a half-dressed man. Instinctively he walked toward the gaunt figure and was about to introduce himself when he realized that he was watching his own skeletal reflection extend a hand in his direction. Two hollow eyes stared back at him. He unbuttoned his shirt to reveal a sharply defined ribcage. Tears came when he realized that his handsome frame had shrivelled to this. His thin shoulders heaved heavily. He splashed water on his face, soaked the sponge and scrubbed the journey's sweat from his neck and chest. Those hollows – his eyes – watched his every move as he patted himself down with the linen towel.

George sat on the edge of his bed. *There is no room for grief or anger here*, he thought. He knew that his remaining energy had to be channelled to his good health. The room was dim. He remained half naked, sitting on the edge of the bed, when he heard a tap at his door. He slipped under the sheets. "Come in."

It was Mary and she carried a small tray. "Mrs. Rhodes made a strong broth and suggested you drink it before it gets cold."

"Thank you."

"Can I get you anything else? A sandwich, perhaps?"

"No, this is fine for now."

After she closed the door behind her, George rose from the bed and sat at the table by the window. It was raining so heavily now that he could not distinguish the sand from the sea or the sea from the sky. The broth was good and quieted his hunger, so he returned to his bed. He hadn't felt like writing for weeks, but a thought came to him and he rummaged through his pockets for his journal. He wrote:

> If this sickness was but a man, I could box him and trample him into the dust. But, this sickness is me, so I must be kind.

At nine o'clock he was startled by the arrival of a nurse. She gave him a tonic, and he was out for the night.

In the months that followed, George was shy in the shell of his illness. He remained on the second-floor veranda, watching the young girls pass below on their way to the dance. When they looked up he blushed, for they casually let their shawls slip to reveal their shoulders, smooth and bare. Then he retreated to his room, but when the music from the pavilion travelled across the night air and filtered into the corners of his mind, he was tempted to descend.

By the spring, he had regained his strength and was starting to feel more confident. He sat out on the lower veranda and watched the young gentlemen callers spending the warm evenings in the polite society of the ballroom dancers. He heard the swish swash of crinoline as the dresses swept the floor followed by the light, quick feet of the men who led the dancers to the rise and fall of the "Savannah Waltz." Lovely. And the smiles. Oh the gay and inviting smiles of girls as beautiful as any of the finest women in Boston. He couldn't help but follow the graceful movements of one girl in particular. She was a dark-haired beauty who silenced the blonde whispers of New Glasgow. She seemed to be the favourite of many men. Her chaperone sat and watched her young charge, who looked to be no more than sixteen. She wore a delicate peach-coloured gown with three semi-circular waves of silk that gathered behind her in an elaborate bustle. Underneath the silk and lace, three tiers of pleated underskirts danced as she moved.

From the safety of the shadows George also followed the confident movements of the men who knew the latest steps and were therefore popular among the young beauties of Tybee. George could see the hopeful eyes of these girls as they waited for a handsome man to sweep them off their feet and take them away from the island to one of the busy cities up north. George did not feel handsome. He needed more time before he presented himself to the company of women. Meanwhile he learned from the other guests that the dark-haired beauty was Adelle and that she was of Cuban descent. Her foreign pedigree and dark eyes only served to make her more attractive to George. The moment he heard her name, he was inspired to write poetry again. Since arriving on the island, he had written nothing but political tirades against the Spanish tyrants who oppressed the Cuban people. Now his passionate voice returned.

> And it is – tho' this all may be ill or be well –
> That perhaps, in the fairer Hereafter, Adelle,
> You and I will be one.

The beach was busy now, filled with the bright red stripes and yellow polka dots of a new season on Tybee Island. George sat in the sun and played with metaphors in his journal to capture the moment. The days, the weeks and months away from the fickle winds of Boston had led to this. He felt some great force, some benevolent gods listening to his liquid voice pour onto the blank pages. This was his *ultima Thule* – his paradise. He was an anchor fixed to the golden coral and salt sea urchins of the reef. Fixed and secure in an explosion of brilliance. He wrote freely now. The angry words had retreated like defeated shadows. Maggie was still. He was content just to sit and write.

The thought occurred to him during this extended period between past and future that he wasn't moving backwards, but he was not moving forward either. He was fastened to this blooming rock of today. Charley wrote often and asked when George would be coming home, and George answered,

"Soon – soon." Charley's question tingled in his fingertips. He pushed tomorrow down.

A shadow fell across the page, and George looked up to see a feminine silhouette under the shade of a wide-brimmed hat. The wind caught her blue scarf and blew it across the sand. "Your scarf." He closed his journal and put his pen aside. He stood and chased the flash of blue until it tangled itself in one of the canvas beach chairs. When he returned the scarf to the woman, he realized that it was Adelle. Until now she had existed only in the pages of his journal.

"You're looking so much better than you were when you arrived in the fall." She looked out toward the ocean. "The breezes are better in the spring. No?"

"Yes, quite." Adelle turned in profile and George thought her beauty was beyond compare. His pulse quickened. He felt he might be able to summon the courage to request a waltz at the next pavilion dance, but before he could ask her, she spoke.

"You should join us at the pavilion tonight. I shall save the 'Savannah Waltz' for you."

George raised his eyebrow. It was as if destiny had answered his prayers for love, yet he knew that he would be one among many young men to share her company. All at once he felt fourteen again, looking at the piles of Maggie's postcards. But Adelle had a way of penetrating the walls of his uncertainty, and he found himself agreeing before he could think things through. The invitation stirred hope. He watched her tie the blue scarf under her chin.

"Will I see you then?"

"I would be delighted."

Back at the cottage George was too nervous to eat supper. He tried on one shirt after another until he settled on the blue. He looked at himself in the mirror and was pleased by the reflection of his former self: tanned, strong and handsome.

Mr. Rhodes was surprised to see George appear in the foyer. "You're not going to take supper, George?"

"I think I shall go for a walk this evening," he said.

"In a suit and tie?"

"Well … I think I shall attend the dance when I am out."

Mr. Rhodes smiled. "It's about time. We wondered when you'd come back to life."

The torches burned brightly in the sand surrounding the pavilion, illuminating the interior with a soft glow. He searched the dancers and found Adelle waltzing with a tall man with dark hair, a high forehead and a pinched look between his brows. *Though he is taller than I, I believe that I have the advantage. I have my voice.* It was the same voice with which he had seduced Maggie so many years ago. George checked his thoughts and willed them to retreat. He shook his head from side to side to rid himself of those other voices. "Not now," he said aloud.

The music stopped and the crowd applauded. The piano player and the violinist accepted the accolades with a simultaneous bow. Now was the moment. George worked his way to the front and whispered into the pianist's ear. The man nodded, spoke to the other musician and they took their places. They started to play the "Savannah Waltz" and couples paired off on the dance floor. George approached Adelle and the tall man.

"I believe this is my dance, Adelle."

She turned to the man. "Martin, I promised this dance to George earlier today. If you don't mind?"

Martin graciously bowed and gestured to the dance floor. "By all means, young man. Enjoy."

George's nose twitched uncontrollably. He perceived an insult in Martin's reference to him as young. George wondered where a man like Martin got the nerve. The confidence. He turned to Adelle and raised his arm, and she took his hand. The up and down movement reminded George of the motion of the sea, and he rode the musical waves smoothly and rhythmically.

"So, George, what is it that you do when you are not a poet?"

"I completed my first year at the Boston School of Law before I fell ill."

"What a coincidence! Martin is a barrister in Savannah. He comes to Tybee to get away from the city during the spring and summer. Will you return to law?"

George suddenly felt inadequate. He had no answer to her question, nor did he have an inkling of the future beyond Tybee Island. The pause was prolonged and painful.

"I didn't mean to suggest that poetry isn't a fine profession. Have you been published?"

Again George shrank in size. "My work has appeared in journals and newspapers. I am waiting to accumulate enough material to publish a volume of verse."

While George had given thought to a volume of poetry like Tennyson or Shelley, he was nowhere close to approaching an actual published collection of his poems. He was forever going back to tinker and revise his work. Write and rewrite.

No, he was definitely not ready to take that step yet. *But what of my social standing?* The waltz ended, but George kept dancing. He was not in the moment. He found himself stumbling into a future that had no shape – no destination.

"George?"

"Yes?"

"The waltz is over."

Martin cut in and for a moment, George saw McQuarrie's face float before him. He wanted nothing more than to connect his fist with Martin's square jaw, but he took his leave instead. Upon returning to his room, George began to pack his things.

Chapter 15

Motherhood

George returned to Boston, planning to resume his studies in the fall. His family greeted him with a flurry of kisses and tight squeezes; even his brother-in-law embraced him closely. McLelland enjoyed having his sister's younger brothers together again in their townhouse on Fourth Street even if it did put an extra strain on their finances and created more laundry for his wife. However, in the final weeks of Christina's first pregnancy, he watched fatigue pull down her fine features. He asked Charley and George to mind their sister.

"We can all pitch in for the next little while, boys. My mother and sister will be helping out. I expect the same from you two."

"Yes, sir."

That night, when he and Christina were in the privacy of their bedroom, McLelland grew increasingly irritated by the laughter coming from the kitchen. Usually he ignored the boys' good-natured squabbles, but sensing his wife's discomfort, he was prickly. His voice boomed down the stairs. "Boys! Tina needs her sleep." That was all that had to be said.

"Sometimes I worry I'm too old for a baby. Isabel already has three children."

"It's only natural to worry, Tina, but you are a healthy woman."

"So was my mother," Christine began and then broke off in tears. "My mother lost three children."

"And, my dear, she had six children who grew up to be beautiful, intelligent and strong."

"Izzie and I were seven years old when our little brother James Richard died. He was so frail and colicky. He coughed and cried and coughed and cried. Poor little thing. My sister and I didn't know what to do or what to say to help Mother. It's cruel, you know. To give life and then have it taken away."

Unlike his Presbyterian wife, McLelland's Catholic faith never waivered, even after he witnessed so much death in war. The Lord had brought him comfort in those dark days. He always felt uncomfortable when his wife railed against God; he tried to soothe her doubts, but she was in the throes of a hormonal storm. He massaged her tight shoulders and kissed her cheek gently.

"What if the baby has coughing fits like George and baby James?"

"My sweet Tina. You will worry yourself sick about things that haven't even happened. Focus on rest. I want you to let Mother take care of things around here until the baby comes."

"You'll get no argument from me. I wouldn't mind being a woman of leisure for a few weeks."

When the baby arrived Mrs. Cameron felt it was her duty to assist her daughter, so the Moore household grew again by two for Jessie brought Lotta. George couldn't help but notice that more than the usual baggage accompanied his mother's visit. She had brought the mammoth trunk from her bedroom in New Glasgow, three leather valises stuffed to capacity and numerous smaller trunks. In addition to the needlework, toiletries and apparel, Mrs. Cameron also brought a fragile and very expensive oil lamp that the family kept in their sitting room in New Glasgow. A gift for Christina, perhaps?

"Boys, boys, careful with that bag now. It has my cosmetics and figurines from Grandmother Sutherland."

"Yes, Mother." Charley's voice was muffled behind his armload of bags and boxes.

"I appreciate your kindness and understanding, Colonel Moore. It will be a full house for sure. A young mother needs her own mother at this time. There's nothing dearer than family." Mrs. Cameron turned to her son. "George, pay the porter. He's waiting on the street. By my count there should be another bag. Make sure he checks the back, George. I do believe I am missing a bag."

With the extra family, Charley and George moved into to the attic on the third floor. Unfortunately the space was not designed for study, let alone two tall young men. Whenever George stood up he inevitably slammed his head against the slanted roof. Books were stacked in the corners of the room, and clothes littered the floor. The dust exacerbated George's coughing fits, and he found himself gasping for air in the middle of the night. Of course this would wake the baby, and the entire household was on edge. The baby's cries travelled like a lightning bolt through George's brain. Needless to say the attic was not conducive to study nor to a good night's sleep.

George and Charley shared the dark, cramped quarters for three weeks before George decided he needed to move out. The problem was the extra cost. He would have to ask his mother for more money to board at the law school's dormitories on Bromfeld. To his surprise, Mrs. Cameron agreed with no questions or an argument.

"That was far too easy," George said to his brother later that same evening as they packed up his trunk with his books and suits.

"I thought so as well. Don't you find it odd that Father did not accompany Mother on this extended visit? She rarely refers to him when she shares news about home. Have you asked her about Father?"

"I have learned one thing about Mother, Charley. Never engage in a conversation when there is the slightest room for histrionics."

"True. I sense we could drown in this subject's depths. Best not to mention it." Charley looked at his brother with a grin that engulfed all other features. "It's good to have you back in Boston."

Chapter 17

Spirits at the Parker

Another night, another day spent in the reading room at the Athenaeum. George's eyes grew heavy, but he shook himself awake more than once to finish his chapters on torts for the next day's examination. *How is it possible that law can drain the English language of all beauty?* George leaned back in his chair and stretched. His roommate, William Crittington, popped up behind him and gave him a start.

"Master Cameron, let's down a few at the Bull and Boar."

"Can't."

"Don't be such a bore. We could hit the show upstairs. Our fair Lydia and *The British Blondes* will not disappoint." Crittington did a seductive sashay and spin. A table of studious young men broke out in laughter at their classmate's antics. The librarian gave them a cold stare and raised a stiff finger to her thin lips.

"Sh! Miss Walsh will bounce us, and I need to study. Howard chiselled me out of ten points on my last examination and called me a flummox in the dining hall. What the hell is a flummox anyway? I want to prove the bastard wrong."

"Everyone knows he's a blowhard." Crittington sat down across from his friend and slapped the palms of his hands on the tabletop. "What you meant to say is you are studying tuh-tuh-tuh-torts for your tuh-tuh-tuh-test in Howard's class." There were more suppressed chuckles from fellow students who were well aware of their professor's speech impediment. The librarian swished to the back of the reading room and shooed out a group of rambunctious juniors. True, Professor Howard stuttered. The man was the bane of George's existence. Unlike William and the others, though, George never made fun of Professor Howard. He held his contempt for the man in empty threats under his breath. But today, after the embarrassing incident in the dining hall, he blurted out, "If I had my druthers, I'd paste him one."

"I know at least five juniors who'd pay to see that, George. Tuh-tuh-tuh hell with old Howard. Let's take a break. I hear Lurline will be in the audience tonight."

Just the mention of her name set George's head spinning. Drunk on the promise of feminine company, he closed the book and slapped Crittington on the back. "The British blondes await."

⊗

George's newfound freedom from the watchful eye of family opened a door into a world of temptation. On Saturdays, like the literary giants before them, George and his poet colleagues stretched out on the lawns of the Boston Common under the dappled shade of its big oaks. This circle of friends was far different than George's usual crowd. His mother would not approve of this gathering. Many of them, four or five years younger than he, were enrolled in Literature Studies at the university. Mrs. Cameron made it clear what she thought of such academic pursuits: "A darn shame! Wasting their parents' hard-earned money on literary excess." Needless to say, George's evenings lounging among young women in the park, his attendance at shows like *The British Blondes* and his extravagant dinners in restaurants remained his private indulgence. And he indulged often.

"Read another, George," said one of the young ladies who circled around the poets in the park.

"One more and then I really have to go."

George obliged then excused himself and made his way to the Old Corner Bookshop at the junction of Tremont and School streets. It was here in William Dean Howells' establishment that they published the legendary *Atlantic Monthly*. George persistently submitted poems to the magazine for the publisher's consideration, but Howells dismissed his work as derivative.

"George, it is in your best interest to go one way or the other."

"Meaning?"

"Either commit to your own voice or cater to the masses. You can't continue to echo the voices of other poets if you want to be considered seriously as a poet in your own right. Have you ever considered journalism? Perhaps you could write for the law review."

"That's not what I had in mind. How can you continue to print the drivel written by Elizabeth Phelps? Perhaps the business is more a matter of nepotism than talent?"

"Now George, you know it is not personal."

Despite numerous rejections, George felt somehow encouraged by Howells and accepted his criticism. In his heart of hearts, this was the place George felt most at ease. Surrounded by shelves of leather spines. He especially enjoyed the frenetic activity of the printing house on the second floor where only those with the utmost devotion to the process of printing books could tolerate the smell of ink, glue and alcohol. The printing house was also a noisy place. While most would be irritated by the thud, thud, thud of the mechanized typesetting machines flapping like fluttering partridge wings, George felt energized by it. He had worked many hours with McLelland on Franklin Street in those days of hope and love. He felt closer to the printed word when he watched Howells' employees churn out this month's edition of *The Atlantic Monthly*. He leaned against the door and thought, *Next time.*

Downstairs, George paid three dollars for his latest acquisition: a copy of Shelley's *Prometheus Unbound*. He opened the delicate tissue frontispiece to reveal the pen and ink likeness of Shelley. He rested his finger on the poet's beautiful lower lip, then turned the page and read:

> One hope is too like despair
> For prudence to smother,

And pity from thee more dear
Than that from another.

After he made his purchase, he set off to meet Lurline Ainsworth at the Parker for dinner. Lurline was his sin devoured in secret. She was a balm for his wounded pride. A diversion, like Adelle, from his ever-present despair – but not a replacement for the young man's memory of Maggie McGregor.

The Parker in its architectural glory stood kitty-corner to the bookshop. It was here that the likes of Dickens, Longfellow and Hawthorne held poetry readings and strolled down the lavishly carpeted halls smoking cigars and drinking brandy. George crossed the street and ascended the white marble steps to the front foyer. Intoxicated by the warm glow of the oak panelling, he took a deep breath. He felt swallowed whole by the hotel's elegance. In the mezzanine he stood before a large arched mirror flanked by two gaslights. He straightened his tie and smoothed back his oiled hair. This was the very mirror Charles Dickens used to stand before in his suite on the third floor when he prepared his celebratory reading of *A Christmas Carol*. George peered into the mirror, half expecting the Englishman to peer back at him.

His attention was diverted by the lithe reflection of Lurline resplendent in a muslin gown in shades of peacock green and blue. The plunging décolleté and absence of sleeves left little to George's imagination. He turned and greeted her.

"My muse has arrived."

He followed the curve of her porcelain neck with the backs of his fingers until his hand rested on her bare shoulders. Here, gathered tulle draped to her cleavage where a cluster of sequined feathers brushed up against her white bosom. With all eyes upon them, George took selfish delight in his companion's social stature among Boston's privileged class. The coquette cooled herself seductively with a large fan of fine ostrich feathers dyed a vivid green.

"Didn't anyone ever tell you that it is the *male* bird who wears the extravagant plumage?"

"By all means, Georgie, slip into my dress, if you think there is room."

She was so stunning. George turned back to his reflection to catch a vainglorious glimpse of their image together. She put her lips close to the back of his ear and whispered, "Hungry, darling?"

"Famished."

"Shall we then?" Lurline rested her hand on George's arm, and they glided into the dining room. Beyond the hotel's luxuriously appointed décor, the establishment was renowned for its sumptuous fare. This was the place to enjoy all that wealth had to offer. Was it beyond George's means? Well beyond. But George ran with a wealthy bunch, and in his desire to spin in the social circles of the well-to-do, he often got swept up by their lavish lifestyle.

Tonight, because George was drunk on Lurline's beauty, or because he succumbed to the fantasy of the moment, he forgot the weight of the bill at the end of the night. He ordered a tomato soup, oysters in aspic and a venison chop. Each date drained George's meagre savings. Last Saturday, he had accompanied Lurline to the opening night of Gilbert and Sullivan's *Iolanthe*. George didn't care for the fairy opera. The pretentious laughter at Selwyn's made him feel uncomfortable and slightly claustrophobic. He missed half the show because two old hens seated next to him cackled hysterically through the entire opera.

"Wasn't Richard Mansfield clever as Lord Chancellor last week?"

"Quite." George's laconic responses were less a matter of having something intelligent to say and more a necessity to curb his cynical views of popular theatre. He even preferred his roommate's taste for the burlesque over the satiric works of comic opera.

"Georgie, *do* have another brandy."

"Go ahead, my darling. I am still working on my first." He sipped his brandy leisurely. Under the table, George felt the coquette's hand rest upon his knee. He flinched and took an unexpected mouthful of brandy that burned when he swallowed it. While he could not help but enjoy Lurline's advances, he knew she was only toying with him. No young woman from Beacon Hill would ever entertain a future with a student from Boston Law, no matter how clever, how athletic or how handsome he might be. Lurline had an underlying agenda in the works. Perhaps these few dates in the public sphere were her way of upping the ante on an unspoken engagement. A little gossip – a modest fling to encourage a proposal from the senator's son, no doubt.

It never ceased to amaze George how Boston's feminine elite accompanied him around town. Scandalous in any other social orbit, but here? At the Parker Hotel? No. Here, it was all a game. Here, they played by their own rules. She did not want a lasting entanglement with a boy from New Glasgow who was barely twenty years old. She had her sights set on a politician or businessman. George was entertainment. Yet it was for this very reason that George acquiesced to the vixen's charms. There was always a rush of adrenaline, followed by a wash of residual guilt. Yet there was no commitment beyond the occasional romantic encounter. No love. No promises to keep – or to break.

"What do you have there?" Lurline gestured with her fan to the small, leather volume George had placed casually next to his silver cutlery on the table.

"Oh ... a book of love potions and other spells."

"Do tell."

"Let me read a bit for you."

"The fountains mingle with the river,
And the rivers with the ocean;
The winds of heaven mix forever
With a sweet emotion;
Nothing in the world is single;
All things by a law divine
In another's being mingle –Why not I with thine?"

"Indeed. I love to mingle." She placed a finger on the stem of her wine glass and stroked it slowly downwards.

"What did I tell you? A love spell."

"You are a curious young man. Let me see your book."

George wasn't so sure. He was not so taken with Lurline that he would allow her to touch the book with her soiled fingers. "Allow me." He opened the cover gently and placed the tissue to the side to unveil the beautiful portrait of Shelley on the inside cover.

"My, he *is* scrumptious!"

"Lurline – meet Percy Bysshe Shelley. He died far too young." George had always wondered what Shelley might have written had he lived beyond his twenty-nine years. He considered the arc of his own existence. When would the public get to hear his voice? Emboldened by Shelley's verse, he announced, "One day it will be my name inscribed in gold on the spine of a leather-bound volume of poetry."

"No doubt. This deserves another round, George."

George was insulted by Lurline's lack of interest in his poetry. He refused to become emotionally attached. *Whatever this is, it is not permanent or lasting. The perfume of a moment.*

"Another round then." He shut the cover, slipped the book inside his jacket and gestured for the waiter to bring more drinks. As the evening of libations progressed, three more couples joined the table. A young woman of George's age and Lurline's social class opened a topic of great interest to all.

"Have you heard about the hauntings in the hotel?" She spoke with the affected Brahmin accent George secretly despised.

"Do you mean that famous androgynous actress, Charlotte Cushman?" said Lurline.

"Yes. She died of pneumonia, here in room 338, if I remember correctly. Some say they have heard her rehearsing her lines as she walks up and down the corridors on the third floor."

"In the words of Sidney Lanier, 'Wronged by death pays life with wrong / And she wakes by night and dreams by day.'"

"George, that is why I adore your company. You are such a quaint and clever entertainer. Such a precise memory."

"A lawyer poet?" asked Lurline's friend.

George wanted to direct the trite comments away from his one true passion. "I read somewhere that Cushman played Lady Macbeth in some performances and Macbeth in others."

"Her talent, though unquestionable, does not extend to her beauty." Lurline ordered another gin sling by tinkling her crystal with a teaspoon. "My mother saw her perform at the Globe and said she was, well, rather unfortunate in her appearance. The look of her alive would be frightening enough."

George lied to bolster his standing at the table. "Our good friends the Cartwrights, wealthy shipbuilders from New Glasgow, stayed at the Parker five years ago and entertained us with their haunted visit on the fifth floor. They woke to the sound of heavy footsteps in their bedroom. The wife, a woman of stoic disposition, claimed that the air grew so icy that she could see her breath. Then slowly – ever so slowly – someone tugged at the sheets and swept the bedcovers off the bed." The young women at the table squealed with delight.

"Who was it?" Lurline, though very drunk, was engrossed in George's ghost story.

"Some say that it was none other than the original proprietor, Harvey Parker himself!" Emboldened by their applause, George ordered another round of brandy for the entire table.

"Come on, Georgie. Just one more…." The woman who pulled George's arm in the direction of the elevator needed no name for she was one of many who, after hours of drinking, blurred into the same blithe spirit. The distinguished guests of the Parker had retired long ago. Asleep in their well-appointed suites, they dreamed of buttered rolls and Boston cream pie. The Harvard crowd had packed it in a half an hour before and made their inebriated way across the river to their dormitories. Teetering on the promise of the woman's invitation, George stood at the far end of the foyer. Suddenly, as if looking at things from the other end of a telescope, the lobby extended into a long, narrow tunnel. The room tilted this way and that. When George tried to take a step, his head felt heavier than he remembered it. That way and this. Three bright orbs danced before his eyes. He followed one of the lights as it floated down the hallway.

"George."

"Maggie?"

"I'm not Maggie, silly. I'm Lurleeene." Her breath retained the acid-sour sweetness of gin. George tried to focus on her features, but Maggie's freckled face and natural beauty danced in front of him.

"Ya' know...." A saccharine breath touched George's ear and he laughed. It was a raucous laugh infused with brandy and cigars. Again.

"Ya' know, we could go up to my suite, but we've got to be quiet. Sh!"

George didn't respond. He followed the bobbing light to the blinding bronze elevator doors. He tried to count the circles in the squares, but he kept losing count and had to start again. Without prompting, the doors opened and George stepped in. His date stood like a bewildered marionette in the front lobby with her pigeon toes and arms akimbo. The doors shut slowly, like the final pages of a chapter before bed.

The elevator jerked into motion, rising to the third floor. George did not remember pushing a button. The car came to an abrupt stop and without provocation the doors opened. George stepped out tentatively, making his way more by touch than by sight.

He heard the door to room 338 open and slam shut.

"Maggie? Is that you? My soul will meet yours in a single kiss. Maggie?"

Chapter 18

To Die Once is Enough

McLelland Moore arrived at George's dormitory, turned the bell on the front door three times and waited. He turned the bell again and was about to leave when he saw through the frosted glass a distorted blur of colour coming down the stairway.

"Colonel, sir. I am afraid George is not home yet."

McLelland took out his watch from his waistcoat and frowned. "I gather he's out carousing all hours of the night with that crowd from Beacon Hill again. Who is it this time, William?"

"Um, Lurline, I believe. You know how it is." He shrugged uncomfortably.

"Well, when he gets home, give him this." He passed an envelope to William. "It arrived to his Fourth Street address. By the looks of it, it's from a friend in New Glasgow."

"I'll give it to him when he gets in. Is there anything else, sir?"

"Not that I can think of." Colonel Moore stepped out of the doorway and into the street below.

"Crittington?"

"Yes, sir?"

"Just let him know that I stopped by and that his brother and sisters miss him very much. If he gets some time in his busy schedule, he could stop by and see them."

"Of course, sir."

As McLelland made his way home across the river, George found himself in the Athenaeum. His head rested on his forearms. When he lifted his eyes, a piercing light cut through his forehead. Still in his evening clothes from the Parker, he blinked at the shafts of punishing light streaming into the large reading room. If it weren't for the fact that he had no books before him and smelled like liquor, Miss Walsh could have mistaken him for any student studying for finals. George sat up and smacked his lips a few times. His tongue was heavily lined with dry fur, and his throat was hoarse, no doubt from smoking too much. *How did I get here? What time is it? For that matter, what day is it?* He looked around the reading room. It was empty save for Takeo Kikachi, who made his home here on weekends to prepare for next week's lectures. His head was buried in *Hilliard's Contracts and Professional Ethics*. Takeo was sound asleep and no doubt had spent the entire night studying. It was Sunday. Last night. He had dinner with Lurline. George checked his billfold. Empty.

No one knew – not his professors, his classmates nor the young women he escorted around town – no one knew that George was squeezed. He cleverly disguised his modest middle-class background from everyone. Even though his mother generously supported him, it was well understood that it was a temporary loan. So he lived the high life on borrowed funds. He had his ways of shuffling funds around so that he always had what seemed to be casual spending money. He borrowed tuxedos from his wealthy roommate, Crittington. He worked as a clerk at the law firm of Dean, Butler and Abbott. He found a way to fund his appetite for fine food and expensive liquor by making frequent visits to the dockyard district. Whenever he found an opportunity, he would offer legal advice at a reasonable price to desperate men in taverns. During his long walks, he would listen for potential clients – off the books, of course. Needless to say there were some dockhands who were well-versed in the intricacies of defamation of character. No matter how hungover from the evening's celebration, his financial hangover would linger for months of after-hours appointments. His wallet needed a break from Lurline. He nudged Takeo awake and then headed home to sleep.

Dishevelled and reeking of liquor, George arrived home to the boarding house. "Well, good night, Cri-tit-ington!" He giggled and threw himself on his bed. He didn't bother to undress.

"Don't you mean good afternoon? I guess it was Lurline who kept you out all night again?"

No response.

"By the way, your brother-in-law stopped by this morning with this." William handed George the letter. "It's from New Glasgow. The person sent it to the wrong address."

"Who's it from?"

"A Mr. D. McQuarrie, I think. It's hard to make out the initial."

George jumped out of bed, almost knocking over the nightstand. His heart beat against his chest and his fingers tingled. Why would Maggie's husband write to him? *Has there been a falling out? Has she left him?* He fumbled with the envelope, tore it open and read the contents.

George's hand dropped limply to his side and the pages floated to the floor. "To die once is enough." His tears refused to fall, as if they knew that they had mourned this loss before. William had returned to his books, so he didn't see his friend's face fall, nor did he hear the strangled sigh escape his chest. Unseeing, George made his way to the edge of the bed and sat silently in a state of suspended disbelief. His friend's figure faded into the periphery of his slowly shrinking world, so when William broke the silence, George did not hear him.

"I should be finished shortly if you want to go downstairs for lunch." When his roommate didn't answer, William goaded him with one of his insulting nicknames, but there was still no response. He turned in his chair and saw a shadow of what was once George. He took note of the pages that littered the floor, picked up the letter and read.

September 13, 1874

To the dear friend of my loving wife,

I am indebted to your aunt for giving me this address. I hope this letter finds you well for you will need strength to steady yourself for what you are about to read. It is with profound sadness that I write to inform you of the sudden passing of your beloved childhood friend, my wife, Maggie McGregor. As your mother may have told you, Maggie was with child when Dr. Grant confined her to strict bedrest in her seventh month.

William did not need to read further. He was well aware of George's first years at the Boston Latin School. No one could really claim that they knew George Cameron because he was always holed up in the library, writing poetry to his young love in Nova Scotia. The other boys used to tease him by making exaggerated kissing noises whenever he walked past them, but William thought it admirable on George's part to keep their long-distance romance going. The solitary young man wrote letter after letter, page after page of promises to return to take her hand in marriage. While he and his classmates revelled in their months away from home, George willed time to pass quickly so he could return to New Glasgow. William recalled when George all but disappeared from school in their final year, just before the final exams. His brother Charley assured everyone that he was indeed alive, but under the weather. Crittington knew that George was paralyzed by the news of his sweetheart's engagement to another man. Heavy clouds followed him for months. He wrote his finals and graduated top of his class, but he seemed hollow inside. It was during their first term as roommates that William witnessed George's irrevocable slide into depression. George changed. His mother sent him south to Savannah for what was supposed to be a month. He stayed on Tybee Island for the best part of a year, interrupting his studies at Boston Law.

When George moved into the dormitory some months after his return, William noticed an unsettling waywardness about his roommate. All he really said was, "Looks like I have some catching up to do." That was that. He resumed his studies, but unlike the reclusive and studious boy he had been at the Latin school, now George was always out. He became uncharacteristically gregarious. He stayed out all night, slept past noon, spent money foolishly and courted several young women at once. To everyone who knew him, George had become a self-centred and promiscuous rake. News of Maggie McGregor's passing was delivered to a hollow man.

Upon his return to Boston from Tybee, George had taken to walking as a way to carry his thoughts from one place to another when he felt the weight of memory begin to show on his face. Walking was a convenient excuse to avoid uncomfortable conversations with his family and classmates – or at least this is how the late-night journeys through the streets of Backwater Bay and the wharf district began. Gradually he grew to crave the unexpected of unknown neighbourhoods. As a matter of course, anonymity soon dissipated when he would frequent a certain well-worn path. Faces became common, and there were knowing exchanges of familiarity. George would tip his hat politely or nod his head courteously to acknowledge the social convention. Then he would promptly cross the street.

It seemed at first that the answer to whatever was bothering George could be just around the next corner or down the alleyway just ahead. More often than not, the troubling thought that propelled him forward was Maggie's betrayal and his feelings of complete loss of control. George angrily thrust his heels into the cobblestone. With each step he felt the vibration of fresh betrayal travel up his spine and click at the base of his skull. Click. There was her decision to accept McQuarrie's proposal. Click. There was the inevitable consummation of that union. Click. There were the subsequent letters of cooling friendship. Click. There was the thinly veiled cheer that skated carefully around the special event of the coming child. Click. There were the mathematical calculations in George's mind that added up to pre-marital relations. Conjecture became his new truth, and it tortured him incessantly. It nagged the back of his mind when he resumed classes and tried to read his chapters on wills, equity and probate. He could not or would not gather the courage to ask Maggie if she ever thought of him. The answer didn't matter anymore. She was no longer his. Some nights George walked as far as Backwater Bay only to wonder how in God's name he could possibly retrace his steps back to his dormitory on Bromfeld.

Hours after receiving the letter from McQuarrie, George woke to the lifting darkness of a new day at least ten miles from the centre of Boston. The sun broke the horizon in thin strips of pink and red to infuse the dawn with a fiery glow. George churned the philosophical complications of the past five years.

Had every hour been a lie? How can an event happen – say the death of a young woman and her stillborn child – and the news of that moment travel from the mourning lips of her husband to make its way across the blank page? In the time between that event and the opening of a letter, George attended classes, joked with friends at the Old Corner Bookshop, flirted with girls at the Parker, studied for hours in the reading room, went to bed, slept, woke at least fourteen times, marked his twentieth birthday – all the while believing that Maggie was alive. She was alive in her betrayal until he read the word *passing*. Her passing from what? And to what? From her life hundreds of miles away to the ground beneath the fields in which they had run in a breathless chase of young love? To the dust underfoot? Or did she simply cease to be? Period. As final as the end of life's sentence.

George took out his journal and a stub of pencil and began to form his thoughts into words on the page.

> Forgetting! Were forgetting
> Done easily as said,
> I should not be regretting
> The days forever dead.
> Forgetting! Were it only
> Exertion of the will,
> I should not be so lonely
> And sad so long, and still.

In the two years since the news of Maggie's engagement to Donald McQuarrie, including the year spent down South on Mother's rest cure, the sentence always ended with a nagging question mark. Will she come back to me? Can I forgive her? But now the sentence ended with a period. Maggie was dead.

George sighed and spoke aloud. "Shouldn't it be enough to die once?" This night he heard her faint reply. He could feel Maggie's hand in his as they walked the fields of Pictou County. "Are you mine?" he asked.

"Pardon me, sir?"

George was startled by the voice of a boy, no more than ten. "Charley?" He focused on this angel standing in the morning light.

"No, sir. It's Tom. Sorry, sir. I didn't mean to break up your conversation with, well, yourself, but when you spoke, I thought you were talking to me. You sounded so sad."

George pulled himself to his feet, put his hand on the boy's head and turned on his heel. He began the long walk home. With each step he muttered, "She is not mine. She's not mine."

The sun had climbed further into the sky, and the day was bright. He gradually recalled what day it was and knew that he would miss George Hilliard's morning lecture on contracts and professional ethics. It did not matter. He did not care.

In the following days, Shelley and Virgil could not console him. Words fell flat on the page. Food was bland on the tongue, and music, no matter how joyful, sounded like hollow winds. Like a ghost, George was lost in the time between the time other people exist in. He walked.

Chapter 19 – 1877

Five Pounds of Leather

In preparation for her son's graduation, Jessie Cameron took George to Henry Tuttle and Co. to purchase a new pair of shoes. The shop came with the highest recommendation from the Cartwrights in New Glasgow. And after all, they should know. On the corner of Washington and Winter streets, George scanned the display of the finest footwear in Boston. Imported from Paris and London, the shoes were far beyond his modest allowance. His mother sensed his reluctance and narrated the script of his hesitation.

"If you're going to walk among men, then money spent isn't vanity but a matter of professional necessity. George, ye have to think in terms of investment."

She settled on the gentleman's Congress shoe. "We'll take one in black and the other in oxblood. Size eleven." Jessie opened her purse and laid a small fortune on the counter.

"An excellent gentleman's dress shoe," said the clerk. "Such divine taste."

George calculated the total and added it to his already burgeoning debt to his parents. Under his arm, George carried out five pounds of fine Italian leather wrapped in brown paper. Mother and son stood a minute on the front step beneath the striped awning.

"What a charming jimmy, don't ye think, George?" Mrs. Cameron slipped her gloved hand into her son's other arm. "Come along. We've a fitting appointment at eleven." She looked both ways. "I shall ne'er get used to the streets in Boston. So many folk. It's a maze. Truly a maze."

At the rear of Macullan, Parker and Company, Mrs. Cameron perched herself on a stool and eyed her son's slender frame in the reflection of the full-length mirror.

"Ye have the Cameron sharpness of mind, but ye certainly inherited the svelte frame and delicate features from the Sutherland side of the family."

As the tailor chalked the lines of a charcoal grey business suit and pinched and pinned the trousers, Mrs. Cameron stood, perused the rack of morning coats and gave the clerk several possibilities for George to try on. She moved to the colourful showcase of neatly folded ties and pocket squares and fingered the luxurious accessories.

The proprietor noticed her interest. "A matching waistcoat, tie and scarf in an understated blue grey will accessorize the jacket handsomely. Please take note of our fine leather gloves." He addressed Mrs. Cameron. "I see you have been to Tuttle's. Such a fine establishment. I can match those exquisite shoes you have just purchased if you like."

"Please do. Thank ye for your kindness." George cringed. His mother positively swooned under the proprietor's excessive flattery. The clerk deferred matters of choice to her and ignored George entirely. Knowing who held the power in this relationship, Macullan ingratiated himself to Mrs. Cameron's purse.

"My son has recently joined the firm of Dean, Butler and Abbott. Or is it Abbott, Butler and Dean?"

"Either way, poor Butler will forever be caught in the middle." The tailor chuckled and continued to pin the hem of George's trousers.

The figures of the day's purchases swam before George's eyes. "Mother, how can I possibly repay you and Father?"

"Nonsense. It's an investment. There is no need to pay me back right away. Establish yourself first. Let's take a break from this money talk and take our dinner at the Parker. And for your own edification, your father has nothing to do with this."

Seven days before George and Jessie Cameron enjoyed a luncheon of mock green turtle soup, thinly sliced ham in a champagne sauce and cream pie, Mr. Cameron – hundreds of miles away – carefully wrapped George's graduation gift in cotton to make its long journey from New Brunswick back to Boston. The last time he was in Boston, the time George fell desperately ill, Mr. Cameron took a trolley out to Waltman Company to escape his wife's incessant mothering. In the large brick building on an expanse of the Charles River, American watchmakers kept pace with the growing trends of their European counterparts. A young apprentice had put the finishing touches on James's gift for George. With keen eyesight and steady nerves, he checked the delicate and intricate mechanism housed within. The young watchmaker closed the case and examined the Scottish thistle engraving. It was definitely a fine example of his workmanship. He read the cursive inscription, a command of sorts: "Make us proud, George." After wrapping the timepiece carefully with a piece of soft cloth, he handed it over to Mr. Charles Waltman, who in turn handed it over to Mr. Cameron.

James had ordered the watch for his son's graduation from Boston Law the very day he dropped ten-year-old Charley and fourteen-year-old George off at the Moores' house. That was almost eight years ago. He picked the watch up the day George wrote his final examinations at the Latin School. For half the price of the European models, James was able to buy the watch and afford the costly engraving. Traditional watchmakers were appalled by the thought of a machine-made timepiece, but Mr. Cameron saw this watch as a symbol of an advancing world; it was a watch of the future. The package from New Brunswick arrived at the Moore house the day before George graduated from Boston Law – the day George and his mother went shopping. Mr. Cameron did not attend his son's graduation.

After lunch at the Parker, mother and son hurried to their next appointment on Winter Street. George never quite felt at ease in front of a camera. Revell's assistant put a metal brace on George's back, positioned his head and, with another metal contraption, held it stock-still, slightly cocked. George held this unnatural position for a full eight minutes. Still as a statue, his thoughts ran wild. In his pocket was the tintype image Maggie had given him upon his departure from New Glasgow. In it she was forever youthful. Forever beautiful. Forever his. He imagined Maggie proudly showing the image of her lawyer husband to her friends. He manufactured their conversation and took a secret pride in the fact that he had done all of this for her.

When Revell handed him his own photograph, George saw the man Maggie never got to meet. It was time. He would take this photograph and the ring to New Glasgow and say goodbye. He would bury them and his memory of Maggie for good.

Chapter 20

Etched in Stone

George took the Intercolonial from Halifax to Pictou Station where his Aunt Margaret and his cousins, now grown men, waited. He half expected them to be the same. The three boys who had waved goodbye when he departed for Boston in 1869 stood before him. Their voices, now deep, represented the inevitable course of time. *Boys grow into men, and women forget promises made at dusk and marry....*

The boys tussled briefly about who would command the reins on the way back to the Cameron farm until Aunt Margaret put a stop to their mischief by threatening the two older boys with a switch if they didn't settle the matter like gentlemen. George breathed in the air, and a rush of childhood memories flooded his senses. His chest was clear, and the clean air felt good. The barns of his childhood rose in the distant fields like grey ghosts. It took all of his strength to push those sweet summers down, deep in his mind. Bury them with the feelings of loss and betrayal.

"George, when you feel up to it, we will take you to the cemetery and pay the McGregors a visit. I know that Gertie is very excited to see you. She's grown to be a rare beauty, George. I am sure the family would appreciate your visit. Such a fine, fine young woman – Margaret. Such a shame. She and her little one are God's angels now."

There was no ignoring the memory of Maggie here, of course. George still longed for her, eight years later. He remembered sitting so close that he could breathe in her sweetness. Looking into those eyes like deep pools. He would get lost in the cool shade of her face as she looked down on him. Smelling the sweetgrass in her hair as they lay side by side on the riverbank. Watching the amethyst sky of dusk gradually deepen. Listening for adult voices to call them in for sleep.

Alone at the cemetery George lowered his head in reverence. He did not feel the closure that he desired when he planned this return to New Glasgow. Before he could gather the courage to visit Maggie's grave, he walked through a small meadow and picked daisies for his sister's headstone. She loved making daisy chains for her little brother. While Louise's features had faded, George remembered her as beautiful, and his memories of the delicate petals were as fresh as this day.

He heard the faint echo of her voice call, "Come let us pick flowers." And George answered aloud, "Yes." He took out his journal and wrote the lines before they were forgotten.

> Stray once again where our footsteps strayed
> Play once again where we once played

He looked at her headstone. A thick green moss covered the dates, so he scraped it away. Mary Louise Stewart, 1841–1861. He wrote again.

> Long since thou and I
> Have been together and it may be
> Ere we shall meet again

"You are death's bride now," he said as he laid the wreath of daisies at the foot of the stone. His sadness gave way to a bubbling anger at the recurring injustice. "Too many brides taken too soon." George looked down at his feet. "How can she be at rest?" Again, he took out his pencil.

> To tumble trembling in a lonely grave?

He turned and walked toward the stone marked McQuarrie. He couldn't bear the thought of being away from Maggie any longer.

Horrifying visions flickered through his mind. That it should come to this. He could not reconcile her soft pink flesh with this cold marble stone before him. He remembered his aunt's words: "They are God's angels now." *No. She is under my feet in the cold ground. No one can mend the loss with feeble words. Hollow syllables of sadness. They all seem so insubstantial.* Try as he might, no words of condolence came forward in George's mind to fill the void left by Maggie's absence, felt so much more acutely now that he was standing on the grass and dirt that separated them.

The tears that had remained locked for so long now found their way. His chest tightened until he gasped for air. He reminded himself to breathe deliberately – in through the nose and out through the mouth. He saw candlelight visions of McQuarrie slipping a ring on Maggie's finger, the two having relations, Maggie screaming during a bloody childbirth. *Slowly. Don't panic. In and out slowly.* He pulled out his graduation photograph and the ring box from his trouser pocket. Before he opened the box, he felt a familiar presence.

Reverend Grant rested his left hand on George's shoulder, a gesture he used instead of a handshake since he lost his right hand in a farming accident when he was a boy. George turned to look in the minister's eyes. His hair had receded and his beard was full, but Grant's eyes were the same – kind and consoling. When George was a boy, Reverend Grant was always willing to listen and guide him in the right direction. He never hesitated to get right to the point.

"My condolences, George. I know you are close to the McGregors. You need not hide your tears." Grant offered him a handkerchief.

George embraced his spiritual counsellor and buried his tear-stained face in the folds of Grant's jacket. He took a deep breath and regained his composure.

"Your aunt sent me. She said you got up early and didn't attend service. She's worried about you. She says you're not sleeping. And I can see by the dark circles under your eyes that this has been the case for some time."

"My breathing fits keep me awake. Some nights I am afraid if I go to sleep I will not wake up."

"Your mind needs sleep, George. We heard that you did well in Boston. You always had a sharp mind for learning."

"I graduated this past year and have secured a job with a Boston law firm."

"I am sure you will be eager to apply your studies to the betterment of your clients."

"It will certainly be more challenging than my position as a clerk for the firm. And you? Are you still at St. Matthew's in Halifax?"

"I see a new challenge on my horizon. I have accepted a position with Queen's University in Kingston. Apparently the previous principal mismanaged funds so terribly that the institution is now on the brink of financial ruin. As the new principal I will have a lot of fundraising to do in the coming years. The community has graciously donated a building to devote to studies in theology. I want to graduate men who are dedicated to service rather than the accumulation of wealth. Can I tempt you to join me?"

"I think my mother would strangle me if I gave up law. And yet, there are days when I wonder if law really is my path in life. I too hear a calling of sorts."

"Poetry? As I remember you wanted nothing more than to be a poet when you were a boy. You drove your mother to distraction."

"Oh, I still do."

"And Charles?"

"He is working with our brother-in-law in Boston but plans to attend university in theology. Mother is pleased, to say the least."

"No doubt. After all, her brothers are both ministers. Perhaps he'll consider studying at Queen's. And you? Do you still seek inspiration in God's word?"

"I still write. It is, in all honesty, the only passion in my life."

"There are no young women in Boston?"

George felt a twinge of sadness. The ring box felt heavy in his hand. Awkwardly, he put it back in his pocket. "No one of special interest."

"Well, don't wait too long. Your aunt wanted me to tell you that lunch will ready at noon." Reverend Grant patted him on the shoulder.

George put his hand in his pocket and felt the ring box. Perhaps Reverend Grant was right. Perhaps a life of service would soothe his conscience. Grant devoted his life to service; he lived frugally and gave generously. Could it be that God was punishing him for being a selfish man? Is this why He chose to take Maggie away from him? He needed to find some reason for all this pain.

Chapter 21 – 1882

The Fly

It is a curious fact that private practices of law assume a collective identity to signify the combined legal training of their senior partners. This specific middle-aged collective specialized in civil litigation. Cameron was not included in the string of surnames painted on the front window of Dean, Butler and Abbott at 42 Court Street in Boston. George had worked at the same small desk in the same reception office off and on as a clerk for more than three years. Now a qualified lawyer for five years, he found himself sitting behind the same dusty desk, under the same dim lights, filing the same type of cases for the triplet of litigators. These lawyers were smaller fish in a much larger sea of prominent legal minds. The biggest fish in Boston's legal pond was Frederick P. Fish whose firm, in its year of inception, represented the giants of American innovation. In March of 1876, six years earlier, patent number 174,465 was issued to A.G. Bell for the claim that his design could transmit vocal sounds over distance. The firm of Dean, Butler and Abbott did not handle this deposition, nor were they involved in any facet of the case, save professional envy.

Since becoming a lawyer, George had made little progress with the publication of his poetry. Yet despite his inability to gain an audience, he continued to write. He wrote editorials in response to every issue of *The Globe*. Some of his letters were rather contentious, and he feared his employers might not be too pleased. Especially since he wrote poetry when he should have been researching legal precedent.

George caught the almost imperceptible movements of a black dot on the inside of the firm's front window. He watched the creature crawl across the backwards B in "Butler" and followed the fly as it made its way to the corner of the windowsill. In a sudden shift of perception, George became the fly. He was travelling across the surface of his life with what he desired most on the other side. He could see it as clearly as the people who walked by the window. His future was before him, yet he could not reach it no matter how much he scurried about. He was a simple ordinary fly, crawling across the giant letters of the senior partners. Below he noticed the crisp corpses of the flies who had spent countless hours crawling across the glass. His would never be a name engraved on a door or emboldened on the letterhead of this firm. This is not where he envisioned himself. How could he devote real time to his poetry when he had meaningless and endless tasks to perform in this crypt?

Beyond the backward letters in the window, he caught a glimpse of fur and jewels. Lurline Ainsworth. She was in an amorous embrace with an older, distinguished businessman who carried her hatboxes and packages. George's pen stopped on the page. She looked through the glass, right into George's eyes, but did not acknowledge their mutual gaze; rather, she turned, threw her head back and laughed. The venomous lines poured onto his foolscap.

> We met with mutual smile upon the lip
> And scorning kiss for each other; when we part
> I do not blame thee that the hate will slip
> Up to the tongue from the more honest heart.
> We hate each other: let us not disguise
> This common feeling; let us rather show
> We know each other as we really know
> Nor hide our bitter looks from other eyes

George watched Lurline fawn over the older gentleman. He felt his jaw ache as he clenched his back teeth and ground them from side to side. He spread his fingers over his eyes and brought them together until he had trapped her figure alone between them. He slowly squeezed them tighter together. She looked his way again, and he busied himself with a fumbling of files and papers. He resumed writing. The nib scratched the paper as he raced to the margin of the next line.

> Time bade me love thee and it bids me hate:
> I do its bidding as my proper fate.
> But while obeying, I will be to thee
> An open hater; be no less to me!

He looked up to see a semi-circular jury peering down at him. His pen stopped on the page, and he could feel the weight of his neglected responsibility press down on the nib until a pool of black ink spread across his last word.

"Mr. Cameron?"

George took out a piece of blotting paper and patted the offending spot.

"Mr. Cameron, it has come to our attention that you are not ... how shall I say?"

"What Mr. Dean is trying to say is ... we have decided to let you go."

George blinked twice and wiped the tiny drops of perspiration on his nose with his handkerchief. "You are dismissing me from my position?"

Abbott cleared his throat. He took two steps back and one step forward before he spoke again. "Though you came to us as a student at the top of your class – a young man highly revered by your professors – you have not demonstrated that same zeal in our practice."

Butler jumped into the waters. "You must understand that our names are on that window. We have our reputations to consider."

George could feel the rising burn of blood crawl up his neck and flush his face crimson. His embarrassment was more a matter of wounded pride than sincerity or an admission that he had done anything to deserve such action. "Very well then, sirs. I shall remove my belongings from the desk immediately."

"Oh no – you have misunderstood. Oh dear!"

"Forgive us. What Mr. Dean meant was ... well ... we did not intend to suggest that you must leave now. We wouldn't want to rush you out the door as it were. Please feel free to finish the week and the files you have started for Mr. Abbott's trial. You have started the Fanshaw files?"

The answer was too painful to acknowledge, so George lied. "Of course. It will be on your desk first thing in the morning."

"Very well then." The three men took a simultaneous step backwards, then headed off in different directions to their respective offices. The doors shut. *Thud* Dean. *Thud* Butler. And *thud* Abbott.

Part Three

Kingston

1882–1885

Chapter 22 – Early September 1882

A Presbyterian Mission

Reverend Thomas Smith's voice rang clear. "Luke 13:3 tells us that honesty is a matter of the will. I ask you this morning, have we truly repented?" The congregation at St. Andrew's admired the singular vivacity of Smith's style that stirred their collective conscience and guided their wandering souls back to the path of righteousness. Among the many attentive parishioners that late summer morning, George sat on the hard wooden pew, fidgeting with his collar. He tried to listen. Red-faced, he bowed his head to conceal his embarrassment from his mother seated next to him. Charley, however, sat riveted to the pew and nodded knowingly as Smith addressed the congregation. George looked at his young brother with envy. Charley's studies were going well. Very well. And what of George? Smith's words scratched the thin veneer of his carefully crafted religious devotion. While Queen's Theology represented a new start, or at least a respite from Dean, Butler and Abbott, it was not going as well as he led his mother to believe. This explained, in part, why the reverend's words on truth and honesty chiselled away at the very facade of his crumbling conscience.

George had studied law with the fervent zeal of a young man who hoped to move men with his words, but the actual application of law fell far short of his lofty desires. At the firm, he felt like nothing more than a glorified clerk, shuffling papers and transferring names and dates to monotonous mountains of meaningless documents. Years of study – not to mention expense – seemed wasted. He longed for the carefree days at the Parker Hotel when he was engaged in drink and debates with Crittington about the week's moot trial. Now, in this pew, he felt, at age twenty-seven, on the downward spiral of his career. The only pleasure he found in life was turning phrases in his mind to find the precise words to capture the feelings of the moment. The word on the tip of his tongue at this moment was *recompense*.

George calculated the figures in his mind: three years at the Boston Latin School, four years' tuition for his law degree, dormitory fees, the rest cure in Tybee, the new suits for Dean, Butler and Abbott, the dinners at the Parker with Lurline, the tuition for Queen's and how much for his poetry books? Each purchase inflated the total beyond his ability to ever repay his family. He underlined the exact figure in his mind twice. George adjusted his focus momentarily and heard Reverend Smith.

"It is quite common to hear ministers rise to the defence of parents whose children have betrayed the gospel."

Betrayed. The word caught George's attention, and he lifted his head to listen.

"You recall the parable of the prodigal son?"

The congregants nodded in unison. Reverend Smith spread his arms wide to fold the members of the congregation into his invisible embrace.

"While the tale acknowledges the responsibility laid upon you for the spiritual care of your children, I maintain it is by no means accurate to assign a life rattled by sin to parental blame and to say that because a child comes to lead a life of impiety, therefore the parents are at fault. Who among us is sufficiently prepared for these things?"

George's mother spoke of sufficient returns on her investment when George began his internship at Dean, Butler and Abbott. But as one year gave way to another and he failed to pay her back, the money he owed became an unbearable moral burden. George shifted in his seat under the weight of debt to his mother. It was this settling of accounts that had kept him for so long under the incessant ticking of the wall clock in the dark offices at 42 Court Street. For five years he notarized letters and listened to the complaints of clients over issues so petty that in an hour they would be forgotten. Indeed – recompense was the very word, the perfect word.

After the service, George and Charley escorted their mother out the doors into the fresh scent of spring rains on Clergy Street.

"Yo ho, young George!" Reverend Smith caught him by the elbow. "I trust today's sermon gave you something to think about for the remainder of the day? Well, well, young man, how are your studies going at our new hall at Queen's?" Smith had a vested interest in the school. St. Andrew's was the instrument for keeping the new institution fiscally afloat, and it was also St. Andrew's that introduced religious studies in the Faculty of Theology.

"Quite well, sir," George lied.

"If you have a moment, George, Reverend Dr. Grant and I have made a few inquiries on your behalf to secure missionary work. The school at Eagle Hill in Deseronto will be your placement this year, if things go according to plan. Mrs. Cameron? May I borrow your son for a few minutes or so? I have a number of details to discuss with him."

"Mother, do you mind?"

Jessie Cameron cocked her eyebrow and drew the tight line of her mouth into a forced smile. "To be perfectly frank, Reverend Smith, I do hope that a placement might restore my son's wandering spirit. He has been dreadfully distracted of late." That was lie too. Mrs. Cameron knew that her son had been distracted since he was a boy in New Glasgow. He was forever writing poetry in his journal – a truth that she struggled to keep in the family. A truth nevertheless that had an incessant way of making itself known time after time.

"I know that George is probably anxious to apply his studies to life," Mrs. Cameron continued. "It is one thing to read about spreading the good word and it is an entirely different kettle of fish when there is someone on the other end to listen. I shall leave ye to God's business. Charley? Where did that boy get to?"

Charley was flirting with a group of pretty young ladies. When he heard his mother call, he bowed and kissed the hand of Margaret Burley. The girls giggled. The young women of Kingston were unaccustomed to such formal demonstrations of affection and blushed when Charley tipped his hat.

"Come along, pupil of mine." Reverend Smith gestured to the manse, so George led the way across the wide green expanse of lawn to the side door of the limestone house.

"Here is the address of Mrs. Fanny Craig," said Reverend Smith once they were settled in his study. "I have written to her husband, Reverend Craig, who is the minister at the Church of the Redeemer in Deseronto. Mrs. Craig has agreed to help you get things settled at the school. She will escort you to Eagle Hill and introduce you to Reverend Anderson at Christ's Church where you will serve your placement for the next year under his mentorship."

Reverend Smith's "few minutes" churned slowly into the entire morning, and George needed time to think before he had to repeat the entire conversation to his mother. Living through it once was quite enough. In a flurry of goodbyes and several handshakes, George found himself at a crossroads of sorts. He looked in the direction of Main Street and down the hill of Queen Street. Seeing it was still early in the day, he headed down the hill and made his way to the wharf. As he walked, he thought of home. Not the cramped townhouse he shared with his mother on Main Street, but the tall pines and the fields of New Glasgow that stretched beyond sight.

He had not been back to New Glasgow in five years. His last visit was solemn and short. He imagined the earth piled on the wooden box and the little coffin with the infant inside. "Dear dead, I will not dig thee up from my memory." George spoke these words aloud though he did not know it. Nor did it really matter if he did ramble on about something that happened thirteen years earlier. No one was listening. The people who passed him on the docks were busy with their own affairs. No one noticed that this soul was dangerously drifting. They cared not for his lost love or his present misery. "Childhood promises!" He winced at his own gullibility – nothing more than an infatuation with a woman so fickle, so false. Try as he might his thoughts always drifted back to the early evening sky on the shores of the East River. Beside her, so close. He had been so nervous. It was there that George had become a man. Fleeting flashes of her mouth on his. Traces of her beating heart against his chest. The painful memories stirred lines of beauty in the poet's mind. A fair exchange. Words pressed heavily on his brain until he released them on paper in his journal.

> I thought that Time would teach me to forget,
> Yet years have passed since last I left thy side,
> And thou art more than well remembered yet
> My beautiful one, my bride!

George sat on the dock and wrote line after line as families unloaded their baggage from the ship and wheeled them down the ramps. It was only when he felt the chill of evening that he took note of the growing darkness. He put his journal in his coat pocket and headed home to his mother. He hoped to get a few hours of sleep before he made the long trip west to Deseronto in the morning.

The Picton stage pulled up to the Deseronto House Hotel after a day's journey. In the distance a thin plume of black smoke rose steadily from the steamship making its way toward the dock at the Mill Point waterfront. The shipyards, piled high with lumber for as far as the eye could see, were buzzing with activity. It reminded him very much of the frenetic activity of New Glasgow's shipyards. The vast empire stretching down the main street impressed George. At the centre of this activity rose a magnificent three-storey clapboard mansion. *This family must be Deseronto's version of the Carmichaels from back home*, thought George. He checked the address Smith had given him and was surprised to discover it belonged to this grand home. Before he could ascend the front steps, a woman in her late thirties opened the door to greet him.

"Mr. Cameron, I presume? You are looking for me." She held out her hand. "Pleased to finally meet you."

"Mrs. Craig?"

"Yes, but Fanny will do just fine. Please forgive my brother, Edward. He was called out about fifteen minutes ago. There was trouble with the blast furnace at the iron works, and he asked me to assure you that he will join us when he can. Hopefully his business will come to a speedy and favourable conclusion. We will meet up with my husband, Robert, at the church, tomorrow. You must be exhausted after your long journey. Perhaps a good night's rest will revive your spirit. I shall show you to your room."

"Yes, if it is no trouble. Thank you."

The following morning, Mrs. Craig pulled on a braided leather cord to ring a little bell in the kitchen. A servant, dressed in full white apron and a freshly starched cap, promptly appeared at the door. "We will take our tea and toast on the west porch, Olivia. While you are waiting for the water to boil, can you ring Jasper to ready the hansom?"

Fanny descended the steps to the front lawn, and George followed her around to the back of the house. He was in awe of such affluence. The park directly across from her brother's house stretched about an acre west to east with gently curving cobblestone paths that led to a central fountain. A gazebo graced its grounds.

Fanny pointed to the empty gazebo. "My brothers William, Herbert and Frederick formed the Rathbun Cornet Band and play there on special occasions and weekends throughout the warmer summer months." She led George to a large circular veranda furnished with handsome wicker chairs and a porch swing. *What must it be like*, thought George, *to live free of financial burden. To buy what ever you want without inquiring the price and calculating the number of salaries saved to make the purchase.*

"Please be seated, Mr. Cameron." Fanny draped her shawl over her shoulders. "Reverend Smith recommended you highly, young man."

"I hope I can live up to his praise." George felt doubt rising. It choked him momentarily. He took a sip of tea.

During the ride to the church, Mrs. Craig pointed out the buildings of interest. She was extremely well-versed in the architecture, materials and styles. "Mr. Cameron, please take note of the clock tower to your right. Our post office features Romanesque details." To George, the four-storey rough limestone castle tower and its adjacent round, red turret were medieval in appearance. They were unlike anything he had seen in Kingston or Boston. "That building also houses the customs office and the local Indian Agent on the second floor. I will introduce you to him later." As they trotted by the massive stone structure, George could see the spire of the Church of the Redeemer pointing the people of Deseronto to heaven. His doubt started to rise again.

"The church serves multiple faiths, Mr. Cameron. Sunday morning sees the Anglican congregation sing their lordly praises only to give up the pews to the Presbyterian parishioners in the afternoon. In the early evening the Methodists make the church their place of worship."

The ashlar limestone of the church was smoothly finished but not polished. As they approached, George noticed the asymmetrical tower. Clearly it had taken significant time and cost to construct this church. "The stone buttresses give the entire structure a rather formidable appearance, don't you think?" said Fanny. "Above the two gothic revival-style front doors, you'll notice two quatrefoils within two large circles. I've always been impressed by the decorative scalloped edges of the belfry louvers." *And all this in the middle of the woods*, thought George.

Once in the church he was surprised to see that it looked more like an ancient amphitheatre than a backwoods place of worship. The pews glistened. "Cherry and white ash. Lovely, aren't they," said Fanny. Reverend Robert Craig was waiting for them. Though amiable, he wore weariness like a badge of honour in his service. After exchanging greetings, he said to George, "The missionary students from Queen's are a welcome comfort to this community. As you will see, there is plenty to do with our young praying Indians." George winced at the expression. No doubt there were worse ways to describe his mission, but the possessive pronoun left him uneasy.

"Mrs. Craig will introduce you to our fundraising committee. They are in the Sunday school room in the basement." Reverend Craig gestured toward a door just off the front entrance, and Fanny took George downstairs.

"Ladies!" Mrs. Craig politely and playfully raised her voice and clapped her hands to catch the attention of a half dozen or so chattering women who were busy sewing tiny stitches on a vast field of red and white circles. Mrs. Craig took it upon herself to explain. "Mr. Cameron, this is a friendship quilt. The members of the town who wish to sponsor our missionary efforts at the school for boys pay for the recognition of getting their names embroidered into one of the rings on the quilt. We will raffle the quilt off during the fall fair."

George did not really know how to respond, so he smiled politely at the women ranging in age from twenty to eighty. The thought that their efforts paid his modest salary made George cry inside. He looked at the hands of the oldest woman in the group, her knuckles gnarled like the roots of an ancient oak. The bony growths and obvious inflammation spoke of unrelenting pain. He watched her labour with blind eyes to create perfectly spaced stitches as she worked her way slowly around the circles. She had not looked up when George and Mrs. Craig entered the room. He doubted that she was even aware of their presence.

Fanny got closer to the old woman and raised her voice. "Grandmother Rathbun, Mr. Cameron from Queen's University is here to meet the Steady Gleaners Guild!"

"Yes, yes, yes. Go on now, Fanny. Can't you see I'm working?" She shooed Mrs. Craig away like an annoying thought and returned to her stitching.

To ease his conscience, George quickly justified her toil in his mind. What would this woman of obvious privilege do with her dwindling days anyway? But he couldn't get the slow, deliberate motion of the old woman's fingers out of his mind. The purple spider veins spread out like crooked roads on a map, the splotches of liver-coloured freckles scattered across the loose leather flesh, the curled white hairs sprouting from the white knuckles. But none of that bothered him as much as the steadiness with which she held that fine needle between her fingertips. It spoke of devotion to God and a clear purpose in life. Her devotion scratched and tore at his temples as his own doubt pulsed just under the skin.

"Reverend Smith tells us that you studied law in Boston prior to settling in Kingston?"

George was startled by the young woman's use of the word "us." *How much do they know about me? What has Smith told them?* He began to sweat.

"Yes, Miss…?"

"Miss Gertrude Craig."

"Miss Craig. It was more of an academic avocation than a spiritual calling."

"I see. My father says that you and your mother attend St. Andrew's. You may know my cousins John and Mary Clements. They never miss a Sunday. They usually sit in the third row to the left. Mary runs the missionary fundraisers at the St. Andrew's bake sales and bingos and such."

"I will be sure to make myself known to her now that I have met you."

Gertrude blushed and then got back to work. George re-evaluated his words in his head and wondered if she took them as suggestive. It was one of many bad habits from his days in Boston. He squirmed a little and turned toward Fanny for direction.

"Where to next? Please lead the way."

"Thank you for your time, Gleaners!" she said cheerfully. She led George past the large quilting frame and the small Sunday school tables and chairs stacked in the corner. "I will get Jasper to take us to Christ's Church."

Reverend Craig met them at the top of the stairs. "Fanny, you will need to make haste at this hour." He pulled out his pocket watch and tapped the glass several times to emphasize his point. "Jasper, take Fanny and Mr. Cameron directly to Eagle Hill."

As the carriage headed west, the factory whistle in the dockyard punctuated the arrival of the noon hour. What seemed like an ordinary mill town just minutes earlier grew eerily silent for sixty seconds, and then a crescendo of male voices filled the afternoon air. Over a thousand hungry men flooded onto Main Street. Workers from the white domes of the charcoal kilns, men from the railway yard, smiths from the iron works and employees from the sawmills poured out like a steady stream of bees from a hive. Some armed with Rathbun currency in hand went to the Empress. Some of the fortunate ones walked home to enjoy the company of their families. Others took their buckets packed by wives and mothers to a quiet retreat on the waterfront or at the edge of the woods.

Jasper missed the exodus by minutes. George caught a glimpse of the daily event when he turned to see the town disappear. Past the dockyard now, the woods swallowed the small carriage. For the first time that morning Mrs. Craig was reflective and silent. She looked across the bay. She began to open her mouth to speak, but stopped and pursed her lips into a soft meditative pout. The ride up the hill to Christ's Church was quiet. George did not understand her silence. As he sat quietly staring at the rising monument before him, she began to speak very softly.

"You know, sometimes I think about things as they were. Before there was Deseronto, before there was Mill Point and long before Grandfather Hugo built this company town, there was the land and the water. Before Captains Deserontyon and Brant brought twenty Mohawk families to these shores, there was the land and the water. Long before Degandawida was born of a virgin mother to perform great deeds, there was the land and the water. The land belonged to no one. It just was." She stopped as if she was stirred from a dream. "I am so sorry, Mr. Cameron. I have said more than I should. Sometimes I have doubts about our work here. Part of me believes that we should just let them be."

George had never heard a woman speak with such poetry, such passion. Her confession of doubt drew his own uncertainty to the surface.

"George, meet Christ's Church," Fanny said in a reverential tone.

As he took in the architecture, George came to understand the tone of Mrs. Craig's words. The church held an aura of indescribable tranquility.

Above the door, a polished white wolf looked down on all who entered.

"The church at Eagle Hill was a gift to the Mohawk Nation for their loyalty to the British crown during the American Revolution."

George felt at ease with Fanny. He felt he could share his thoughts with her. He paused and then confessed, "I am afraid I feel somewhat overwhelmed."

Fanny could see the look of despair in her new friend's eyes. "I would like to give you a small gift to help you if you ever find yourself adrift, in need of reassurance." She reached into her coat pocket and pulled out a slim green volume entitled *The Anxious Reader.* "My mother-in-law brought this back from her visit to London last year. Reverend John Angell James has a way of addressing one's doubts straight on, as it were – without the intimidation that can come from sermons delivered in person. All you have to do is close the cover if you don't agree."

"Really, I simply can't. I am grateful for the offer, but…." George opened the delicate cover to read the directions for the "profitable reading of the treatise."

"I insist. Consider it my investment in your education, or if you like to think of it another way – your salvation. If Reverend James cannot satisfy your questions, then you may have your answer after all."

"Thank you, Mrs. Craig. I shall give your Reverend James a read tonight."

Jasper brought the horses to a halt, jumped down and helped Fanny out of the carriage. George flattened his unruly hair with his hands and stepped down. A small group of Mohawk residents had gathered to greet them.

"Ah, here is Reverend Anderson and the other church elders. *She:kon*," she said as she approached them.

"*She:kon, skennonkowa ken!*"

"I do, my friends." Mrs. Craig seemed perfectly at ease. She turned to George to explain their greeting. "For centuries the five nations of the Iroquois were at war. Eagle Hill was the birthplace of Tekanwita – the keeper of the Great Peace who brought an end to war and formed the Five Nation Confederacy. I have been entrusted to carry on the tradition of peace with the Church. It is an honour I take very seriously."

A tall young woman had been listening intently as Fanny spoke. She turned to a distinguished-looking gentleman and spoke to him in Mohawk.

"That's Eliza Sero," Fanny told George. "She's Reverend Anderson's assistant and translator." Reverend Anderson smiled warmly at George and Fanny.

The elders greeted the new missionary student with warm handshakes and toothless grins. Reverend Anderson spoke and pointed to a small girl. She was pale and quite delicate in stature. Eliza translated. "Reverend Anderson is introducing his daughter, Mary. She works with the young ones on Sundays. She decorates our church for special occasions. It is quite a sight!"

"Presently we are preparing for the spring festival," Mary said. She coughed a little, and then tried to stifle it, but the fit was upon her. She held her hand to her chest. It was a deep, painful cough. George knew the pain of such a cough and immediately his heart went out to the girl.

Anderson turned to his translator and spoke. She said, "Please excuse his daughter for a minute. She has the grippe. It comes and goes. She will recover in no time." A female elder guided Mary inside to wait until the spell had passed.

"Come," said Reverend Anderson in English, and he beckoned for George and Fanny to follow him into the massive church. The grandeur of the church's interior matched the magnificence of its exterior. A massive triptych of the "Lord's Prayer," in Mohawk, graced the front altar, extending to the full height of the rafters. George took a deep breath and inhaled the sweet smell of fresh-cut pine and linseed oil.

Fanny pointed out the communion service on the front table. "It was a gift of Queen Anne, and it stands as a beacon of goodwill."

Reverend Anderson came directly to the point of the visit. His tone had changed, but Eliza's translation did not echo the seriousness of his facial expression or his lowered register. "We are not interested in the mission style of the residential schools in our sister nations. The work of the Mohawk Institute in Grand River is not the model we wish to follow. We do not want to separate the children from their culture or from their parents. Most of their instruction will be delivered in Mohawk, save your lessons. We want a peaceful marriage of cultures."

George stammered a bit before he managed a response. "Of course, Reverend Anderson. My role is to educate, not to assimilate."

Anderson's eyes narrowed slightly at the mention of the word that hung suspended in the air despite its charged gravity.

Fearing he had insulted the reverend, George turned to Mrs. Craig for assistance.

"The purpose of your visit to Christ's Church is to impress upon you that very point," she said. "You will be a spiritual advisor and an academic guide."

George nodded sincerely to emphasize his understanding. Mary, now recovered, gently took her father's arm, and he softened under her touch. A smile returned to his face. "Mr. Cameron, please join me. I shall show you your classroom and give you copies of the boys' lessons."

"You will have to forgive my father's vehemence in matters pertaining to the education of our youth," said Mary. "He is the spiritual caretaker of the Tyendinaga and the keeper of the Great Peace. It is a heavy burden at times as more and more young members of the nation seek adventure elsewhere. In part, an education in English facilitates that transition. Nonetheless, he is grateful to you and our sister church in Kingston."

As George and Mrs. Craig made their way back into town, it was now his turn to be silent. He needed to meet with the boys. He needed to hear what they had to say before he could commit. Doubt was shouting in his ears. Yet it was not fear that fed his doubt. It was respect. A sincere reverence for a people who belonged. People who had roots. Respect and a feeling that he had somehow violated the sanctity of their church by his very presence.

Chapter 23

The Stranger

Two weeks into his placement, George arrived at the British American Hotel to catch the early stage to Deseronto and was told there would be an unexpected stopover at Millhaven. "There is an important delivery that must go to Trenton by train, and we'll have to wait a half hour or so until the Prince Edward County stops at the Odessa station. I warn you, there's not much to do there, so I hope you brought some reading with you."

The stopover gave George time to explore the rocky shores of the lake. It brought him a measure of familiarity and peace. He sat and began to write. Before long, the splashing of oars hitting the water caught his attention, but he couldn't see a boat. Curious, he ventured off the shore in search of the source of the sporadic dipping. He jumped from rock to rock, hoping to see beyond the point. He heard a sweet melody dance across the water. The sun, now high over Amherst Island, blinded him, so he raised his hand to his face and squinted through his fingers.

The splashing stopped and the tune faded beneath the chattering of the gulls along the shore.

"Mind your step, or I shall have to rescue you." The voice was bold, young, playful.

"At the rate you are navigating those rocks, I shall drown before you reach me."

Her laughter was unexpected and defiant. Then he saw her face. Beneath the shadow of her wide-brimmed hat he could tell that she was beautiful. She sat patiently in the boat as it drifted closer to shore. It was a fair face, an unusual complexion for a farm girl. It was a face that made him think of summers past. George checked his emotions. He laughed at himself and cringed at the secret power women held in their beauty.

"Well then." Her voice broke the uncomfortable pause. "I am Ella Mae. I live up there." She pointed up the small cliff to a brick farmhouse. "You must have passed my house on your way down here."

"Yes, I did. Your house is charming." George teetered on the rock upon which he was precariously balanced, checked his footing then cautiously stepped back to the security of the shore.

Ella Mae drew in the oars and rested them on the seat in front of her. Confidently, she steadied herself. To George's surprise, she slipped one naked foot at a time into the shallow waters. She lifted her dress and the eyelet ruffles of petticoat above her calves and walked to the front of the boat. She deftly pulled the rope hand over hand until the bottom of the boat scraped lightly over the sand. Grasshoppers buzzed in all directions. Ella Mae skillfully tied the rope around the broken branch of a fallen tree and sat in the shade. She gave her petticoats a shake to loosen the sand that clung stubbornly to the fine eyelet hem. She pushed her bonnet back to reveal a crown of thick flaxen curls. She was no more than a child of sixteen, but her tight-fitting bodice revealed the mature curves of a woman. Her grey eyes were fixed upon George's feet. The waves lapped over his fine leather shoes. She giggled.

George thought, *Girls giggle. Girls and the many coquettes who graced Beacon Street.* He watched the expression on her face change from one of amusement to a hint of anger. Friends had mentioned to George that he had a tendency to stare – unconsciously judging others with his silence. "Excuse me. My apologies," he said, stepping up onto a rock out of the water. "I was deep in thought when I heard your song ... and then I couldn't see you." He gestured toward the sun rising further in the sky. He was spent. For a man who lived and breathed words, they failed him miserably at this moment. Her beauty stirred something in him he believed had long passed. Before he could dazzle her with his wit and win her with his charms, he heard someone calling from above and he lost his footing. As he stepped back up on the rock, he caught the hem of his trousers on a branch.

"Ella Mae!" A voice broke through the brush. Twigs snapped underfoot. "Woo hoo! Ella Mae!"

"Annie, I am down by the shore." A flash of black and white charged through the brush and stopped abruptly on the edge of the cliff overhanging the water. The friendly face of a collie looked down. The dog cocked her head to one side and then the other. She barked.

"Come, Daisy." A young Black woman of twenty or so grabbed the collie by the scruff of the neck and guided her to a safer path. She treaded down the steep trail to the shore and put her hands on her broad hips. "Miss, you gave us a fright when you didn't show for breakfast. Come up now. Your father will be sore if you keep me from my morning chores." She let Daisy go and the curious dog sniffed her way to George's feet. All the while Annie kept a keen eye on the young man.

"Annie, I am not a child. I was rowing along the shore when I ran into Mr...."

"Cameron," George offered.

"He is lost."

"I can see that." Annie looked at the man who was wringing out his wet socks. "You shouldn't speak with strangers."

"Annie, how can we ever meet anyone new if we always think on them as strangers?" Ella Mae retrieved her shoes from the boat and was about to climb back in.

"Leave the boat now and run up to the house before your father throws a fit."

Ella Mae rolled her eyes, pulled her bonnet down on her head and trudged up the hill in her bare feet.

"Goodbye to you, Mr. Cameron. I hope you find your way. Take care not to fall in. Come on, Daisy." And with a final giggle, she made her way up the rocky shore. The dog followed, playfully jumping on her companion. George caught a final glimpse of the flaxen-haired girl when she turned and waved.

That evening in the tepid waters of his bath, George washed the day's journey from the back of his neck. The late days of September swirled with dust along the road that stretched from Kingston west to Mill-haven. His suit would have to be brushed tomorrow and his shoes, well, his shoes were ruined. He could hear the girl's giggle and smell the starch of her fresh-ly pressed blouse. Virginal. White. He squeezed the sopping sponge over his head and muttered, "Bah! Love is for fools."

"What's that ye say, George?"

He had forgotten that his mother was on the other side of the screen, sewing the hem of his torn trousers by the lamplight of his reading chair. Had he really said that aloud? Sometimes he wasn't sure what was thought and what passed from his lips as speech. He squeezed his eyes tight and pressed a cloth against his face. "Nothing, Mother."

Nothing? Ella Mae's cheeky retorts made him smile. The nerve! She was flirting with him; he was sure of it. He had known the veiled glances, per-fumed arms and moistened lips of many women in Boston. Unmistakable signals. Her body had not gone unnoticed. Hardened by thoughts of her calves and tiny, perfect feet, George began to stroke himself softly but firmly under the water. It throbbed, eager for rougher play.

"Ye have been in there for ages, George. Ye must be a prune by now." When her son did not reply, Mrs. Cameron spoke again. "George?"

But he was drowning in thoughts of Ella Mae. Her firm bosom. He closed his eyes and touched those golden curls and stroked her pale cheek with the back of his hand. The imaginary caress brought him to his climax. He grabbed the side of the tub to steady himself. It had been months since he'd felt the rush and shudder of his manhood. He leaned back and sighed.

"George. I insist that ye get out now. You'll catch your death."

It was settled. He would return to Millhaven. Was this his recompense? Would a young fertile bride settle his accounts? He owed his mother this much.

"I'm finished, Mother." George looked at himself in the glass, still vital, still hard. Then he caught a glimpse of his pocket watch on the washstand behind his own reflection. Furtively he tucked it deeply into his handkerchief drawer. He then wrapped himself in his dressing coat and peeked from behind the screen.

His mother looked up and smiled. "Well, now. I thought ye drowned in there."

"I feel much refreshed." He kissed her on the cheek. "How goes the mending?"

"Good as new." She removed her wire-framed spectacles, put down her sewing and rubbed the back of her neck. George understood this gesture as a request, so he stood behind his mother and gently loosened the tight muscles in her neck. While he rubbed her shoulders, he devised a legitimate reason to return to the shore. He cleared his throat.

"Mother, I seem to have misplaced my watch. I am certain that it must have slipped out of my pocket when I stumbled on the rocky shore in Millhaven."

"Ye have been so absent-minded since we left Boston. I insist that ye return the morrow to search for it. Your father gave ye that watch. Aye. I insist. What if someone should find it and pocket it? Ye must return to Millhaven in the morning."

"As you wish, Mother. I shall have to rise early. Mother, if you please, could you ask the cook to wake me before six so that I have ample time to take breakfast?"

Chapter 24

Finding What Was Lost

The proprietor of the Picton stage looked up from his accounts. "That will be fifty cents." He recognized the young missionary from previous coach runs to Deseronto. "You're not due out Millhaven way 'til Monday."

George blushed beneath the weight of this accusation. He fumbled with his story. It got caught on his tongue and twisted a bit before he could get it out. He was hoping that by the second time even he would believe the lie.

"Coach leaves in fifteen minutes, but you wouldn't know that given the fact that you lost your watch and all." Ellsworth took George's money.

George could feel the faint ticking of the watch in his pocket even though he had wrapped it in his handkerchief. He wondered if Ellsworth could hear it too. That would explain his strange remark about the facts.

"Jonas will be your driver today. Next!" The young couple behind George moved forward in line.

George could tell that it was going to be another humid day, so he took off his jacket, rolled up his shirt sleeves and sat on the bench of the British American under what little shade the porch offered. Despite the heat, he was fully awake and felt rested for the first time in months. To his surprise, he had slept through the night. He took this as a good omen. Lately he'd been sleepless, turning over phrases from the *Presbyterian Reader* in preparation for his next meeting with the boys at Eagle Hill. Next week's lesson was coincidentally on the topic of doubt. How could he pretend to lecture young minds about the evils of uncertainty when he dwelt at doubt's doorstep every day?

For years sleep had taunted him. It was an elusive tune in a dance with no partner. His painful memories of New Glasgow were right under the surface of his mind. One scratch, one crack could release a sea of regret. Maggie's ghostly voice would call him from a distant shore. *Not now*, George reminded himself. *I cannot think of her. Not now when I am about to move forward.* He pushed these thoughts back into the recesses of his mind where they continued to skulk and wait.

"Where you stopping, sir?" Jonas broke the spell.

"Millhaven."

"What brings a fine gentleman like yourself out Millhaven way? Legal matters?"

"I am going back to retrieve a lost pocket watch."

"Why not save yourself the time and trouble and buy yourself a new one?"

"It is a very special watch."

"Indeed, it must be." Disappointed with the mundane nature of his passenger's visit, the garrulous driver turned to the travellers in the rear. George stopped listening. The journey seemed longer this time. This time anticipation mingled with fear to produce an intermediary sense of doubt. *What if she thinks me a fool? Worse yet, what if she is engaged to another man?* George grew jealous of Ella Mae's fictitious suitor and then sad when he remembered Mr. McQuarrie's proposal. He knew what it was like to lose love to a rival. His fear intensified when they passed the sporadic farmsteads on the outskirts of the village. *But surely she's too young to have any serious suitors.*

Despite the Grand Trunk Railway stop a mile north of the village, Millhaven did not see its population swell the same way Bath, a village further west, did. For most, the village was little more than a brief stop along a route of greater importance. However, for others, Millhaven was the destination, and the families there who worked closely with the land took root like the clusters of lilac bushes that lined the road. Their roots travelled just under the surface of the clay soil and stretched northward to Camden East.

I want this, thought George. His mind was now resolved: he would win the young girl's heart. No doubt. No doubt at all.

When the coach stopped at the post office in Millhaven, George blinked several times. Dust lined the creases in the corners of his eyes, making him look older than his years. He stepped down and made his way toward Ella Mae's farmhouse on the shore of the north channel opposite Amherst Island.

As he approached the large brick house, he could hear the clank of pans and the clink of jars in the back kitchen. Sounded like Annie was busy preparing lunch. Walking to the front entrance, he realized that this was no ordinary farmhouse. Its intricate gingerbread was carefully carved and lined both the front porch and the second-storey gables. The windows and doors were arched, and the door was elaborately decorated with a complex design of Celtic knots cast in iron. Expensive, and curiously out of place. The fine brick house would blend in on any street in Kingston or Boston for that matter, but it stood out among the clapboard farmsteads in the rest of the village. Disappointed that Ella Mae was nowhere to be seen, he decided the direct approach was best, and he went to the front door and rang the bell. What did he plan to say when someone answered? He had neglected to include dialogue in his well-rehearsed ruse.

A man answered the door. He looked to be approaching sixty, but his age was difficult to discern given the thick grey beard that grew several inches past his chin. "Can I help you? You seem lost. I think you may have the wrong house." Billings Emigh stood five-feet-seven inches tall. He wore a clean white shirt, freshly starched and pressed. His dress trousers were held up with black suspenders.

"I've come to call on Ella Mae."

"Have you now?'

"I understand she lives here."

The clanging in the kitchen stopped. A minute later, Annie made her from the back kitchen until she stood a few feet away from the front porch. Her skin was the colour of coffee beans and her piercing dark eyes pinned George to the spot.

Wiping her hands on her apron, she greeted the visitor. "Good morning, Mr. Cameron. What brings you back to Millhaven? And so soon?" Annie knew very well why George was there. She was more than familiar with the dumbstruck glimmer in the eyes of Ella Mae's many gentlemen callers. George tried to hide that smitten look of the young with a straight face, but Annie wasn't finished with him just yet. She pressed him a little further. Like a barn cat, she decided to play with the field mouse. She took tremendous amusement as she tossed her prey up in the air and then stared at him knowingly.

"You know this man, Annie?"

"Yes, sir. His name is George Cameron. He is a missionary with St. Andrew's in Kingston. Ella Mae and I encountered him down by the shore yesterday while he was waiting for the coach to Deseronto."

George gave Annie a nod. *Ah ha! So Ella Mae's guardian talked with the postmaster. Well, she's no match for me.* Accustomed to the games of open courting in Boston, George cleared his throat and faced this opponent, who was clad in a white apron and clogs. Out of the corner of his eye, he spied Ella Mae through the ironwork grate.

"Yes, I have returned today to search for my pocket watch. It must have slipped out of my pocket when I lost my footing on the rocks. My mother insisted that I return immediately to look for it lest it be exposed to the elements or pocketed by some lucky soul who stumbled upon it by chance."

Billings assessed the stranger who had at least ten years on his prized daughter. He compared this man to the pimple-faced boy who had asked his permission to take Ella Mae to the dance at Finkle's Tavern in Bath. Of course he declined the invitation on behalf of Ella Mae. No daughter of his would be caught dead dancing in the company of drinking men. Billings knew he could not so readily dismiss a young man of George's obvious education and social graces, so he resolved to invite the young man into his home. He drew himself up to his full height and instructed Annie to get their guest a glass of water.

"You could have saved yourself the time and money on coach fare to replace the watch, Mr. Cameron."

"It is George, please. Funny, the driver made the same observation this morning. While I realize that replacing the watch may be the commonsense thing to do, this watch holds sentimental value. You see, my father gave it to me after my graduation from Boston Law in 1877. It is engraved with a message from him, and I hold the watch dearly."

Billings was impressed. Here was a man of means and stable influence for his headstrong daughter. "Please come in and sit down after your long journey this morning. Ella Mae and Annie will help you search the shore for your watch after lunch."

He led George to the parlour, where he gestured to a straight-backed chair. George took a seat, and Ella Mae and her father sat opposite him on a horsehair divan.

"Tell me, young man, what brings a promising young lawyer from Boston to Kingston?"

George began the story of his life, all the while acutely aware of the judge and jury in the room. "I am Nova Scotia born and raised. My family, supportive of my academic promise, decided to send me and my brother Charley to Boston from New Glasgow when I was only fourteen. After I graduated from the Boston Latin School, I then attended the newly opened University of Boston School of Law."

Ella Mae must have detected a strain of emotion in his voice when he said the phrase "only fourteen."

"How difficult for you to leave friends and family." Ella Mae could not even entertain the thought of being in the same situation. Her little family was all she knew and loved.

Could she read his thoughts or was the pain of this childhood parting so obvious?

"I can hardly remember it." The truth was that he did not want to remember the pain he had buried so deeply. *No*, he thought. *Not now*. He reined in his emotions and focused on his mission: to win Ella's heart. Or what was his mission again? Yes, to find his watch. He felt it ticking in his pocket and was certain that everyone in the room could hear the incessant rhythm of his lie.

He turned to Billings. "To speak truly, sir, I found law to be a rather – how shall I say this without sounding ungrateful? – I found the practice of law a hollow enterprise. I longed for something of more substance in my life. My mother and I thought we would join my younger brother Charles who had decided to study theology here in Kingston. I heard a calling – let's say – stronger than justice. I was also accepted to Queen's Theology. Part of my program requires a year's placement, teaching young boys the Bible. My placement is at the reservation school in Deseronto. I was here yesterday on a forced stop-over."

George deliberately left out his year in Tybee. While it was a necessary break in his academic path, revisiting it now would open up painful thoughts kept in tiny boxes at the back of his brain. He paused, peeked under the lid of one of those boxes and then shut the lid quickly. *I shall not go there. Not now. Not in the company of Ella Mae.* He let his eyes wander around the room to avoid eye contact. He cleared his throat. Satisfied that he had given a good account of himself, George brought the conversation back to the matter at hand. "I think I shall start my search. I must admit, I am anxious to find my watch. Ella, will you join me?"

"Of course." Her cheeks grew pink and then red under the promise of a well-to-do suitor. She was tired of the boring conversations of farm boys. She wanted to hear of George's adventures.

Billings weighed the story and decided that George was indeed an honest man. But not so honest that he felt comfortable leaving him unchaperoned with his daughter, so he revised George's plan. "Annie, set another plate for our guest. Ella Mae, please help Annie with lunch. After we've eaten, you and Annie can join George in the hunt, if he hasn't found his watch by then."

Annie laughed. "Yes, Ella Mae loves to help in the kitchen."

"Not fair, Annie!" protested the girl.

"Now, Annie. Ella Mae does love to bake." Billings wanted to bolster his daughter's domestic abilities.

"True, sir." Annie turned to George. "Mr. Cameron, you really should try her pumpkin pie. Without exaggeration, it is far better than mine. She has a delicate way with pastry."

"I shall be sure to leave room for such a praised pie. Your hospitality is most unexpected, I mean, most welcome. Now I shall head down to the shore before any more time passes."

Billings rose to his feet and saw the young man to the door. Daisy lay in the shade of a giant maple. When she heard voices, she perked up her ears, wagged her tail and decided to join George. She trotted alongside the stranger as he made his way to the shore.

After the pretense of half an hour, George returned to the house.

"Any luck?" Billings called out from the barn where he was getting his wagon ready for a trip.

George held up the watch by its chain and dangled it in the air. "It's no worse for wear."

"Good boy, good boy." Billings patted the horse's neck and steadied him to manoeuvre the bit into his mouth.

"Going out?"

"Yes. After lunch I have some business to tend to in Bath. Lincoln here needs to feel the bit for an hour or so to be comfortable. He's new to the rig and spooks a bit is all. It's a good thing your watch didn't fall in the water, or you would completely lose time. I think the ladies have lunch almost ready. You'll probably need to wash up a bit after your long search through the rocks. Please just let yourself in. I shall follow shortly."

George stopped in the dining room where he marvelled at the craftsmanship of the beautifully carved crown moulding and the precisely cut lines of the wainscotting. It was not what he expected of a house stuck in the middle of nowhere with no tavern or shop within miles, save the post office. Billings broke his reverie.

"You seem surprised by the intricacies of my handiwork. I carved all the woodwork you see. Oh, my brothers helped a bit, but what you see is the labour of my hands for my dying father. He spent one summer here before he passed and willed the place to me."

Ella Mae had entered while her father was speaking. "My grandfather, Joseph Emigh, had this house built for his third wife when he turned eighty."

Billings corrected his daughter. "I'd say it was more for himself, since Margaret never cared a whit for the lake. I carved all of this in the winters when the chores were lighter."

"His third wife?" George said.

"Yes. He could not stand to be alone. Grandmother Margaret wanted a brick house with all the city trimmings," said Ella Mae.

George wondered whether Billings was alone. He wanted to ask where Ella Mae's mother was but thought that might be too forward.

"Father could never say no to Margaret," said Billings, "even when she refused to set foot in a house built by the lake." The memory of his stepmother was obviously a sore spot; he changed the subject just as Annie came into the room, wiping her hands on her apron. "My brother William is your age," said Billings. "He is studying medicine at Queen's. Perhaps you may have run into him?"

"Can't say that I have."

"Not all farmers are poor and uneducated, Mr. Cameron," said Annie. "I bet he didn't tell you, but Ella Mae's father is a trained lawyer."

George was taken aback. He raised his eyebrow. A farmer who was a qualified lawyer like himself? Interesting indeed.

"Now, Annie, I'm sure Mr. Cameron doesn't have the time to listen to the details of property transfer and the like."

George was keenly aware that he and Ella Mae hadn't had one moment alone since the first time they exchanged words down on the shore. He was energized by her presence but didn't want to reveal his attraction in front of the girl's father. He turned to examine the mantle and noticed a curious pair of rather old candlesticks displayed there.

As if conjured by his thoughts, Ella Mae came up behind him and brushed lightly past like a kiss of gossamer silk. The imperceptible threads between them quivered with energy. She picked up one of the candlesticks and traced its curves with her fingers.

"My great-grandmother brought these Dutch *kaarsenstandard* with her when she and our family fled Bachway, New York, in 1796. She died in childbirth at Miramiche on the St. Lawrence. My grandfather remarried soon after they arrived on these shores. I cherish these pieces as a reminder of the sacrifices my family made to settle here. This land is important to us." Ella Mae handed him the candlestick.

It was so heavy. George wondered what would possess the woman to carry such a weighty and seemingly unnecessary knick-knack if they had to flee.

Again as if able to read his thoughts, Ella Mae added, "These are among the very few things in my family that can be traced back to Holland. My grandfather's grandfather brought them to New York when he settled in Backwater Cove. My great-grandfather had eleven children, nine of them sons. His brother Jonas had seven of his own sons. My family stretches from the lake to Wilton and Camden and beyond."

"Do you have family here in Canada West?" asked Billings.

George could feel the light brush of downy hair against his hand when he passed the heirloom back to the girl. "No. It's just my mother, Charley and me. My father and two of my sisters live in New Brunswick. My other sister, Christina, lives in Boston with her husband, Colonel Moore. I lived with them for four years when I went to school in Boston. I must admit, I miss them terribly."

"I can't imagine being away from my family," said Ella Mae.

"Please join us at the table for lunch," Annie said as she placed a platter of cold ham on the table.

"I would like to wash up first if you could direct me to the water closet."

"No need to put on airs here, Mr. Cameron. You can wash up in the kitchen." Annie pointed to the door.

When George returned, Ella Mae put pickles and cheese and freshly baked biscuits on the table. All eyes fell upon him as he seated himself. "I'm sorry to keep you waiting."

Billings bowed his head in prayer, and the table followed his lead, punctuated with a chorus of "Amen."

"Let's eat." Billings passed George the ham from one direction and Ella Mae passed him biscuits from the other.

Flustered, he deferred to Billings' offering and smiled at Ella Mae. George concentrated on eating as best he could.

"Are you enjoying the Queen's theology program? You must find it to be quite a change from the Boston School of Law," said Ella Mae.

"A friend from my home in New Glasgow, Reverend Grant, recommended Queen's when he saw that I had become disenchanted with the legal profession. It's a funny thing – he knew five years before I did. I guess he sensed that I was lost, spiritually speaking. I had encountered losses—." He stopped. He did not want to go there. It was sufficient to say loss without going into the details of betrayal and his subsequent years of depression. George sat his knife and fork on his empty plate and wiped the corners of his mouth with his napkin.

"I think the pie has cooled enough to serve now, Annie," said Billings.

Annie rose to bring the pie from the sideboard. "Ella Mae here is one of only a handful of girls in the family over several generations," she said. "All beauties – but who am I to judge?"

George heard giggles coming from behind the kitchen door.

"Can we come in for pie?"

He turned to see two adorable fair-haired children, their eager faces peeking around the door. The girl, no more than five, was a younger version of Ella Mae. The freckle-faced boy with his toothless grin might have been four.

"Annie said we could come in if we didn't 'rupt."

"Of course you may, my pretties. Mr. Cameron, this is Miss Maudie-Lynne and Master Sanford Emigh, Esquire."

"I like your…." Maudie searched for something, anything, to like about the stranger. "I like your shoes. They're pretty. Like you."

"Thank you, young lady. Your shoes are also very pretty."

"I like pie," the young boy chirped. He didn't want his sister to forget why they were there. "My sister has a dil-kut way with pastry. Just like Mother. Right, Papa?"

"You are absolutely right about that, Sanford," said Billings tenderly.

Maudie and Sanford had successfully weaseled their way to the table and sat casually, waiting to be served.

"Just you wait, Mr. Cameron. One bite and you will ask Ella Mae to marry you!"

"Maudie!" Now it was Ella Mae's turn to blush. "Slow down, you two. Have you washed your hands?" The pair held out their pudgy pink hands for their older sister's inspection. Ella Mae checked front and back. Satisfied, she asked Annie to cut the pie.

"Well, I'll have to have my pie when I return from town." Mr. Emigh excused himself from the table and looked at his youngest children. "You two better leave a slice for me. Excuse me, Mr. Cameron. It was a – a pleasant surprise to meet you. We hope you'll visit again." And with that he left Ella Mae under Annie's watchful eye.

The pie sat on the table, golden orange and beautiful. Ella Mae had twisted the pastry in fine braids around the crust. Annie cut into the thick pumpkin centre, carefully navigated each slice to the pretty white china plates with their delicate red flowers and poured a small dollop of thick cream on each portion.

One bite and George was transported to bliss. His tongue caressed the creamy morsel, still warm. It tasted of nutmeg and sweet maple syrup. It was beyond anything the Parker had to offer or anything his mother's cook had prepared for the family when he was growing up in New Glasgow. He must have uttered a guttural sigh, for Annie stopped to comment.

"My, my, Mr. Cameron! We've never heard quite that same reaction before."

George was too preoccupied to take note of Annie or Ella Mae or the children. Maudie, however, had decided that it would be great fun to squish the pie between her fingers and lick them one by one with loud smacks and exaggerated sighs of pleasure.

"Look at me, I'm Mr. Cameron!"

"It's George, please." He winked at her.

"Maudie!" Annie took the girl by the ear and directed her to the kitchen.

George was finally alone with Ella Mae. She came up behind him and slowly took his plate. The gossamer threads began to tingle when her breast brushed his ear. George felt the blood pulse through him as he grew uncomfortably hard, the watch ticking in his pocket, keeping time with his own pulse. His desire for Ella Mae blended with the sensation of the velvety pie on his tongue. He wanted to kiss her hard and thrust his tongue in her mouth to taste her, but a little voice broke the moment.

"Can I have more, Ella Mae?"

George had completely forgotten that little Sanford was in the room.

"You will get a bellyache if you eat any more, and then the pleasure of your meal will be lost."

Annie stepped back into the dining room with a sour Maudie in tow. Annie cleared her throat. "Miss Maudie has something to say."

"I do?"

George stifled a laugh, barely managing to keep a straight face.

"I am sorry for being naughty. I am a wicked child who ought to be whipped with a switch." She stopped to remember the exact words Annie had fed her for the spontaneous apology, but the next few were new to her and she stumbled on *respectable* even after several attempts.

"It was all good fun. No harm done." George picked up Maudie and looked her in the eyes. Ella Mae's eyes. The little girl kissed him on the nose. She had the same look of cheeky defiance. *I wonder what her mother was like? Or is it Billings who coddles this little miss?*

"It's alright," Ella Mae assured her little sister. She moved in closer to George and kissed Maudie on the top of her little head, inches away from George's mouth. George watched Ella Mae's lips pucker and felt their softness in his mind. *Focus!* He sat the child down with a mock spanking. "So your father went to Bath on business?"

"Yes, to trade barley. And milk and eggs and cheese and wheat. There's a flour mill just over the bridge."

The turn in the conversation brought George back to the reality of his own situation. Though tempted to remain in the pleasure of Ella Mae's company, he did not want to overstay his welcome. *I need to leave her wanting more.* He pulled out his watch and tapped on the glass. "The stage will be arriving shortly to take me back to town. I really must thank you for a lovely day."

Maudie pouted. "So soon?" The remark may well have come from Ella Mae herself, for it was she who now wore her emotions on her face.

"I should like to stop by for another visit, as your father suggested."

"That would be lovely. I'll walk you to the door." While Annie was busy clearing the table, Ella Mae escorted George to the front porch. "I am glad that you found what you were looking for."

George was puzzled, then caught himself. Of course. The watch. He had forgotten the entire pretense of the visit.

"Now your mother will not have to fret." Before George could respond, Ella Mae kissed him gently on the cheek, turned and walked back into the house.

"To crumble with one kiss," George whispered to himself. He stood for a moment, touched his cheek, then headed off to meet the stagecoach.

Chapter 25

Pumpkin Pie

George walked through Market Square, dodging the decaying manure left by the day's cattle auction. The boardwalk, though incomplete, provided a temporary reprieve from the mud. He could not rest his mind. The oppressive humidity of the day folded round him like a thick cloak of wool. He had been walking the streets of Kingston in the late evenings, in part on the advice of his physician. He felt that if he could navigate these streets, he could find his way, at least in his mind, to a place of rest.

As soon as he turned up Brock Street, he could hear the distinctive sounds of the Telgmann concert party in full swing at the Queen's Inn. He quickened his pace, crossed the street and followed the music. When he walked through the doors, Oscar Telgmann was at the piano leading the Queen's rugby team in a lively march as they drowned the day's loss to Ottawa in pints of Staley's ale under the queer glow of electric lights.

The piano stopped when Oscar saw his good friend George Cameron at the bar, but the rugby players were too drunk to notice, so they kept singing.

"*Meine feines libretto!*" shouted Telgmann. He pushed his way through the hulking shoulders of the players and slapped George on the back. "Well, well. Can't sleep again, my young librettist? I say to hell with sleep and the spirits that haunt you!"

"Save the liquid spirits," George joked.

"How about a rendition of 'Ghost Tappings' for my spirit of the walking dead?"

George always enjoyed Oscar's company. Their friendship had started several weeks ago in this very bar where the two had lively conversations about the foolish trend in musicals and the insatiable appetite in America for the Savoy opera. Both concluded that a mock opera was in order. George himself would play the poet, Wind, and poke fun at his own thwarted attempts to be heard. Though George felt that he was betraying his artistic principles, he remembered what Howells had said in Boston: "If you want to make a name for yourself you must cater to the masses." George cringed at the thought of selling out, but Oscar's enthusiasm and talent drew him in.

Oscar turned to the proprietor and motioned for another by turning his mug upside-down over his head. He pointed at George and held up two fingers. Staley nodded. Oscar and George headed to their usual table at the back. Perspiring and red-faced, Telgmann loosened his collar, pulled out a limp white handkerchief and mopped his brow with several quick taps. He wiped the back of his neck before returning the cloth to his trouser pocket.

"Is Alidia here?" George had to shout even though Telgmann was a foot from his face.

"No, she is at home staying up with Mignon who has caught a croup. Terrible cough."

"What about your sister? Is Elsa here?"

"She went home ages ago."

Staley brought two mugs filled to the brim and sat them on the table.

"*Danke.*" Telgmann wrote his imaginary tab in the air with a broad smile.

"Yeah, yeah, yeah," Staley replied. "You'll be singing 'til dawn to settle accounts at the rate you're drinking, Oscar."

Telgmann turned back to George who was turning a folded piece of paper in his fingers. "Have you given more thought to our little opera?"

"Indeed I have, I have…." George began to unfold the paper.

"Well, then, do not keep me on tenterhooks. What have you got?"

"I thought you might be interested in the lyrics for our young heroic baritone."

"Have you included alliterative phrases to keep the tongues wagging?" Telgmann joked. His new friend had made it abundantly clear that he despised light opera.

George was now riding a low buzz that energized him. "I assure you, I am alive with alliteration! Now hold your laughter awhile and listen. The song I have written is about a pumpkin pie. When asked how much he loves our heroine, he should extol the virtues of her pumpkin pie."

"Ah ha! I will laugh, but only because we want the audience to do so as well. It is indeed a fitting ballad for our young soldier. Leave the words with me, and I shall patter out a proper tune when next we meet. I shall not sleep, my friend, 'til the job is done. Tell me though, how did you come about such a witty verse?"

George could still taste the thick sweetness of Ella Mae's pie, his first bite warm and soft. "I believe we should call her Ellie. It is a wholesome country name for our sweet soprano, don't you think?"

"Ellie, Nellie – pie it is. But do tell. There's more to your restless nights and plastered grin than the desire for pastry. Am I not right? *Mein freund*, confess!"

"She is, shall I say, an exquisite beauty of rare wit and intelligence for a girl of sixteen."

"*Sechzehn!* I shall have to hide my little Mignon, you rascal. An exquisite beauty you say?"

"She is sweet and fair for a country girl, yet has an ample figure that tests my private conduct."

"Privates indeed!" joked Telgmann. "But she is not a city girl? I would think a man of your taste would gravitate toward the elite lasses of our fair town."

"Enough of my love life. What think you of the verse?"

"I can work with it, no doubt in my mind. An ode to pumpkin pie for my lusty lad, but you'll get none of the topsy-turvy nonsense of our boys to the south."

Staley caught Telgmann's eye and pointed to the piano. Telgmann nodded, excused himself and resumed his place at the keys.

Chapter 26 – May 1883

A New Direction

The decision to leave Queen's was made for George. Principal Grant called him into his office to counsel the man he had known since a boy. A man who, in his opinion, never intended to commit to the study of theology despite his regular attendance at his mission placement in Deseronto. His work at Christ's Church, though appreciated, had been lacklustre at best, according to Reverends Craig and Anderson. There were rumours about George's off-the-books lectures about poetry and philosophy and Mohawk traditions. Despite numerous letters from the principal, George had not pulled up his socks. His mediocre grades were not enough for Grant to keep him on. Reverend Dr. Grant needed to bring this matter to some closure for all concerned. Unpleasant as it may be, he had to dismiss George from the college.

"It is not that you are not academically capable; your first-degree standing from Boston Law is sufficient testimony to your intelligence."

George sat silently in the hard wooden chair in the office of the principal, a man born in Stellarton a short distance from where George himself was born in Pictou County. A man twenty years his senior. A man he had known his entire life. He knew of Grant's achievements and he felt hollow in comparison. He told himself to stay focused. *Do not wander down the hallways of regret. Do not visit graves of lost love.*

"Theology appears to be an unfulfilled quest to provide you with meaning or perhaps direction. But you need to answer a divine calling – not project devotion's visage." Grant rubbed the stump of his mangled hand on his jacket and signed some papers with his left.

George began to physically squirm under Grant's knowing eye. Had he heard of George's late night pub-crawls or nocturnal activities on campus? George knew everything the good reverend was saying was true, so he did not reply. He merely nodded in solemn respect for the time he had wasted in pursuit of an answer to fill the void in his life – a void that could not be filled with alcohol or women or with prayer. While all this shame was churning in George's mind, he realized that he would have to break the news to his mother. He wasn't sure that she would understand, but he knew Mrs. Craig, on more than one occasion, had hinted that perhaps it was time to pursue his true passion: poetry.

The principal's mouth continued to open and shut. His eyebrows moved up and down with each expression. "It is our responsibility to train young men in the academic study of religion and to educate theological students for academic training and ordained ministry in the Christian faith tradition. We want to graduate men of service."

Try as he might, George could not stay focused on Grant's words. He was too busy treading water. He needed to keep his head above the surface, but the undertow of his own failure pulled him down. Still unpublished, he did not feel like a writer. The songs he had written for the new Queen's rugby team and the prize he won in the Queen's annual poetry contest were not enough. Nor was his new job as a writer at the *Daily News*. The only saving grace was that his father was not here in Kingston to witness yet another humiliation to add to his dismissal from Abbot, Dean and Butler. "Make us proud" burned in his conscience every time he opened his watch. There was one thing James Cameron would not tolerate: another moment of wasted time. While George had inherited his father's Scottish Presbyterian work ethic, he did not share his father's intrinsic admiration for respectable middle-class professions. His parents did not value poetry, nor did they see the point of pouring out one's feelings on paper for the world to read.

Grant stood up and put his hand on George's shoulder. "Remove the splinter and move on." George mirrored his actions with no real sense of what the man had said. "We wish you the best in your literary pursuits at the *Daily News*," said Reverend Dr. Grant. "Please send your mother my best."

Each note of Oscar's tune floated across the tavern to underscore the poet's burgeoning sense of guilt. Charley broke the spell.

"How did it go with Grant?" Charley had completed his studies at Queen's and started part-time work at a publishing house. It was a temporary position until he could find a proper placement.

"I got the sack. It is for the best really." George paused a minute and then added, "I felt somehow unworthy."

"Does Mother know?"

George did not answer. Charley took another sip of ale and put a comforting hand on his brother's arm. "There will be a part-time position at the publishing house when I leave."

"I'll leave the publishing to you, little brother. I had my fill working with McLelland in Boston. I want to write. I am confident that my position at the *Daily* will allow me to reconnect with that passion. It's not poetry, but...."

George looked at his brother. He had always been so jovial, so carefree. He had grown into such a fine young man, his steadfast companion. George was secretly jealous of the comfortable way Charley wore his life like a perfectly tailored suit. "The problem is I've been chasing a dream that isn't of my own making." George stopped short of dragging his mother into the conversation. A minute passed, then two. He was afraid to confide his fears aloud, but Charley was the one and only soul in the world who would not judge him. He broke the silence.

"I feel like am constantly on the outside looking in – standing on tiptoe."

"Tipsy do you say? We're all tipsy."

"I'm serious, Charley. I feel so temporary about myself. When I was a boy of ten, I had an unusual dream. It was strange in part because it was a recurring dream. For as long as I can remember, I have been standing on tiptoe in a garden with high hedges all around. I can see the vision of myself so plainly. I stretch as tall as I can, but I can only see just above the top of the boxwood hedge. There is Mother, Father, Maggie and you, of course."

"You just haven't found your place yet. Be patient."

"Patient? I am twenty-eight years old! I've been patient. All I want to do is write, but you know how Mother feels. Perhaps she is right: poetry doesn't put food on the table."

After another slow round, George left his pint on the table half empty. It was time to pack it in. He waved to Telgmann and embraced his brother. "I love you, Charley. You know that, right?"

"Forever and a day."

George staggered out of the Queen's Inn and headed up Brock Street. When he got to the apartment, he fumbled with his keys in the half-light of morning. The house was quiet, waiting for the day to begin. He sat at his desk and began to write.

Standing on tiptoe ever since my youth
Striving to grasp the future just above.
I hold at length the only future – Truth,
And Truth's Love.

Chapter 28

The Change

George prepared every syllable of his breakfast conversation with the vigour he had invested in closing arguments during the moot trials of his university days. He even anticipated his mother's potential arguments during her cross-examination. There were so many things to discuss, so many changes to their routine on Main Street.

Mrs. Cameron began the morning meal as she always did, with a short prayer to acknowledge their good fortune and the food before them. George said his own silent prayer: *Please God, let her understand and accept the decisions I have made and the changes that are about to occur in her life. Amen.*

George opened the conversation with his first witness: the principal of Queen's University. "Mother, I met with Reverend Grant earlier this week to discuss my progress in my studies."

"What a bonnie man! He's made a name for himself in this town. Honestly though, George Munro Grant was the clumsiest of students back home. Who would have guessed that he'd do so well for himself? Our Reverend Dr. Grant received his doctorate from the university."

"Yes, Mother, we are all so very proud of this remarkable man's achievement. Reverend Grant owes his success, in part, to his firm and unshakeable resolve. Mother, the principal and I came to a mutual and quite separate conclusion that I lack this resolve in my studies in theology."

Mrs. Cameron had heard this very argument in Boston barely a year ago. She felt a rush of embarrassment. Any concern for her adult son's future was shoved aside by the burning shame of another step off the social ladder.

"What will Reverend Smith say? He has gone to considerable lengths to accommodate your missionary placement." Mrs. Cameron thought of her family back in New Glasgow. They would no doubt hear about her son's shortcomings through Reverend Grant's family. Her mind was racing, grasping at anything that would soften the blow of another failure. Perhaps it wasn't as bad as she imagined it to be. Perhaps George would tell her that they were returning to Boston, and that he was going to resume his position at Dean, Butler and Abbott.

Receiving no reply, she took a deep breath, remained outwardly unruffled and countered her son's last remark with a sincere inquiry. "And the principal has decided on what course of action?"

George thought to himself, *Ah ha! She is taking the moral high ground and will not engage in her typical histrionics.* Very well then, he would present his next witness: Mrs. Reverend Fanny Craig.

"My work at the mission day school – though highly rewarding of course – is, in the words of Mrs. Reverend Fanny Craig, 'Below my station and obvious abilities.'"

Mrs. Cameron did not expect this turn in her son's testimony. She gathered her own resolve to add, "Quite. Nine years' training in the field of law is no doubt wasted on teaching young men who have no more ambition than to chop wood and fish for pickerel."

"So you understand my position. Two of my spiritual advisors have suggested that my noble pursuit is, well, not suited to my temperament. Who am I to argue with their sincere evaluation of my abilities? The ministry requires a steadfast temperament to fulfill the obligations respectably, as it were."

"Quite."

George was slightly thrown by her terse agreement. He treaded cautiously and placed the next plank of his carefully constructed defence. "You know that I have always shown a natural facility for the written word. Others seem to agree since my poem 'Adelphi' won the poetry prize at the university this year. Well, capitalizing on the momentum of this honour, I've decided to submit an application to the *Kingston Daily News* to be editor-in-chief."

"And? Do ye anticipate a favourable outcome?"

"I do, Mother. I believe in exercising God's gifts rather than denying them or feigning a religious calling when I have heard no such voice."

"And your talents as a gifted advocate and student at the top of your class in Boston?"

George had not predicted that his mother would move backwards. Had he not made it perfectly clear that law was *her* dream for him, not his own desire? He would lose all control if she started to cry over broken promises. He began a fresh assault in a completely different direction.

"I have wonderful news, Mother. News that will be sure to please you."

"George, I am not certain that I can take any more of your good news."

"I plan to ask a young woman to marry me."

Mrs. Cameron grew unusually flushed. A sudden surge of blood crept up her face and she turn a brilliant crimson.

"Jenny!"

"What is the matter, Mother?"

Between gasps for air, she managed to say, "It's the change, George. I shall need a cold cloth, or I shall surely faint. Jenny!"

"Mother, I can get your cloths, just breathe calmly." George had to postpone the momentum of his advantage. *Damn her theatrics.*

"Jenny!"

Seated in the kitchen, a young woman of nineteen heard Mrs. Cameron's frantic call. She waited until the old woman called her a third time before she decided to move. It was her secret power over her tyrannical employer.

"Jenny!"

"Yes, ma'am. I am coming." She ran into George in the doorway. He was obviously in a foul mood, so she excused herself and moved past him.

"Jenny, I shall need cold cloths now or I shall faint. George, open a window, I need air."

"Yes, Mother."

The young woman returned to the kitchen where she dipped the cloths into a basin. She was in the process of wringing them out when she heard her employer at the kitchen door.

"Jenny! I am having one of my episodes. Get the doctor. Go! Now!"

Within the hour the doctor arrived and tended to George's hysterical mother. Once the sobbing tapered to an intermittent sniffle, he packed up his bag and left the room quietly. George met him at the bottom of the stairs.

"Well then, Dr. Saunders, what is the verdict?"

"Our patient will be fine. Nothing a bit of rest and a strong tonic won't cure. She will no doubt sleep straight through until morning. The poor dear. George, I will caution you not to upset her. Women who experience the change can be – how shall I say? – sensitive. She would do well to remain in bed for a few days. I have instructed Jenny to prepare her a good, strong broth in the morning. I shall be by in a few days to check on our patient." And with these instructions the doctor took his leave.

The worst is over, thought George. At least now it was she who must approach him about the new woman in his life. His next move would be to convince her that Ella Mae was really not like the others in Boston. This was indeed serious. He knew his mother had hoped and prayed that he would bring home an heiress or at the very least a woman from a good family. And to Mrs. Cameron, "good family" meant a family of wealth and social standing.

He decided to remain undisturbed by his mother's unfortunate display of emotion. He would adhere to his usual custom of taking the Saturday morning stage to Millhaven to see Ella Mae. He would invite her, and a suitable chaperone of course, to take tea here at his home with his mother. Then he would ask Billings for his daughter's hand. Before that, he had to secure the position at the *Daily News*. He had to make a name for himself.

So the next order of business in the new direction of George's life was to inquire ever so casually about the editor-in-chief position. But how? He did not want to appear too desperate in his inquiries, nor did he want to seem too aloof. What was the right course of action?

He was contemplating the most effective strategy at the breakfast table the next day, when his mother made her first appearance downstairs since the previous morning. He placed his napkin beside his plate, rose to greet her, walked five paces to the other side of the table and pulled out her chair. When she was seated, he kissed her gently on the forehead. "Good morning, Mother. I did not know you would be joining me or I would have waited. Does Jenny know that you are down?"

"Good morning, dear. Yes, Jenny is well aware that I shall attempt to resume my regular diet. Ye will have to forgive me. The doctor stressed that I required several days' bedrest. What is one to do with the time? A waste really. I refuse to spend another idle day. Now, George, when do I get to meet your fine young lassie? Is she someone from our church perhaps? Am I already acquainted with the woman who has stolen my son's heart?"

"Mother, are you sure you are strong enough, or rather, have given yourself enough time to regain your strength to enter into such a stimulating conversation or entertain the possibility of company?"

"Nonsense, George. Do not be so dramatic. I am perfectly capable of having.... Forgive me, George, but given my episode, I cannot for the life of me remember your young lassie's name."

"Miss Ella Mae Emigh."

"My, my! What a sweet name."

"She is a sweet girl."

The word *girl* did not go unnoticed, and Mrs. Cameron leapt upon it at once. "Please, George, if ye will, how old is your young lady?"

"She is seventeen, Mother. Now I know what you must be thinking, but you were younger than that when you married Father."

"True, but times were different then. Please, what is it about this young Ella Mae that has ye certain that she is a suitable match for ye?"

"She comes from one of the oldest, most respected Loyalist families in Millhaven. Her father, Billings Emigh, has a legal degree and a sizeable tract of land just ten miles west of Kingston. Ella Mae is extremely well educated despite her gender and lack of higher learning. To be honest, Mother, she is one of the most natural of beauties I have ever met. She lives with her father, younger brother and sister in a charming brick farmhouse."

"High praise indeed. What does her father say about this rather sudden engagement? I assume ye have asked for his blessing to pursue this commitment?"

"I am confident that we will have his blessing once I secure the editor-in-chief position with the newspaper. I shall make my usual visit this Saturday to invite Ella Mae here to afternoon tea so that you and she can have an opportunity to share a laugh or two at my expense." From George's point of view, this conversation was going better than he had anticipated. "I believe, Mother, that you and Ella Mae will get on famously. Now if you will excuse me, the hour is late and I have plans to meet with my employer." With control back in his hands, George felt emboldened and intoxicated by the possibilities that lay before him. Yes, he felt the jagged pieces coming together.

Chapter 29 – August 1883

Charmed or Cursed

As she awoke early on Ella Mae's wedding day, Annie felt dread creep up her spine like a cold draft seeping into the house. The sensation had a sound, like the beating of soft wings. She turned and caught a glimpse of something, but she did not turn fast enough to catch its fluttering image. She set about to rid the house of this evil presence. Before the rest of the household was awake, she rearranged the furniture in the parlour to confuse any evil spirits. She dare not tell the nervous bride of this feeling, but as Ella Mae's maternal guardian, she knew it was her duty to dispel it.

Three days earlier, Annie and Ella Mae's Aunt Catherine had baked a three-tiered wedding cake. The top layer was a rich fruitcake that would be wrapped up and given out to the guests at the end of the celebration. Annie, Miss Maudie, Telgmann's daughter Mignon and his unmarried sister Elsa would place this cake under their pillows that night to dream of a future love. The bottom layer was a heavy chocolate flour cake baked to signify the financial stability of the groom. The delicate middle layer was a light vanilla cake to represent the bride's pure heart.

It was between the bottom two layers that the bride now carefully placed her silver charms. Each Christmas since Ella Mae was thirteen, Annie had given her a tiny silver charm. She had collected them from weddings she had attended. The first gift was an anchor, for a love that is steady and true, the next was a heart for a life filled with love, the third charm was a treble clef for a life of harmony, the fourth was a tiny silver horseshoe for luck. Wedding charms had not always been so favourable. Annie remembered her grandmother telling her that besides charms signifying good fortune, there were tiny miniature rocking chairs for a long life of spinsterhood, little silver crosses for losses and little bird charms for fate. Annie instructed Ella to tie the clasp of each charm with a ribbon long enough for the bridesmaids to pull them from the layer of vanilla butter cream between the bride's and the groom's layers. Annie retrieved the charms from Ella Mae's trousseau. They were wrapped in one of the handkerchiefs that Ella Mae had embroidered with "E.M.E." in tiny blue silk threads. Alice Emigh taught her sweet Ella Mae to smock and crochet and embroider two years before she passed away. It was a gift that no one could take away, their special time to pass on traditions from mother to daughter.

"Annie? Shall I include the butterfly that I pulled out of Charley and Margaret's cake last month?"

"No, dear. That one is yours, to ensure lifelong beauty."

Annie went into the parlour to check on the little girls. Miss Maudie and Mignon Telgmann had made tiny little bundles of sugar covered almonds for their guests: one almond each for health, wealth, happiness, fertility and long life. Maudie and Mignon had, of course, eaten a few more than their fair share. As punishment the two little girls had to retire to the parlour to rest their tummies. While the girls groaned dramatically, Annie was distracted by the fluttering of wings and a soft thumping against the parlour window.

"Annie, why is that bird trying to get into the house?"

Annie pulled the curtain shut before she spoke. "Nonsense! Birds are just birds."

At Ella Mae's tea shower a week earlier, Annie had presented the bride-to-be with a wooden spoon for luck, and Ella Mae laughed at Annie's irrational traditions.

"Really, Annie Appleby, you are, without exception or embellishment, the most superstitious of women."

While this was true, today of all days Annie shared only the most accepted superstitions; she kept the other, more ominous, omens a secret. All day long she battled the strong evil presence. Folklore was one thing to share with others, but her sincere and profound belief in haunts and spirits was better kept to herself. Annie repeated a rhyme to herself about the choice of wedding day: "Whoever married in August be / Many a change is sure to see." *It is an ambiguous prediction at best*, she thought. *Isn't change part of life? It cannot be good or evil. It is an honest rhyme. A realistic way to view marriage.*

She returned to the immediate day. It was long past the season of peonies and lilies. While she and her neighbours often quarreled about the exact meaning of each specific flower, they were in unanimous agreement that the rose was indeed the perfect bloom. But peach-coloured? Was that not the colour of lust? The colour of flesh? Annie worried that perhaps Ella Mae's marriage was one of necessity, for Ella Mae did not have bleeding cloths this month or last. Time would tell. No use dwelling on what could not be undone; there was work to do.

After Ella Mae and Annie finished with the cake and favours for the guests, it was time to get dressed. Annie instructed Ella to put a coin in the toe of her left silk slipper. Once she'd done so, Annie slowly spun the young bride in a circle and instructed her to utter a wish for wealth.

"Annie, really! Don't be so silly. What does wealth have to do with love?"

"Well, my little goose, it does no harm. Speaking of silly geese, how do you two find your belly aches now?"

"We're all better. Ella Mae, look what I got. It's a dolly bag." Maudie held up the lace bag proudly and tapped the bottom. "It's rice. Me and Mignon get to throw it at you and George for your fur-til-a-tea when you climb into the carriage."

"It is Mignon and *I*, little Miss Maudie." Annie looked out at the sky over the lake. No rain – a good sign. She spotted George and watched the groom as he made his way up the path from the shore. He seemed distracted, but that wasn't unusual. She still couldn't shake the niggling feeling of dread.

"Annie, whatcha lookin' at?" Maudie pushed up beside the only mother she had ever known. "Oh, it's George. Stay back, Ella Mae. Annie told me it is bad luck for the groom to see the bride."

At the edge of the shore, George looked out across the north channel. The water was a deep cobalt blue, and the sky grew cerulean as the sun crept higher. *August is a strange month*, thought George. Indeed on this day the grass was dull green and snapped like brittle straw underfoot. The cicadas sang incessantly about the summer heat, and grasshoppers clung to fragile grasses blown by intermittent breezes. On the edge of a small cliff, just above the shore, Billings, Charley and a handful of Ella Mae's uncles made a beautiful canopy of lilac branches while the women – Ella's Aunt Catherine, George's new sister-in-law Margaret and Telgmann's wife Alidia and sister Elsa – wove in wildflowers and bunches of apples and pears tied with bright ribbon.

It was his wedding day. It was just over a year ago that he had acquiesced to the likelihood that he would be a bachelor for the rest of his life. The day reminded him of his childhood summers on the shore of the East River, passed in the blissful ignorance of what life held for him. *This is my wedding day*, he repeated silently. *It is not a funeral. Not a day to mourn a woman who has now turned to dust.*

A bird flew up above him, swooped down and caught him off guard. Like a whisper blowing in the field of phlox, she flew up the path to the house. Curious, George followed. The small bird – a house sparrow – came to rest on the top branches of a ma-

ple tree just outside Ella Mae's window. Here it chir-
ruped and cheeped so sweetly that George searched
the foliage to find it. "Whither whilt thou lead me,
little sprite?" When he looked beyond the branch,
he saw into Ella Mae's bedroom. Miss Maudie was
looking down, waving her little hand fiercely to catch
George's attention. He pretended not to see, but he
caught a glimpse of a delicate white moth in the mirror. Ella Mae. At first, he dismissed the gravity of
what had just happened. Then the bird took flight. It
was too late. George had seen his bride.

The afternoon was bright and cheerful. The bride approached the shore in a little red rowboat decorated
with sprigs of myrtle and wildflowers. Billings manoeuvred the oars, and little Maudie scattered daisies
in the water behind them. All were resplendent in
their wedding clothes.

"Really! What a flair for the dramatic!" Mrs. Cameron sat among the other guests who were standing
on the little cliff above the shore, awaiting the bride's
arrival. She sat on one of the dining chairs Billings
had made for his wife for their wedding eighteen
years ago. Jessie was one of the few who sat; most
of the guests formed a semicircle around the beautiful altar made by family and friends, waiting for the
young couple to join hands. The guests clapped as
Billings helped Miss Maudie out of the boat first. The
adorable little sister held Ella Mae's nosegay as the
proud father helped the young bride step from the
boat onto a little wooden bridge he had constructed
for the occasion. The little red boat was Ella Mae's

idea. It was her little joke, and George could not be more delighted.

"What on earth was that girl thinking? Such an indulgence," griped Mrs. Cameron quietly to herself. When Ella Mae stood beside George, Jessie took note of the girl's softly protruding belly and concluded that George's motive to marry her was more a matter of his own premarital activities with this farm girl than true love. Then she was hit with a sudden realization. A thought so powerful that she felt it necessary to share it with Charley. She gestured for her son to come closer, and she whispered, "Why, Charley! This Ellie is the spitting image of Lassy McGregor from New Glasgow. Don't you think?"

"Mother, quiet."

"My, my! She's as plump as a pregnant pigeon!"

"Shush."

Telgmann played a sweet tune on the violin while his sister sang.

George looked at his bride and knew that there was no mistake. No doubt. Her beauty was undeniable. Her sense of whimsy, a delight. Her strong will admirable. In her eyes he could see their sons: healthy and strong. He wished his father was present to see her beauty and to share in the promise that his name would move forward in time. This thought led George to the anticipation of their wedding bed. In a voice that he did not recognize as his own, he heard, "I will" and then "I do." As he slipped the tiny ruby ring on Ella Mae's trembling finger, he thought: *with Maggie's ring I thee wed*. When Reverend Smith gave him permission to kiss his bride, he felt the luscious mingling of their breath. He inhaled deeply. He felt the journey of his own breath searching the unfathomable depths of her soul. He was drifting out to sea. He thought of sweetgrass braids. He thought of Maggie. *"Remember me, George. Soon we will be together again. Soon."*

A small, uninvited guest tilted her head this way and that. No one noticed her watching the ceremony from above. She made no sound, but Annie felt her presence.

Chapter 30 – January 1884

Dust

Mrs. Cameron looked at the letter in her lap. She recognized the hand at once. It was from Christina, yet there was something smeared and rushed about the words. There were large spaces of hesitation like bridges of contemplation on the page. As Mrs. Cameron deciphered her daughter's words, her heart beat heavily in her chest.

January 25, 1884

My dearest Mother,

I know no words to capture God's ways. It is beyond my comprehension how a man can rise in the morning for work, kiss me goodbye as he has done a thousand times before and never return. How can the finest of men be taken? I say taken for I am robbed of his presence.

The Boston Globe gave him a glowing account this morning. The paper mentioned his esteemed military career as one of Governor Andrews's first commissioned officers. I am heartsick beyond these mechanical words. I find no comfort in my hollow prayers. God saw fit to take away my darling son Alfred and now, my husband. Please be gentle when you share this news with Charley and George, for they looked to McLelland as a father. I shall write again when matters are settled here in Boston.

Your Loving Daughter,

Christina

Mrs. Cameron changed into her mourning attire, drew her blinds and took to her bed. She sent for her sons and waited until she heard them at the door below. Then she wept.

After the words – words so abrupt and raw – George felt ill. He embraced Charley, bent over and kissed his mother's forehead and said, "I must be alone to write."

"Where are you going?" asked his mother.

"My study."

She gestured for Charley to help her out of bed. "George, you must mourn with the family. Your sister needs her family."

George's face fell into furrows. The inside of his lower lids burned with tears that he was holding back. When his breathing became laboured, he steadied himself against his mother's dresser. "My feelings are beyond me. I feel a fit coming upon me. Please, I beg of you. Let me be excused."

His mother waved her handkerchief toward the door and buried her face in the folds of Charley's jacket. George opened his mouth then closed it. No words.

George descended the stair. Each footfall heavier than the last. He retreated to his study and locked the door. Sitting behind his desk, he stared at the blank page, pressed his hands over the paper's smooth whiteness and waited for the words. An hour passed and the room glowed orange and pink. Dust floated in the shafts that streamed through the window and spilled onto the floor.

Oh brother! Dust and ashes – dust
Upon the tongue so sweet a song.

Another fifteen minutes passed. How could it be that a man so vital should come to this? He stood and stretched. The thin lines of yellow and orange glowed behind the silhouette of Main Street until a greyness settled in the room. Life setting into darkness. He heard the bustle in the house above as Charley pulled out his mother's travelling trunk. Then he heard the huff and grunt as Charley carried the trunk down the stairs. Thoughts began to spin again in the darkness.

I look aloft – the stars are cold
But in the East I see the sun.

He took out Maggie's tiny photograph and descended into a deeper level of sadness. He craved despair.

"George?" Ella Mae rapped lightly on the door of George's study. She tried the doorknob. Locked.

"Cook has prepared a light supper. Surely you must be hungry. George? Answer me please."

"Go away." George was in his own world, and Ella Mae was not invited.

George and his mother picked up the fragments of Christina's life as if they were fragile shards of a broken teacup. Each piece a tiny moment of anguish beyond the comforting words either could offer. Christina was inconsolable. George's sister hid beneath the black crepe and veil in a lace tent of denial. The shutters were closed and the blinds drawn, creating a perpetual night. Stifling. A fitting shroud for a mourning wife. The burial was delayed until spring when they could break ground. *The ceremony of death in America is elaborate and exhausting*, thought George. The steady stream of mourners who passed through the Moores' home to share their memories of the deceased served as a constant reminder of death's reality.

"If I have to respond to one more letter of obligatory condolence, I shall rip myself to bits."

"You know as well as I that we must respect the protocol of mourning." Mrs. Cameron slid the letter opener under the sealed flap of another letter. "If you like, I can take these matters into my hands while you rest. Perhaps some time away will ease the loss."

"Mother, loss follows one no matter how far you travel. It's in me."

George knew of this loss. Time might ease the pain, but it never really went away. He thought it best to keep this knowledge to himself.

"Excuse me. I need some air." George opened and closed the door quietly, but a rush of cold swept into the house. The black crepe cloth that was tied to the knocker fluttered away in the harsh winter wind. George chased it down the street like he was chasing death itself away from the house. But there was no escaping death. He tied the crepe ribbon back onto the door.

Chapter 31 – March 1884

The Pin

Ella Mae listened to the sounds of morning. They were always the same in this strange house on Main Street. Each morning like clockwork George got up for breakfast, kissed her gently on the forehead and began his grooming regimen. Through the fine feathers of her long lashes Ella Mae feigned sleep as she watched her husband. She heard the familiar swish, swish, swish of his shaving brush as he lathered up the soap, the rasping scrape of thin metal against stubbled flesh and the staccato tap, tap, tap of the blade against the wash basin. Each time he tapped the blade exactly four times. She could see his figure turn in the mirror to check to see if he disturbed her. She did not move but took a deep breath and exhaled slowly to mimic the rhythm of sleep. Still in his nightshirt George continued his toilet ritual. Every morning for the past seven months since she joined George and his mother to live on Main Street, it was the same performance. He rubbed oil deep into his roots and massaged his scalp. He felt that his full head of auburn hair was the chief attribute of his personal attractiveness. Ella Mae hated the fuss. *Pure vanity*, she thought. Following his every move through veiled lids, she watched him brush his hair. First he used a hard-bristled brush to stimulate circulation. She counted to fifty. He switched to a softer brush for polish. She counted to fifty again. It was never forty-nine or fifty-one. It was always fifty. Once finished he examined his reflection from every possible angle. Satisfied, George got dressed.

Ella Mae rolled over. *Why does he waste the morning with toiletries when he could play under the billowing sheets with me?* The answer was obvious when she felt her hard, rounded belly. In the final month of her pregnancy, Ella Mae had learned that she disgusted her husband. With her back to George, she knew that he was folding the towel twice before he hung it on the washstand as he did every morning at the end of his grooming session. He picked up his pocket watch and fastened it to his vest then left the room.

She heard Mrs. Cameron greet her son at the foot of the stairs. "Good morning, my son. How did ye sleep?"

"Terrible, Mother. Maybe three hours at best."

"Ye work too much. I tell ye, all of this poetry nonsense cannot be good for ye. Don't ye remember Dr. Putnam in Boston warned you of the dangers of feeling given your tendency to melancholia? I'll call on Dr. Saunders to see if he can give ye something to rest your mind."

"Mother, I am fine." George hated the tonics doctors had given him in the past. They clouded his thoughts and feelings so much that he could not write.

"Sit awhile. Jenny made scones, following my recipe of course. Sit awhile and take some tea with your mother before ye rush off to the paper." And then the same question she asked every morning of her son: "Is Ella Mae still in bed?"

"Yes, Mother."

"Pity. It would do her some good to get up and about and socialize a bit with her family."

Ella was not in the mood for a family breakfast. One morning shortly after she moved to Main Street, Mrs. Cameron turned to her and touched her lightly on the arm. In confidential whispers she shared the secrets to perfect eyebrows. "It's truly a pity that your brows are like bleached straw. Too much sun, I say. A lady's complexion should never be exposed to direct sunlight. Do let me clip your brows, aye? I recommend that we rub brandy liberally into your roots each night and apply some vitriol as a matter of habit to encourage a darker growth. After all, brows frame the face! Don't you think, Ella Mae?"

More grooming tips. It quickly became obvious to Ella Mae where George had acquired his obsession with appearances. Every eruption in her skin, no matter how minute, ended in balms and salves mixed with witch hazel. Mrs. Cameron insisted that Ella Mae wear her hair in the city fashion. Ella Mae loathed the tight centre part, and the chignon gathered at the nape of her neck drove her to distraction. She examined her comic reflection with a frown. The silly tendrils on each side were ridiculous. "I look like a pampered lapdog!" This only made George laugh at her, and Ella Mae grew less and less rebellious with his condescending amusement.

Mrs. Cameron was not impressed. "I know in the country there is no time for fashion, but in Boston this is the way 'twas done." Each morning Ella Mae's mother-in-law laid out her attire for the day. There was no choice. Ella Mae preferred the delicate prints of her cotton dresses to the dark hues of these heavy garments. Mrs. Cameron insisted on a sturdy undergarment of whalebone and wool throughout Ella Mae's pregnancy. Its rigid front busk gave a single rounded breast to minimize the size of her waist. Perhaps she pressed the issue in part to disguise her daughter-in-law's sudden and rapid weight gain in the early days of her marriage. When Ella Mae first voiced her protest concerning the corset, Jessie tried appealing to the young woman's own sense of vanity. When that didn't work, she echoed Dr. Saunders' recommendations. "Only wool should be worn next to the skin, dear. The animal fibres will prevent the retention of odour."

When Ella Mae and George were alone that night, she asked for her husband's assistance to remove the offending garment. She wanted – no, needed – to make herself perfectly clear. "George, I can't wear this." She held the heavy wool garment up to his face. "I look like a giant spoon when I wear it. Besides, I can scarcely catch my breath. It can't be good for the baby. Please, George."

"What does Mother say?"

"She thinks..." Ella paused to put on her mother-in-law's heavy brogue. "'It's the gay height of fashion in Britain.' I don't really care what fashion dictates; I refuse to wear it."

"Shh! Mother will hear you."

"Let her hear me, George."

"Perhaps you can wear it when you leave the house. For church and such."

She gave up. "I thought it would be just *us*."

They had this same conversation many times and it always ended the same way. "Where is she to go?" Since the Camerons' divorce, Jessie preferred to tell everyone at church that she was a widow. No one knew that James had left her to live with another woman in New Brunswick. George felt somehow responsible for their troubles. Their arguments always centred around money. Guilt had a way of winning every argument, and Mrs. Cameron knew it.

All Ella Mae could hear now were the muffled exchanges between mother and son downstairs. She slipped out from under the quilt and relieved herself in the chamber pot, which was increasingly difficult to navigate in her ninth month. Then, she tiptoed out of her bedroom and across the hall to the banister where she slid down the wall, sat behind the spindles and listened.

"I shall be late for dinner this evening, Mother. Oscar, Charley and I plan to meet after work to discuss the next act."

"Ye and Oscar have been at it for two years now. Surely this wee opera will come to an end soon? Why don't ye bring Oscar and Charley here for dinner, aye? I haven't seen your brother in weeks."

"Very well, Mother." He paused. "You have to understand that poetry takes time. The libretto must fit the narrative and coordinate naturally with the musical score. We revise, scrutinize and revise again and then in the next minute reverse all the changes, so we are back where we started."

"Sounds to me like you're working in circles."

"It is the creative process, Mother. We will be in my study, so please do not disturb us." George continued to ramble on about the opera, but he was speaking more to himself than to his mother. "I fear I have too many characters and the audience may get confused, but Oscar assures me that he needs their voices to balance the soprano and the baritone. I am off, Mother. Do try to take it easy on Ella Mae. The baby is coming soon, and she needs her rest. Billings is bringing Annie Appleby from Millhaven to help. Perhaps, when you have time, you can ready her accommodations in the back kitchen. I leave all matters domestic in your capable hands, Mother."

The truth was that if Ella Mae didn't listen in on these conversations, she would scarcely know what was going on in George's life or remember the sound of her own husband's voice.

"What your wife needs is fresh air, exercise, fish liver tonic and a tepid bath."

Between the clinks of cutlery and the clunks of the cups, Ella waited patiently for George to defend her, but he rarely did. In response to that particular observation, he said very little. "Now, Mother, you must understand that old Billings dotes over his children, and they are, well, to be frank, they are spoiled."

Not true! Ella screamed in her mind and bit down on her tongue. *I want to go home. Yet here I am, in a stuffy house where everything is dark and ancient.* There was no end to Ella's list of complaints, but who could really blame her? Mrs. Cameron was the lady of the house. However, the mention of Annie's name lifted Ella's spirits. How Ella Mae missed Annie's sharp wit and wicked tongue. She also missed the boisterous play of her collie in the fields. Tears welled when she thought of little Maudie and her innocent truth about absolutely everything. Everyone around the breakfast table at home spoke from the heart. There was none of this "Well..." pause, reflect on social convention, speak again and so on. Now, every word that came out of Ella's mouth had to be weighed and measured against convention and public appearances.

Ella Mae refused to call her mother-in-law Mother or Jessie. She was nothing *like* her mother. The memory of her loving mother made Ella cry. Just as sad was the complete change in George when he was in his mother's presence. The spark that had raced between George and Ella Mae when they first met was extinguished by his cold reserve in this home he shared with his mother. George said Ella had become the "angel of Mrs. Cameron's house" on Main Street, yet she felt more and more like an uninvited guest.

Ella Mae felt the stretch and kick just under her skin. Her belly was so taut that she could see the formation of a little fist. Her breasts hung heavy from her frame. She had become lost in this heavy suit of motherhood. She missed running with the children along the fence where her father kept the cows. She missed rowing in her little red boat up and down the shore. Most of all, she missed being Ella Mae.

From her perch upstairs in the cold hallway, Ella Mae heard the scraping of chairs below as George pushed his seat back and stood up. She counted George's five steps to the other end of the table, where he pulled the chair out for his mother. She knew she had to make her way back to the bed in the slight chance that George had forgotten something or came up to kiss her goodbye. Getting up from the floor at this stage in her pregnancy proved difficult. She rolled onto her side and lifted herself up until she was on her hands and knees. By steadying herself on the railing with one outstretched arm, she managed to push up with her legs and straighten her back until she was upright. She tiptoed into the bedroom and crawled back into her cocoon. She listened. The door opened and closed twice. First for George and then twenty minutes later for Mrs. Cameron and her cook. She was alone.

Ella Mae felt lighter. She got up again and wrapped herself in a blanket. Jenny, under Mrs. Cameron's orders, had placed a breakfast tray on the table outside the bedroom door. Ella picked up a scone, broke it in half and slathered it in strawberry preserves. She washed it down with a sip of tea. Ella Mae knew that she would have at least two hours to dance and sing. In the midst of song, a strange feeling swept over her. Curiosity. At first it was a faint whisper in her ear. The little voice got louder and louder still. *Just what does he write in that journal of his?*

Ella Mae made her way down the stairs to George's study and tried the doorknob. It was locked. She returned upstairs and opened the door to Mrs.

Cameron's bedroom. Carefully, ever so carefully, she opened the woman's jewellery box and found exactly what she needed. She giggled when she shut the door and made her way back to the study. She took Mrs. Cameron's hatpin and jiggled and poked, jiggled and pushed until she heard a click. She turned the knob slowly, opened the door a crack and peeked in. She stepped into the dark room. She felt giddy with the adventure of it all.

George's study was lined from floor to ceiling with books: law books, theology books and volume upon volume of poetry. The walnut desk was littered with copies of *Atlantic Monthly* and old copies of the *Daily News*. "Where is it?" Ella searched under the scattered papers, looking for the leather journal that George wrote in night after night.

Once, in the middle of the night, Ella had silently crept downstairs and hid in the dark to watch her husband in his study. Between sobs, he wrote in his journal, page after page, into the early hours. Ella's eyes had grown heavy and her feet cold as she sat on the step in the darkened hallway. Afraid she would fall asleep, Ella Mae had tip-toed back up the stairs to their room. She stirred when George came up to bed. "Is it morning?"

"Shh, darling. It's early. Go back to sleep."

The room was filled with sunlight. Ella Mae wondered how he could write all night, sleep for two hours and then get up in the morning to work at the newspaper all day.

Now in the study Ella Mae could not see the journal. Perhaps he took it to work. She opened the heavy curtains. She tried the long centre drawer. Locked. Mrs. Cameron's hatpin was pressed into service again. Ella pulled the drawer out slowly. There they were. At least half a dozen black leather journals. The next threshold in this journey was opening the journal and turning that first page. She read page after page of enigmatic metaphors. As she untangled the images, she was certain that very few of these lines were about her. She came across one poem titled "To Lurline," but the vast majority of the poems were addressed to "M." or "M. McG." She read one line aloud: "Last love is sweet, but first love is dearer still." *He does not love me!* It was curiosity that had pushed her this far, and it was curiosity that kept her turning page after page, journal after journal. She got lost in the phrase: "I cannot kiss a stranger." *Am I that stranger?*

Before Ella Mae closed the drawer, something blue caught her eye and renewed her hope that love might conquer the ghosts of former liaisons. After all, her husband had a life before he met her. The tiny blue gutta-percha case she had given George on their wedding day featured an intricate carving of two doves. She smiled when she remembered his surprise. "Oh!" he said. "I love it wondrous well." And then he smothered her with sweet kisses. Why he kept it locked in his desk was a mystery to Ella Mae, a mystery until she opened the case. She fully expected to see her own face peering back at her through the delicate gold frame inside, but in the panel where she had placed her own image less than a year ago, George had slipped another tiny tintype. The young woman was holding a book, her finger marking a certain page, and on the table was what looked like a stack of postcards and letters tied with a ribbon. Her smiling eyes were frozen in time. On the left-hand panel, two colours of hair, auburn and gold, were woven together under the glass. Engraved in the gold casing in a simple cursive script were the initials *M. McG*. Ella Mae's face fell and she clutched her chest. The narrative of her romance was rewritten in an instant.

Ella Mae was startled by the booming voice of her mother-in-law at the front door. Had it really been two hours? She closed the journal and placed it in the drawer with the others, exactly as she had found them. She shut the drawer, slipped out of the study into the hallway and put her foot on the bottom step.

"Ella Mae! You're up and about."

Ella Mae turned to greet her mother-in-law as Jenny hustled past, juggling various bundles, packages and fresh flowers. Still dressed in her nightgown, Ella Mae unscrambled her thoughts to manufacture a suitable lie. "I came down to get a glass of milk."

"Are you unwell, Ella Mae?"

"No, Mrs. Cameron." She bit the inside of her cheek.

"Will ye be down for dinner? Charley and Oscar Telgmann will be joining us."

"We'll see. I am feeling so large and full," replied Ella Mae. She started up the stairs.

"Lassies these days," said Mrs. Cameron as she headed down the hallway to remove her hat and gloves, "so worried about their figures. Look at me! I had nine children – God rest the souls who are in heaven – I'm past fifty and I still have my figure yet. Do not deny your appetite, Ella Mae. The secret is portion control. Portion control and a sturdy undergarment."

Ella Mae forced a smile. She went up to the room she shared with her husband and shut the door. She couldn't help but feel that something was missing. What had she forgotten? She drew the lace curtain back to reveal a beautiful afternoon. She returned to her bed and slept.

Dinner was late that evening. George and Telgmann were going at it again at the piano in the parlour. When they eventually emerged, George was clearly surprised to see his very pregnant wife seated at the dining table. He moved behind her and rested his hands on her shoulders. "What a lovely surprise, darling. I gather that you are feeling rested?" He kissed her on the top of her head. In the presence of his mother, George was merely a cut-out of his former self – monotone and soulless; however, with Telgmann in the room, he was animated, almost his old self. He smiled.

"Mother said you had a bad day. If you are up to company, I have asked Oscar to join us."

"Oscar is always welcome at our table. How is Mignon? And Alidia?"

"Both well. You are ready soon, no?"

"Yes, very soon. Have you and your brothers and sister had an opportunity to perform much lately?"

"Not as often as we would like." Telgmann sat at the table and grinned widely. "George and I have been *bis spät in der Nacht arbeiten.* How do you say this in English? 'Burning the midnight oil.'"

"It is more like burning the candle at both ends," Charley added as he strolled into the room. He gave his sister-in-law a big hug and rubbed her belly with gentle hands. "Hellooo in there!"

"She moved! Charley, talk to her again."

"So you think it will be a girl?"

"No doubt in my mind."

"Time will tell. I am hoping for a boy myself."

Ella Mae smiled. This was the first time George had expressed any interest one way or the other in her pregnancy. There was so little left of George after work, after the opera, after his journal. It was almost as if he had used up all of his words and had nothing but silence and impatience left for her, but with Charley and Oscar present George was sweet and attentive.

"George, I don't mean to intrude on your chat." Mrs. Cameron looked directly at Ella Mae when she said this. "I can see you're busy with serious matters, but have you seen my amethyst pin? Ye know the one with the Scottish thistle that your Grandfather Sutherland gave to me when I was a wee lass?"

Ella Mae flinched. The pin. She retraced her steps in her mind. Had she left it in the drawer? Ella Mae pinched herself as hard as she could. It took the edge off and allowed her to sit quiet. Now she pinched herself like a silent scream. Ella Mae let go of the tender flesh on the inside of her arm and folded her hands on her lap.

During dinner Charley kept the table entertained with tales of boyhood adventures in New Glasgow. Ella caught herself laughing unapologetically at George's unfortunate encounter with a raccoon in the outhouse.

"Who is ready for dessert? Jenny has prepared a lovely pie. My recipe, of course." Mrs. Cameron rang a small bell and the young woman appeared.

"Yes, ma'am?"

"You can clear the table now and bring out our bonnie pie."

"Yes, ma'am."

Ella Mae got up and started to help Jenny clear the plates.

"Do sit down, dear. You're in no condition to exert yourself this way. "

"Ella Mae, listen to Mother."

"I am not used to being waited on. I really don't mind."

"*We* mind, dear. Just make yourself comfy and enjoy the pie."

Ella Mae resumed her seat, and Charley rested his warm hand on her trembling one. "Ella Mae, did George ever tell you that he devoted an entire song in our opera in honour of your pie?"

Telgmann laughed and winked at George.

"No, George did not tell me." Ella blushed and looked down at her hands folded neatly on her lap. She wanted to pinch herself.

"Sing us a few bars, Georgie boy," poked Charley.

"I wasn't aware that ye baked. Please, what particular type of pie could inspire our George to write an ode to a dessert, of all things?" Mrs. Cameron turned to look her daughter-in-law in the eye.

"Pumpkin."

"How sweet."

But not as sweet as the first, thought Ella Mae. George's words to the mysterious *M* plagued her. He was living an entire secret life without her.

Mrs. Cameron pushed back her chair like the grinding of teeth. The Cameron matriarch placed her napkin on her now empty dessert plate and rose from her seat. The men stood. "Need I remind you, George, of the hour? You gentlemen should mind the time. You'll need to rise early to catch the train."

Ella Mae let out a gasp. "George? Train? But the baby."

"Ella Mae, have ye forgotten, dear? George and Oscar will be visiting Ottawa to present their composition to our prime minister. Charley is going as well."

Charley caught Ella Mae's eye. "We'll be back soon. Don't worry. I'll keep him out of trouble."

George laughed as he took a long, slow drag on his cigar and exhaled a puff of billowing blue smoke. "I am sure the baby will not know the difference."

"But I want you to be here. I need—"

"Don't make such a fuss, dear. George has more important matters than waiting on babies. Jenny and I can manage perfectly well."

Ella Mae sighed audibly and let her hands fall in her lap. "Of course you can."

Chapter 32

A Momentous Debut

"Annie!" Billings shouted from the drive shed. When there was no answer from the back kitchen, he turned to his nine-year-old nephew, Timothy. "I need you to finish hitching Lincoln to the buggy. Thread the reins through the rings on the harness and loop them over the rein hook. I'll be right back." He patted Lincoln on the neck and headed for the house.

Annie appeared at the door carrying her small valise and Maudie's favourite toy. "Little miss forgot her doll. Should we drop it off at her grandmother's place on our way?"

"She'll have to make do without it. I just received word from town that George has already left for Ottawa."

"But the baby is so close. George should be here."

"You needn't remind me of the fact, Annie."

Billings put Annie's bag in the back of the buggy while Annie climbed up onto the seat beside Timothy. Billings had asked his brother to spare the boy from work on the farm for a while so he could help his cousin, Ella Mae. "You listen carefully to your cousin, boy. I want you available to fetch me when it's time for the baby," said Billings. It gave him peace of mind to know that Annie and Timothy would be with his daughter before and after the birth of his first grandchild.

From her bed, Ella Mae could hear Annie's familiar laugh ringing through the house and a stranger's laugh like the whinny of a small colt. Who could that be? Her curiosity was overruled by the regular tightening of her abdomen. Her sheets were wet with perspiration, so she rolled to the empty side of the bed. Her room smelled faintly of her home by the lake, and she drifted off to sleep dreaming of the farm.

When she awoke, Annie was sitting by her side, stitching the final decorative touches on a baby's bonnet. By shifting her buttocks an inch at a time, Ella Mae was able to roll onto her side and tuck a pillow between her knees. She wedged another one under her heavy breasts. Now Ella Mae could see the entire room. She smiled when she saw the beautiful bouquet of violets that her father had brought in from the farm. It was lovely. She was happy, surrounded by these touches of home and with Annie by her side. Another tightening of the abdomen. Ella Mae rubbed her huge belly in slow circles. "Soon. Soon I shall meet you, my precious little one," she whispered.

While Annie rubbed her back, Ella Mae turned names over in her mind. "I've always been partial to Joseph, my grandfather's name, but I'm absolutely certain this baby is a girl. I'd like to name her Phoebe, for my great-grandmother." Yes. Phoebe Cameron. Perfect. Her baby should be named for this strong woman of Dutch descent who had braved the difficult days of settlement on unfamiliar shores. To herself, Ella Mae wondered yet again when George would return; she wanted to share with her husband the names she had chosen. She braced for another tightening.

"Well, Miss Ella Mae, we'll soon meet baby Phoebe, unless it turns out to be baby Joseph after all."

"When, Annie?"

"Before the day is done, I expect. I shall heat up some clear broth. You will need your strength to work through the pain." Annie kissed the expectant mother softly. "Remember the waves on the shore at home, my sweet. Each wave rises slowly, crests and then gives way. I shall be back quick as a wink. I'll have Timothy sit outside your door to help if you need anything."

In the kitchen Annie and the cook chatted by the woodstove as Jenny heated the chicken broth. Today was the first day Jenny had laughed in the Cameron household. It was an unusual laugh of three different registers punctuated by a snort. Her unabashed amusement made Annie Appleby laugh in turn, so the kitchen was alive with laughter.

In the parlour, Mrs. Cameron busied herself with the final embroidered touches to a christening cap. She flinched with agitation each time she heard the clucking hens in the kitchen. While she took it upon herself to discipline Jenny, it was not her place to reprimand Annie Appleby. She couldn't for the life of her understand why Billings gave this young Black woman free rein over the affairs of his household. She set down her work and opened the kitchen door, letting in a surge of cool air. Mrs. Cameron followed.

"Miss Appleby. How kind of ye to tend on our wee mother to be."

"I prefer Annie. Just plain Annie, and it is my pleasure, Jessie. I brought her brother and sister into the world. It seems natural that I deliver Ella Mae's child. Jenny is heating some clear stock for her now."

Bristling at being addressed by her Christian name by this woman and horrified by Annie's discussion of her deliveries, Jessie Cameron thought it best to set things straight right away. "I shall see to it that the doctor attends. I'm certain ye will be of tremendous help."

"To be honest, Jessie, Ella Mae and I decided that I will deliver the baby."

"Did ye now? I was unaware that ye had a licence to practice medicine. Are ye familiar with the use of forceps? Chloroform?"

"No, ma'am, but I have delivered ten live births with nothing more than hot water, a fresh supply of clean cloths, scissors and prayer. Mind you, I have used a needle and thread on occasion when the baby comes too fast."

"Well! I am certain there will be no need for ye to take out your sewing basket." Mrs. Cameron turned to Jenny. "Ye have your own chores."

"Jenny, I am at my wit's end without my daily chores." Annie filled a cup with broth. "Thank you for your help. I'll take this tray up to Ella Mae. It will be best if she rests afterwards. I shall pull her blinds and instruct her cousin to sit outside her door. Timothy! Yo ho ho, Timothy!"

"Perhaps he will hear ye better if ye go to him," Mrs. Cameron offered.

"Yes, Annie?" The fair-haired lad poked his head in the kitchen. "Is it time? Should I fetch Uncle Billings?"

"Not yet, my sweet. Come with me, Tim. Carry this basin up the stairs and be careful not to spill." She held the door for the boy as he slowly walked with the basin of cool water. "You will be looking after your cousin this morning while I do some chores for Mrs. Cameron. Take this cloth and wipe her forehead to keep her calm and cool."

"Very well," said Mrs. Cameron. "Jenny, I suggest that the two of you do the week's laundry this morning, for there will be plenty of foul wash to do after the birth." Mrs. Cameron retired to the parlour where she picked up her needlework to settle her nerves. While Jessie felt above all matters domestic, she did have a steady hand for embroidery. She put on her spectacles and returned to the delicate stitches on the tiny cap.

In the backyard Jenny filled the agitator tub with three buckets of hot water. Annie helped by carrying the pails back and forth from the back kitchen. While Jenny added the soap flakes and turned the wooden paddles, Annie prepared the rinse water. She unwrapped two packets of Reckitt's Blue and dissolved them in each bucket of cool water. Annie marvelled at the cold water pumped into the house on Main Street through lead pipes. It was so convenient to turn on a tap instead of walking back and forth from the pump at the well on the farm.

Ella Mae was stirred awake by the waves of contractions. She was rowing in her little boat, but she felt like she was hitting a storm. She braced for the pain. "Timothy." She spoke calmly but firmly. She felt a flood of warm liquid burst between her thighs. "Fetch Annie now."

Timothy ran down the stairs two at a time. "Annie, something is happening! Annie!"

Ella Mae could hear the *trop trop trop* of Annie and Jenny as they ascended the stairs. Annie rolled up her sleeves, pulled back the covers and removed the sopping wet pillow from between Ella Mae's legs. All the while she moved with a calm confidence that only experience can bestow. She instructed Timothy and Jenny to rearrange the pillows behind Ella Mae to support her in an upright sitting position. She manoeuvred the mother's legs into the birthing position and checked to see how many fingers she was dilated. All the while she gave instructions and imitated the breathing exercises she had practiced with Ella Mae.

"Jenny, remember what we discussed in the yard? Now calmly go downstairs and get the items I requested."

"Yes, Annie." Jenny was a little frightened, but she repeated the items over and over under her breath as she made her way down the steps.

Annie turned to the boy. "Timothy, go to Market Square and fetch your Uncle Billings."

"Yes, ma'am!" He was out the door and down the stairs. He ducked under Jenny's arm and scooted past Mrs. Cameron.

"Jenny! Get Dr. Saunders. Now!" Mrs. Cameron shrieked.

"No time, ma'am. The baby is coming now."

"All the more reason to hurry then. I order ye to get the doctor!"

"No, ma'am. Annie needs certain items we prepared in the kitchen." And with the quiet calm of Annie, she brushed past her employer and retrieved the hot water, cloths, string, candle, brandy and scissors. As she made her way back up the stairs, she heard the front door shut.

Mrs. Cameron walked out on the street and waved down her neighbour. "Fetch the doctor immediately. My son's wife is about to deliver a baby." Satisfied that the doctor would be there soon, she turned and climbed the front steps. On the way back into the house, she heard the powerful wail of her new granddaughter.

At that moment, George was on the *Chaudiere* with Charley and Oscar, returning from their meeting in Ottawa with Sir John A. Macdonald. They made the transfer from the Prescott to the St. Lawrence railway line the moment George's daughter took her first breath. George and Telgmann were basking in the accolades they had received from the House for their composition "Our Premier."

Charley was buzzing with the success of the trip. "The press coverage is sure to build anticipation for the launch of your opus, gentlemen."

Oscar slapped George on the back. "Our little fairy opera will now be as momentous as the birth of your child!"

His friend's comment triggered the memory of Ella Mae's imploring eyes. Secretly, George wanted to be there for his wife, but his fear of losing another woman to the dangers of childbirth plagued him as the date crept up on him. He was so consumed by the opera that he had paid little heed to her changing body and incessant complaints of swollen ankles and puffy fingers. The closer Ella Mae got to the date, the more George thought of Maggie. He imagined Maggie's pain and vicariously shared her suffering, though not his wife's. While he lauded childbirth as the most noble of duties a wife could perform, he wanted to maintain his romantic notions of motherhood separate from the blood-stained cloths, tearing flesh and the uncertainty of a safe birth. His trip to Ottawa, though planned weeks prior to the birth, would keep the beauty of his bride intact.

George watched the landscape chug past. Trees, farmland, more trees and red granite outcroppings. *Why does Ella Mae have to be so forward?* Billings's endless indulgence of his daughter's bold nature had ruined her for George. The day of their wedding, he had been taken aback when the old man warned his future son-in-law, "You may use moderate correction on Ella Mae – Lord knows she has tried my patience more times than I can count – but by no means will you lay a hand on her in anger, or you will answer to me. Do you hear?" George was too appalled to answer the man in words. He nodded his head gravely.

As the train snaked its way through the Canadian Shield, Charley and Oscar nodded off. George pulled out the blue case Ella Mae had given him for a wedding present last year. Maggie peered up at him from beyond the grave with unblinking eyes. "My heart forever entwined with yours." He touched the glass and stroked the delicate braid. *Memento mori.*

Chapter 34 – September 1885

Autumn Closes

George looked out at Amherst Island through the window of the bedroom he had been sharing with his young wife, the room that was hers before they were married. In the gathering darkness the far shore seemed so close that he could touch the pines. And yet…. He held his hand up to the pane of glass. *I have always been on the shores of my life looking out. My future is that island, right in front of me, but there is forever this cold, deep stretch of grey between me and it.* Leaning against the wall, he opened his journal, flipped back a few pages and read to himself:

> My spring is over, all my summer past:
> The autumn closes, winter now appears.
> And I, a helpless leaf before its blast,
> Am whirled along amid the eternal years
> To realize my hopes or end my fears.
> The autumn closes, winter now appears.

At that moment, looking out the window, George felt the weight of his age. In one week, he would be thirty. He had thought that his position at the *Daily*

News would somehow satiate his appetite for writing. He had anticipated a career that would allow him to provoke his readers with his words, but how he loathed the mundane articles about errant lightkeepers, the farm reports and melodramatic obituaries. *Where do I turn now?* He felt the weight of his own failure crushing his chest. He could not face those that looked to him for something he could not give. Idle chatter. Hollow words.

As he looked out over the channel, memories of home floated on the surface of the water like steel grey ghosts. Johnny MacIntosh appeared before him, the deaf and blind boy who ran round and round in a well-worn path, digging himself deeper and deeper into the dry earth. Going absolutely nowhere. The boy's circular journey made George dizzy with the futility of his own life. He felt like a bear baited by elusive fame. Tethered to the stake, he snapped and tore at invisible enemies. Wounded and stuck in one place, he turned to confront his foe. Biting, clawing, roaring, he wound himself around the stake in a show of controlled violence. *My pride devoured by the insatiable appetite of indifferent spectators. I will be revenged. Who are they to judge me when they cannot write a jot?*

> He is a poet? Never! I deny
> He hath a portion of the sacred rage.
> All flowers of speech may bloom upon his page,
> His soft words on my senses idly fall:
>
> Not having any utterance for his age,
> He hath no power to stir my blood at all.

I know it is the destiny of the poet – or at least any poet worth reading – to suffer. But I'm tired of suffering. "I am exhausted."

"Then go to bed."

"Pardon me?"

"You said you are exhausted."

"Did I? I didn't realize I said that aloud."

He turned from the window to see Ella Mae seated beside the small bed, working on the intricate smocking of Jessie's dress. The glow of the lamplight softened her face seductively. He watched her chest rise and fall with each breath. A vision of naked thighs spreading in front of him stirred his manhood. She was such a beauty. But that day had passed. Once, her smile was sunshine, and wherever she went the summer lingered there. But now? A frost settled on those beautiful features. He could see the curve of her breast through the thin white fabric of her nightdress. He touched the nape of her neck and traced the line of her cheek to her mouth. He tried to kiss her, but she turned to the side so that he kissed her ear. She looked down at Jessie's blue checkered dress and continued to work. How she had changed since that first morning on this shore. Who would have thought that a bosom so warm and so inviting should have a heart of ice within?

"I shouldn't have to beg my own wife for affection."

"Affection? What you mean is relations. That's different than affection."

"You make me feel like a thief, stealing morsels."

He pulled her out of the chair and embraced her, but she remained limp in his embrace. When he held her at arm's length to look at her face, she refused to look at him. He pushed her down on the bed and began to unbutton his trousers, but she turned toward the window and began to cry.

"I am the thief."

"For crying out loud, Ella Mae. What does that mean? Stop being a child. Perhaps Mother was right. We rushed—" He stopped. As the words left his lips, he realized the real reason they had hurried into marriage. He was only thinking about those ecstatic moments before she told him she was pregnant, not the long string of moments to follow. Once the words hung suspended in the air between them, he wished he could take them back. He buttoned his trousers and turned to leave the room when she spoke.

"I have your mother's hatpin."

"Pardon me?"

"You know, the one she asked you about before you went to Ottawa."

"Then return it. Ella Mae, this really is trivial." George walked to the door. He turned the knob but stopped when his wife spoke again.

"In fact, you had it all along. It was in your study drawer."

He stood there as awareness dawned. This simple fact explained everything.

"Pity Mother had to go so long without it."

Ella Mae listened as George descended the back stairs to the kitchen. She picked up her smocking and searched for her needle. She hesitated a moment and then dug the needle into the soft, white flesh of her forearm.

The next morning, a neighbour helped Billings carry George's lifeless body from the north shore to the farmhouse. Dr. Nash examined the corpse.

"It's the strangest thing, Billings. I really don't know what to tell you. He seems like a healthy man in his prime. There's no outward cause. Had he been sick of late?"

"Not that I could tell. Annie? Did you see him this morning?"

"I heard him stirring in the kitchen before sunrise. What hour I can't really say, because I went back to sleep. Ella Mae told me a while ago that he hasn't slept all that well since the passing of his brother-in-law over a year ago. Apparently he and Colonel Moore were very close."

"Grief has its way of weighing heavily on the heart." Dr. Nash wrote a few notes in his book for the official cause of death. Seeing that there was no outward cause and no recent illness save a family history of asthma, the doctor pronounced the cause of death as heart failure. In his estimation, the young man's early passing could only be the result of a hereditary weakness of the heart.

As Billings and Annie spoke with the doctor in hushed tones out in the hall, Ella Mae approached the lifeless man on the bed. She could hear Maudie sobbing in the kitchen. In the pale morning light, George looked as if he was sleeping. Ella Mae thought it strange. From the time they were married, he always retired late and woke early, so she rarely saw him asleep. This was the first time she actually saw the thin veil of wrinkled skin over his eye sockets. They created a blank gaze toward heaven. It was morbidly fascinating. She spent a long time just star-

ing at his motionless face. To the young widow, this
calm was a good thing, but she dare not speak these
words aloud. Gone were the deep furrows in his
brow that marked his incessant fretting over exactly
the right word. Gone was that look of disapproval in
his eyes. Gone was the tutting of his tongue when
she used some colloquial expression in front of his
mother. Gone was the placating smile when she used
the wrong fork at the dinner table. It suddenly occurred to her, like a clear note breaking the silence,
that she must maintain his dignity and the illusion of
their happy marriage. She needed to locate George's
journal.

She glanced ever so slightly out of the corner of
her eye to see if anyone was watching. When she was
absolutely certain that she was alone, she slipped her
hand into George's pockets one at a time, searching. Her movements were not hurried or anxious.
She was calm as she glided her delicate white fingers
into the breast pocket of his morning coat. It was
cold. There was no telltale heart beating. Ella Mae
removed her hand when she heard her father's footsteps and steadily smoothed out the lapel of George's
jacket. To an observer, Ella Mae was merely saying
goodbye. An observer wouldn't see the twinges of
panic that tightened her chest when she did not recover George's journal. It was his custom to tuck the
thin leather book into his breast pocket whenever
someone approached him.

She gave a sudden and audible gasp when Billings rested his strong, tender hands on his daughter's shoulders. He pulled her tiny fragile frame to
his chest and held her quietly. He did not say a word,

but simply gave his daughter a safe place to cry. No tears came.

"Father, I need some air."

"Annie, take Ella and the children outside and sit with them by the barn. Wait for the undertaker. I sent for my brother to take the children to Uncle William's farm. I will ride into Kingston to inform Mrs. Cameron of this most unexpected, most tragic turn of events. She shouldn't have to hear this news from a stranger." Billings recalled when Annie told him of Margaret's passing, a moment from another world. It was not that Billings was callous, but he had very few feelings for his son-in-law. What was past was past. He couldn't change the facts. His immediate concern was to ensure that Ella Mae and little Jessie remained at the farm. The thought of Mrs. Cameron having any hand raising his granddaughter made him shudder. He was adamant that he alone must set things right for his daughter.

As he hitched Lincoln to the gig, he thought of Ella Mae. He was worried. Each visit, though few in number, brought a paler, stiffer and more silenced version of his daughter. He did not suspect physical violence; he was sure he had made it perfectly clear that he would not tolerate anyone raising a hand to his daughter. Still, she had withdrawn further and further into herself. Even Annie's cheerful disposition could not provoke a smile from Ella Mae's lips. No doubt the days to come would be difficult for her. He would see to it that she and her daughter remained on the farm.

Annie turned toward the drive shed and saw Mr. Emigh take the gig in the direction of Kingston. She followed his progress until he disappeared around the point. "Your father is on his way."

"Where did Jason Parrott find him?"

"I am not certain."

Ella Mae headed down to the shore. Annie turned to Maudie and Sanford. "Stay put. Do you hear?"

"Yes, ma'am. Where's Ella Mae going?"

Annie didn't answer. She ran to catch up to Ella Mae. "Are you sure you want to go down there in your bare feet and nightdress?"

"I must find it, Annie."

"There is nothing that can't wait a day or two."

"Annie, no one else can find it. It will be the ruin of me – and then there is poor Jessie to think of. No one can find it, Annie. For God's sake, help me look!"

Annie had witnessed grief before, and this display of desperation definitely was not it. Nor was it shock; there was something so unsettled in Ella's tone that Annie grew fearful for the young widow's soul. It was pure panic.

"Please, Ella Mae. Tell me what we are searching for."

"His journal. It is a small black leather journal. George kept it on his person at all times. It was not on the body."

Annie sensed the urgency of Ella Mae's search, so she saved her questions for another time. Ella Mae was now on her hand and knees, searching through the weeds. She pushed up her white lace sleeves as she worked her way to the water's edge.

"It has to be here, Annie. I must find it."

Annie noticed the faded scars and fresh wounds on the young woman's inner forearms. Crimson scratches laced the white flesh. They were deep and infected. Again Annie knew that now was not the time to confront her. A wave of nausea swept over her as she watched the crazed widow fumbling about the shoreline.

"Where did they find the body?" Ella Mae was now standing in the shallows as tiny waves lapped up against her ankles and soaked the hem of her white nightgown.

"Come up, my sweet. You might slip on the rocks. Here, give me your hand. I doubt George went wading in the water this morning. Let's look further down the shore by Parrott's property line. Perhaps he did not even have the book on him this morning. Perhaps he left it in his room or at home in Kingston."

"No! Impossible! Keep looking. It was always his practice to write first thing in the morning."

Just as Annie was going to stop searching, she spotted the dull black leather binding and fluttering pages of the little book. "Ella Mae? I found something."

The widow's eyes were wild. Ella Mae scrambled up the rocky ridge. "Where? Give it to me now! Do not read a word of it, Annie!" She wrestled George's soul from Annie's grasp. As soon as she had what she was looking for, she began to run back to the house. She fell in the tall grass.

By the time Annie caught up with Ella Mae, she had scrambled to her feet and was frantically flipping through the pages. She was sobbing uncontrollably, so Annie kneeled down beside her and with her hand on Ella Mae's back, tried to encourage the young Mrs. Cameron to sit. Exhausted, Ella May fell limp into Annie's arms.

"He's gone, Annie."

"Sh, sh. There, there. Let it out. Let the tears wash away the sadness."

But Ella Mae was not crying. "He can't write any more secrets."

Annie wasn't really sure what she was hearing. A confession? Regret? Despair? Relief? She wondered what secrets George was keeping from everyone.

Ella Mae started to sing.

"But Pauline would not take advice.
She lit a match, it was so nice!
It crackled so, it burned so clear,
Exactly like the picture here.
She jumped for joy and ran about,
And was too pleased to put it out."

Annie decided that she could not keep this from Mr. Emigh. While she loved her sweet Ella Mae as if she were her own sister, this was not the girl she remembered. Something had happened to change her, and the answer to this something must be contained between the thin leather covers of that book. While it wasn't her place to read it, perhaps Billings could convince his daughter to tell him of the volume's contents. She resolved that she would tell Mr. Emigh of her concerns for his daughter.

Chapter 35 – November 1885

Counting Knives

Dr. Nash visited the Emigh residence in Millhaven no less than a dozen times in the fall of 1885. Broken bones heal. A splinter can be removed. A cold will eventually pass. But a shattered mind? There was no way he could even pretend to know how to help Ella Mae. The young Cameron widow was mad, no doubt, but how to restore her to her senses was beyond his skill and training. He sat at his desk in his Bath office and composed a letter to Dr. Clarke of the Rockwood Asylum in Kingston. Billings may not like it, but he had done all he could for his daughter.

Dr. Nash took note of Ella Mae's prolonged fatigue brought about by severe insomnia. He added that she had become aphasic since the day they discovered her husband's body. How permanent this loss of speech, Nash could only guess. The most disturbing of symptoms was the woman's obsession with self-mutilation. He wrote:

> Family members have trimmed the patient's
> nails and wrapped her hands in gauze to no

avail. She continues to stimulate herself by gouging deep chunks of flesh from her face. Night wandering has led to multiple secondary injuries: cut feet, numerous lacerations requiring stitches, frostbite. The passing of her young husband and the recent birth of her year-old daughter appear to be the exacerbating causes of her melancholia. Without Ella's will and desire to recover, I am at a complete loss as to how to cure a mind diseased. I hope that you will take some time to meet with Ella Mae and her father in the near future.

Professionally Yours,

William T. Nash

Billings and Annie accompanied Ella Mae to the imposing limestone building overlooking Lake Ontario. Annie knew this place and she shuddered with fear. It was here in the Cartwright Stables that she, her mother and sister were kept after her father's death. Her father was financially burdened from the day he came to Canada. Try as Appleby might, he could never keep his head above arrears. Instead of debtors' prison, the Appleby women were brought to Rockwood. Annie could not think of those dark days before Billings Emigh came to fetch her to work at the farm as his housekeeper. A close friend of her father's, Billings heard of the family's plight and made arrangements. He paid their debt and she never looked back. As they approached Rockwood now, Billings sensed her hesitation.

"You'll never go back to the Cartwright Stables, Annie, so get that thought out of your head. Dr. Nash assured us that there have been many changes since then."

As the carriage pulled up to the formidable building that had been commissioned by Sir John A. Macdonald twenty-five years earlier, Billings had to fight the urge to keep going. He looked at his daughter's frail figure. She had lost so much weight that she was skeletal. Then there was the baby. Ella Mae cried whenever Annie brought the child to her. She cried so much that the baby would start as well. Then there was his daughter's tearing of her flesh. He felt so helpless in the face of this ... he had no name for what this was.

When they walked through the central entrance into Rockwood Asylum, a stout nurse with thick ankles and a heavy gait went down a hallway to get the chief of staff. An amiable man appeared from one of the many doors that lined the long hallway. He held out his hand to Ella Mae first and introduced himself as Dr. Clarke. There was no response.

"Mr. Emigh, if we could discuss Mrs. Cameron's case in my office while Ella Mae tours the facility, I shall share the letter sent to me by Dr. ..." he opened and closed Ella's file quickly, "...Nash."

"He's a good man and a trusted friend, Dr. Clarke. I know he wouldn't send us here unless he was certain you could help my daughter."

"Nurse Train, call Poppy down to accompany Miss Appleby and Mrs. Cameron to the recreational hall."

"Yes, Dr. Clarke. This way, ladies, please." Nurse Train escorted the visitors to the nursing station where they met with a young woman about Ella Mae's age. Poppy led them into a large room, where patients of all ages were gathering for the afternoon's entertainment. The staff also attended, so the hall was crowded.

Annie hesitated. "We might better sit by the door in case Ella Mae has an outburst. They can be violent at times and unpredictable."

"I thought Ella might feel better if she could see the water. Dr. Clarke says she lives by the lake in Millhaven." Poppy turned her attention to Ella Mae. "We are going to hear some music. They're really quite good. Do you like music, Ella?"

Ella Mae mumbled something under her breath, but to Annie and Poppy the words were incomprehensible puffs of air.

Poppy was undeterred. "What's this? Ella Mae? Did you say something?"

Annie answered for her. "Most of the time I believe she is trying to talk, but I don't recognize any words."

"It's early, and I realize you don't know me, Ella Mae, but I really want to help." She turned to Annie. "Dr. Clarke always encourages us to speak with the patients directly. He really has changed things around here for the better. Music's only one of the pastimes that Dr. Clarke encourages. Mind you, some of the new policies are a bit experimental, but the patients certainly seem to enjoy the music."

Poppy and Annie quietly continued their conversation while keeping an eye on Ella Mae. They paid no heed to the makeshift stage where a young woman was seated at the piano next to a man, her older brother. He stood and touched his bow to the strings of his violin. He played with such sweetness that the once rowdy assembly grew quiet immediately. Ella Mae listened. She tilted her head. The violinist seemed vaguely familiar, but she couldn't quite place him. Then her eyes grew wide. She recognized the man as Oscar Telgmann.

"Oscar?" The word formed distinctly in her mind, but it sounded like a grunt when it reached her lips.

"Oh look, Annie. Look at Ella Mae. She's smiling!"

To Annie's surprise, the music transformed the blank stare she had witnessed for the past two months to a slightly animated shadow of what Ella Mae used to be. Annie looked into Ella Mae's eyes to see if her other senses were restored, but her hope fell slightly when there was no sense of recognition behind her pupils.

The young widow looked beyond Annie. Absorbed by the music, nothing else existed for her. Nothing but the rise and fall of slow waves breaking.

When he and his sister were finished, Telgmann lifted his bow gently from the strings, lowered his instrument and opened his eyes to eager applause and the anticipation of something more. He and his sister took a quick bow. Oscar looked around at the smiling faces and then stopped when he came to Ella Mae. Ella squinted her eyes as though trying to sharpen his image, but she looked to be heavily sedated. Oscar spoke to his sister who smiled and rose from her seat. He took her place at the piano, and Elsa stood and sang. Oscar looked up now and again from the keys and watched Ella Mae's lips move to the lyrics.

> "And my Love – my little Nell,
> The apple of my eye, I
> To thee how can I say farewell?

I love thee more than I can tell;
I love thee more than"

"Pumpkin pie," said Ella Mae, though the words were completely indecipherable.

"The patients seemed to really enjoy the music," said Annie. "Ella Mae seemed particularly moved by that last song."

"The music was Dr. Clarke's idea," Poppy said. "He's a musician himself. He introduced music to his studies of the insane in the Hamilton and Toronto asylums. Only he prefers to call asylums 'hospitals.' He feels if he changes the language, perhaps the stigma attached to these afflictions will also change."

Annie was curious. How could a girl, perhaps a year older than Ella Mae, find herself working in an insane asylum? She had to ask, and that led Poppy into another story.

"The answer is simple: my brother, Joseph. We tried to take care of him at home, but he wandered off something terrible. My mother and me was always looking for him. He'd finally come home and sleep for days on end. The doctors said he had paresis on account of his untreated syphilis. As time went by, he couldn't remember what he just said or did. When he got angry and had the fits, Mother said, 'That's it, Joseph. I love you, son, but you is scaring me something awful.' She's never been here – I mean, to visit. I came and helped when I could. The doctors said Joseph always seemed better when I was here. When he passed, Dr. Metcalf and Dr. Clarke offered me this here job. I live on the floor with the patients. Mostly I stay with the patients in the dining hall, walk with them along the lakeshore for exercise and talk to folks like you about what we do here. Dr. Clarke believes in exercise and fresh air. Dr. Metcalf always said I should have been a nurse because of my extraordinary patience. I can't read or write, but Dr. Metcalf said, 'You can't teach patience.' Joseph was a lot better here than what we could do for him at home. I don't know if you are finding it hard at home with Ella here, but I can imagine you're getting tired. I can see it in your face."

"I just don't know what to do with her. Her little brother and sister are scared of her. Who can blame them? Her father is devastated. The way she tears at her flesh like that. He lost his wife about seven years ago – now his sweet Ella Mae."

"How do you account for the change in her?"

"Oh, I doubt that there was ever really one cause, but her husband died two months ago."

"Was it some sort of accident?"

"No one really knows. Dr. Nash thinks it was heart failure."

"So young. Now this poor dear has a broken heart too."

By this point, the entertainment portion of the afternoon was ending. Poppy directed Annie and Ella Mae to the basins to wash. Ella Mae was calm and cooperative. It seemed as if the music and the company of others was having a positive effect. She washed her hands and dried them on the towel. She folded the towel twice as she always did and placed it carefully over the rack. There were no mirrors. Even if Ella Mae wanted to see her reflection, it was doubtful that she would recognize herself. At the dining table Annie and Ella Mae were joined by Poppy and two other female patients. They were served generous portions of beef and barley soup with large chunks of meat and potatoes.

"It is a far cry from the strained vegetable gruel they served two years ago. Dr. Clarke and Dr. Metcalf introduced this new diet when they arrived to make changes here at Rockwood. Some of the older ladies help out in the kitchen as part of their therapy. It makes them feel more at home. They're pretty good cooks."

"Ella Mae loves to bake pies."

Poppy turned to the young woman beside her. "Maybe when you're up to it, Ella Mae, you can make some pies for the other folks here."

Nurse Train made her way across the dining hall and gestured to Poppy.

"Ella Mae? It's time to see Dr. Clarke now. If you'll let me, I'll take your hand and guide you to his office. He really is a good man, Ella Mae," said Poppy. "He'll be so pleased to hear that you enjoyed the music."

Ella Mae gave the young woman her hand and obediently followed Poppy down the hallway.

Ella Mae sat in the high-backed leather chair and stared at the man behind the desk. He was sitting in front of the window, which created a perfect silhouette. She traced this shape in the air with her finger. Why the man was sitting in the rectangular patch of light was unclear to Ella Mae. In the background she could hear the steady rhythm of *clink - stop - clink - stop - clink - stop*. She *did* know that she was Ella Mae. Of that she was certain. So when the shape addressed her, she looked at it. She turned her face toward the voice that poured out like warm honey. She decided she liked the voice, but the clink-stop-clink-stop-clink-stop behind her made her shrug and tilt her ear to her shoulder. Inside she was singing:

"Now see! Oh! What a dreadful thing
The fire has caught her apron strings
Her apron burns, her arms, her hair;
She burns all over, everywhere."

"Ella Mae? I know you can hear me. You do not have to say anything if you do not feel like talking. When I ask questions, I want you to think about the answers." He stood up so the voice stretched upward in the big white rectangle. The voice travelled from behind the desk and across the room. Ella Mae watched the shape move and listened to the golden voice. She could see the man now. He was a nice man. He sat down beside her. She was not scared, nor was she anxious. Her arms hung limply by her sides and her shoulders slumped forward. *Clink-stop-clink-stop-clink-stop.* She wanted that sound to stop. She wanted to simply stop. Her eyes were heavy. Her breathing became slow, regular, deep. She was drifting, drifting into the warm waves of summer. She slipped under the water and woke with a start. How long had she been asleep? She was still sitting in the leather chair with the high back. The voice was still there. Soft, so soft.

"We'll wait a little longer for the medicine you took before you came here to wear off. For now I would like to examine you. May I touch you, Ella Mae?"

Ella Mae made no sound, but she did not object. She was used to Dr. Nash examining her almost ev-

ery other day. Someone else was in the room. Out
of the corner of her good eye, she could see a short,
round ball of white floating behind the man.

"Patient has irregular pupils."

Ella Mae heard the quick *scratch, scratch, scratch,
scratch, dot.* The white ball was writing something.
Are you writing about me? This thought was clear,
sharp and painful. *No more writing, I say. Stop writing.*

"Patient is now agitated by something in the
room. Obvious physical response. Pulse racing, body
thrashing, low moaning, irregular breathing. Seda-
tive effects of opiate tapering off."

Scratch, scratch, scratch, dot.

Stop writing! Ella thought that if she held her
breath long enough she would disappear. A sudden
rush of violent air expelled from her lungs and she
gasped. She took another deep breath and held it for
the count of one, two, three, four, five. She felt her
lips tingle and her cheeks puff out. Her eyes were
burning, so she held her hand up to her cheekbone.
The pain registered immediately. She exhaled violently and cried out.

"Numbing effects of local anesthetic are now
completely worn off. Patient beginning to feel physical distress from self-inflicted wound to the right
eye."

*Scratch, scratch, scratch, scratch, swish, scratch,
dot.*

What did that sound mean? What was the word
that meant that sound? She began ripping at her
hair and pulled out a handful by the roots. A firm
but gentle hand softly pulled her hand down, slowly
stroking it. Calmly. It was a familiar hand.

"There, there now, Ella Mae. She does this when the medicine starts to wear off, Dr. Clarke."

Ella Mae recognized that voice and the gentle touch. *Annie? Annie are you there? Make it stop, Annie.* The words were trapped in her throat, now dry and sore from screaming.

"Patient's screams seem to vocalize recognition."

Scratch, scratch, scratch, dot!

Clink - stop - clink - stop - clink - stop.

"Ella Mae gets upset sometimes at things we don't see or hear, but that sound.... What is that noise?"

"The ladies in the dining hall are counting knives. Freedom is one thing, but precautions must be taken."

"Yes, I see."

"Ella Mae? Do you know where you are?"

Ella Mae's shakes became worse. She tried to tear at her wounded eye. *Where's that other sound? Where did it go?* Ella Mae heard the scratching noise and became frantic. She screamed. *Someone is writing. I can hear someone writing!* Ella Mae tried to rise from the chair and grab the nurse's pencil. Dr. Clarke called for restraints.

Ella Mae wanted to crawl back in the cupboard she used to hide in when she played with her brother and sister. The safe cupboard. The cupboard of no feeling, the cupboard of no sound. *Where is my medicine? I need my medicine. Annie? Annie will you get the spoon? Give me my medicine. I'll be good. I will stop crying now.* Imploring with her eyes, she looked up at Annie.

"Sir, she will go into a shaking fit soon."

"I am sure she will, but we must be strong during her delirium tremens. If you need to leave, say so.

Nurse, record the symptoms of detoxification. Miss Appleby, please trust us. Can you stay? She seems comforted by your touch."

"Yes, sir."

"Restrain her firmly."

Ella Mae started to break free and tear at her face. The wound under her eye was open again and bled down her cheek and into her mouth. Restrained, she started to bite her tongue violently so that it too started to bleed. Ella Mae tasted the salty iron liquid, thick and warm, until someone shoved a damp cloth in her mouth.

"Won't she choke, sir?"

"She can breathe through her nose. The cloth will absorb the blood and prevent her from biting her tongue and from biting us."

"Help me! Please help me!" The voice shook itself free from her throat and made it past the wet cloth and out the corners of her mouth, but it was unintelligible.

"Nurse, prepare the morphine. Half her regular dose." The doctor removed the cloth and put a clean one between Ella Mae's teeth. "Careful she does not bite down on your hand. Talk to her, Annie. She can hear you now."

"What do I say?"

"Anything calm. Try to hum. Stroke her calmly, slowly. She'll tire soon. Nurse Train, are you ready to inject the dose?"

"Yes, Doctor."

The first attempt was an abysmal failure. The hypodermic skidded across the tile floor. The doctor ordered the nurse to soak a cloth with the medicine. "Let her suck on it, Annie."

Ella Mae could taste the familiar bitter fluid on her lips. She licked her chin – then she began to suck vigorously on the cloth. Bliss. She crawled into the quiet of the cupboard and curled up in the corner. Dr. Clarke dictated his closing observations. *Scratch, scratch, scratch, dot!* From the safety of her cupboard, Ella Mae looked out.

"Stop him, Annie! George is writing about me."

"Did you hear her doctor?"

"I did."

"She spoke!"

Chapter 36 – 1889

Letting Go

Charley stood at the front door of the Emigh farmhouse in Millhaven. Billings did not let him in the house. He spoke in hushed tones through the half-opened door. "I warn you, she's not ready to talk about it. It's best you go now."

"It's been four years. We're about to bring *Leo The Royal Cadet* to the Martin Opera House. I thought—"

"That may be so, but there's still something un-settled in her mind about your brother. I don't want to stir things up again. You weren't here, Charley. You don't know."

"I'm caught in the middle, sir. Mother believes that you're keeping young Jessie from her father's legacy."

"Charley, Ella Mae has always been fond of you, but with all due respect, your mother has never, well, she's never been kind to my daughter, nor has she shown any interest in Jessie – 'til now."

Charley searched his pockets and pulled out four tickets to the opera. "Well, I'd like to give you these in case you change your mind. I'm sorry there isn't one for Annie. If I had my way, she'd be joining us. Anyway, the curtain rises on July eleventh, one week from now. That should give you plenty of time to think about it. The prime minister will be in attendance. It really is an honour." Charley was about to leave when he heard Ella Mae's familiar voice.

"Who is it, Father?"

Charley hesitated. The look in Billings' eyes silenced him.

"Father?"

"It's me!" Charley shouted past Ella Mae's gatekeeper.

Ella Mae moved past her father and embraced her brother-in-law warmly.

"Charley! I haven't seen you since...."

"It's been awhile." Charley hesitated. Billings did not take his eyes off him. "I visited you in the hospital, but you were in a bad way then. I guess we all were. You look well now."

Ella touched the scar under her eye. She turned at the sound of her daughter's rapid little steps as she ran through the front hall to see who was at their door.

"Jessie, my sweet. Come meet your Uncle Charley."

The little girl appeared at the door, then retreated behind her grandfather's leg. She didn't remember her uncle, but she peered with curiosity at the jovial man standing in the doorway.

"Let's go for a walk, Jessie. Don't be shy, silly. Let's show Uncle Charley your wee boat." With the promise of a boat ride, Jessie cast away her shyness and stepped out into the shade of the front porch.

"I don't think it's a good time right now." Jessie's grandfather was adamant that Charley should leave. Yet, the girl was magnetically drawn to her kin. She warmed to Charley's smile and gentle nature.

"It's all right, sir. I shall keep them safe."

Jessie pulled Charley down the path to the lake, and the two ran like drunken butterflies through the long grass with Daisy the collie bounding alongside. Ella Mae meandered down the path behind them with the stoic stride of a patient parent. While Ella Mae had absolute trust in Charley, Billings kept watch in the upper field. Worry had its way of holding Ella's father in a suspended state of disbelief and mistrust.

On the very shores where George had met his bride and married her, Jessie rowed in her own little boat. In the very shallows where a neighbour had found the corpse of her father, the child splashed the oars in an awkward attempt to move forward. Her efforts were thwarted by her size, so she ended up rowing in circles. Charley absentmindedly skipped stones across the surface of the water. He was startled by Ella Mae's direct question.

"Did you know her?"

"Maggie, you mean? I did. Are you sure you want to talk about this? Your father made it very clear—"

"My father is only doing what he can to protect me, but I think it's time I talked about it."

"Well, I was too young to know what was going on. I do remember after she died though. George was in law school at the time. He had a breakdown."

"He never seemed content to just be."

"I miss him, Ella Mae."

"To be honest, I don't think I ever really knew him. It all happened so fast."

"I miss him less when I work on publishing his poetry, and of course there's the opera."

"Of course. The opera. If there was ever another woman in our bed during our marriage, it was that opera." Ella Mae had a strength of mind now that her father didn't understand. She needed to bring those years to some ending. "I was so angry when I learned that you had published his poetry, Charley."

"I know."

"It was too private to publish. He never really loved me, you know. I didn't want anyone to know those things about him." She pointed to Jessie who was still navigating the shallows with tremendous determination. "Especially her."

"You can keep her from those truths until she is old enough to understand." Charley knew that his argument was weak, but he also knew that his mission was greater than any perceived embarrassment. "I need you to know something about my brother. On the outside he never settled on anything, but inside, well, that was different. Inside, his voice was always there. He struggled so hard to be heard. No one listened. I am sharing that voice now. People will listen.

It is my way of honouring him." He picked up another handful of flat stones and flicked them one at a time across the surface of the water.

"I've come to accept that it wasn't, I mean, it wasn't anything I did or said. The poems are about her, not me. Did you know that?" Ella Mae mirrored Charlie's actions. She picked up a stone that was far too large. She tried to skip it, but it plunked into the shallows.

Charley took her hand and made a few adjustments to the angle of her wrist.

"You're trying too hard Ella Mae. Relax a bit. You've got to pick the flat ones. Hold them like this. Now bend your wrist and flick." Ella Mae pushed up her sleeves and Charley saw the fine scars lacing her inner arms. "Try again."

"I can't."

"Just let it go. Plant your feet on the shore, look out into the distance where you want the stone to go and let it go. You'll get it. Come on, Ella Mae. Try again. Just let it go. Like this." He sent a stone flying. "Remember to snap your wrist sideways at the end." Charley looked up toward the house and saw Billings walking toward them. *No. I'm making progress. I can't stop. Not now.* He handed Ella a stone.

She tried again. *Skip, skip, skip, plunk.* "Charley! Did you see?"

"I did."

He turned to see Billings standing on the outcrop above them. "Sorry to keep your daughter so late, sir. We've had a very nice chat."

Billings did not look convinced. "It's time for Jessie to get ready for bed."

"Grandfather!" It was clear Jessie did not want to leave this magical time with this man who had flecks of gold in his green eyes, just like hers.

"We'll be up in a minute," said Ella Mae.

Billings smiled at his daughter and headed back to the farmhouse.

Dusk descended on the three figures as Ella Mae managed to skip a stone farther out onto the calm surface of the water. They climbed the rock face to the outcropping of land overlooking the expanse of Amherst Island. As they set out for the farmhouse, a cluster of bobbing fireflies filled the air.

"Look, Uncle Charley. Look at the dancing star flowers."

Charley stopped on the path and examined his niece's up-turned face. He stooped to pick her up. He searched her eyes and found George. Charley brushed back Jessie's auburn curls. "It sounds like we have another poet in the family."

Packed to capacity, the Martin Opera House was abuzz with the excitement only an opening night can create. Sir John A. Macdonald, seventy-four and entering another election, welcomed a temporary diversion from politics, though many in Kingston would argue that his attendance at the premiere of *Leo the Royal Cadet* was nothing more than an opportunity for the old chief to gain the popular vote. His wife, Agnes, in her early fifties, was a different woman. With her hair now fully white, the gossips pointed out that the poor dear had aged decades in a single year. Agnes's brother, Hewitt, carried their frail daughter Mary up the stairs into the balcony box and lowered her gently into the seat beside her mother. Seated directly behind the Macdonalds, Charley and Jessie Cameron watched their honoured guests get settled. Mrs. Cameron put her hand on Lady Agnes's shoulder to get her attention.

"We are ever so pleased, Lady Agnes, that you and your husband can attend this evening. We do hope you enjoy our little opera. My son would have been honoured. Truly honoured."

Lady Agnes gave a curt little nod over her shoulder.

Mrs. Cameron sat back and surveyed the audience. "I see *she* decided to make an appearance," she said to Charley. She nodded her head toward the balcony box across the theatre. "It's been four years. Surely Ella Mae can move past petty grudges. And that dress is hardly suitable for such an occasion. Doesn't she realize that this is an important day for George?"

To Mrs. Cameron's surprise, Lady Agnes turned in her seat and looked her in the eye. "My dear Mrs. Cameron. Since your son is not with us, I can't imagine he'd mind what his wife is wearing." She did not wait for a reply but turned in her seat immediately to speak with her daughter.

Dumbstruck, Mrs. Cameron fanned herself with the program.

The band began to play, under the direction of Oscar Telgmann. This signalled the crew to roll up the enormous stage curtain to reveal an elaborately painted backdrop of the Royal Military College. Macdonald tapped his cane against the balcony to the opening number. On the stage below, the baritone belted out the lyrics to a rousing drinking song:

"Fill up the bowl, boys, fill it to the brim. The liquor is Burgundie, drink with a vim!"

In the balcony across the opera house, Ella Mae clutched the wooden armrest of the maroon leather chair to steady her nerves. Billings sensed his daughter's uneasiness and placed a reassuring hand on hers. Gaslights illuminated the opulent interior, giving it the soft amber glow of a waking dream. The elaborately decorated stage curtain was a work of art in itself. Framed by a giant scallop-edged valance and flanked by two fringed tapestries on either side, it suggested a certain pretention. George's widow watched his daughter Jess, Oscar's daughter Mignon and Ella's sister Maudie peek over the balcony and point out the funny feathered and bejewelled hats of Kingston's finest. Then she looked up, way up, at the intricately carved plaster dome that rose thirty-five feet above them.

As the opera unfolded, Ella Mae recognized her late husband in the character of Wind, the opera's comic poet, who hid under the table, unperceived by the other characters, feverishly writing everything down in a simple black notebook. The actor playing Wind spoke directly to the audience: "Aw, by Jove! What a doocid pwetty scene! Just the thing for my new faewy opewa! Aw! I'll just wite it down befoh I fohget it."

Laughter rose in the opera house in response to the character's exaggerated lisp, but the clown made Ella Mae cringe with mortification. He represented everything Ella Mae hated about George. His hours of incessant scribbling, his secret study, his drawer filled with journals and secrets. Ella Mae struggled to focus on the opera, but her thoughts were dragged time and time again back to those years on Main Street. A clapping thunder broke the spell. At the end of the opening scene, the actors, bolstered by enthusiastic applause, gained confidence – especially Wind, who pranced about the stage, a caricature of a failed poet.

When the curtain was raised for the next scene, Maudie cried with delight, "Look, Ella Mae! It's you! It's your white dress!"

To friends and family, Maudie's observation was a quaint truth. Only Ella Mae knew that young Nell wasn't really her. She was and she wasn't. The sweet soprano was, after all, an actress who was merely a reflection of a woman who was the echo of another's reflection. She was like the photograph placed over her own image in George's little frame. A substitute bride.

Little Jessie pushed her aunt to the side. "Maudie! I can't see."

Maudie, now a mature young lady, put a maternal hand on Jessie's back. "Here. Let me help. Stand on tiptoe. Better?"

The child strained upward, but she could just peek her little nose over the brass railing. Billings whispered in her ear, "Come, my sweet. Come sit on Grandfather's knee. Best seat in the house." Jessie scrambled eagerly onto her grandfather's lap and gasped when she saw the bright red uniforms of the RMC cadets and the pastel ruffles of the pretty parasols. The picnic scene began. Nellie, the sweet soprano, sang her opening lines.

"It is strange how a fellow forgets, when he wishes,
The girl he has held in the country so dear;
Whether at the piano, or washing the dishes,
He'd love her forever. Yet, in less than a year,
He forgets."

Charley, stirred by the truth of the script, looked across the theatre at Ella Mae who squirmed in her seat. Perhaps Billings was right. This was a mistake. He kept looking across the theatre, willing her with his steady gaze to look in his direction. She raised her head, and he caught her eye. With a little wave, he captured her attention. Then he made a pantomime gesture of skipping a stone across the water. "Let it go," he mouthed to her.

Ella Mae smiled and flicked an imaginary stone in return.

Author's Note

The story behind the story unfolded in a most unusual manner. It began when I found a mud-caked ruby ring on the property of my parents' house in Millhaven, Ontario. As I stood on the shores overlooking Amherst Island, the ring begged me to tell its story. After I rinsed the band in water, I noticed a fine inscription to Ella Mae. It was this simple clue that led me on a two-year journey to find its owner. During my research at the local archives I uncovered a small photograph of a young woman in a rowboat. The woman, all dressed in white, stared back at me from under a wide-brimmed hat. When I flipped over the photograph, she was none other than Ella Mae Emigh. As the pieces started to come together I realized that I was living in her house. I also discovered that she was married, at seventeen, to George Frederick Cameron, a Confederation Poet who was also the librettist of Canada's longest running opera, *Leo the Royal Cadet*. My journey has taken me from Nova Scotia to Boston, Massachusetts, and home to Kingston again.

I am grateful to Reverend Charles Cameron who published his brother's *Lyrics on Freedom, Love and Death* and brought *Leo the Royal Cadet* to the stage. Much of the personal information came to me after I visited the Cameron fonds at the University of British Columbia where George's hand-written journals are now housed. While I used historical names, dates and places when they were available to me, the interpretation of these events is fictional.

I would like to acknowledge the unconditional support of my husband, Brian Rombough, and the patience and keen eye of my editor, Marianne Ward.

A graduate of Queen's Faculty of Education, Tracey has devoted thirty-three years to her teaching career in the areas of Literature and Fine Art. During her time as an educator in Kingston, Ontario, she has worked with students to create set designs for many drama productions and community events and continues to do so. She was awarded her school board's Outstanding Service Award (2013) and Queen's Teacher of the Year Award (2000) for her work as a mentor. Tracey won the Royal Reel Award at the Canadian International Film Festival in 2014 for the screenplay based on the manuscript for this novel.